# KING OF THE COURTS

# KING
## OF THE
# COURTS

**TYLER CHAMBERS**

Copyright © 2024 Tyler Chambers

The moral right of the author has been asserted.

Apart from any fair dealing for the purposes of research or private study, or criticism or review, as permitted under the Copyright, Designs and Patents Act 1988, this publication may only be reproduced, stored or transmitted, in any form or by any means, with the prior permission in writing of the publishers, or in the case of reprographic reproduction in accordance with the terms of licences issued by the Copyright Licensing Agency. Enquiries concerning reproduction outside those terms should be sent to the publishers.

This is a work of fiction. Names, characters, businesses, places, events and incidents are either the products of the author's imagination or used in a fictitious manner. Any resemblance to actual persons, living or dead, or actual events is purely coincidental.

Troubador Publishing Ltd
Unit E2 Airfield Business Park,
Harrison Road, Market Harborough,
Leicestershire LE16 7UL
Tel: 0116 279 2299
Email: books@troubador.co.uk
Web: www.troubador.co.uk

ISBN 978-1-80514-448-9

British Library Cataloguing in Publication Data.
A catalogue record for this book is available from the British Library.

Printed and bound in Great Britain by 4edge Limited
Typeset in 10.5pt Adobe Garamond Pro by Troubador Publishing Ltd, Leicester, UK

*To Lauren, Emelia and Mason - for their continued love and support.*

*'Secrets and lies threaten his perfect record,
but what happens when his secret becomes the biggest
threat of all?'*

## 01

# TUESDAY 13TH OCTOBER, 10:55 P.M.

The familiar New York background noise of hustle and bustle filled Daniels' ears as he opened the car door and stepped out onto the wet sidewalk. Towering over the quiet residential street in Lower Manhattan, the clear night sky was filled with stars as light rain nestled on the shoulder of his dark, wool coat. He signalled to his driver to park and as he closed the door a cab whizzed past sending a puddle of water in every direction. After giving way to a young family to continue their journey, Daniels walked up the stairs of his managing partner's three-storey townhouse and firmly knocked three times on the door. He stood for a few seconds before a light switched on and Macpherson peered through the side window.

"I certainly did not expect to see you at my front door at gone 11 on a Tuesday night," she said as she opened the door to greet him.

"Neither did I," Daniels replied. "This isn't really a trip that I wanted to make but I thought it would be better if we had this conversation in person. May I come in?"

Macpherson stood to one side and allowed Daniels to walk past her into the house.

"The library would be best for this chat, I assume?"

She shut the door and followed after him down the hallway. Before Daniels could even take a seat in one of a number of dark green leather chairs that filled the room, Macpherson started the conversation because she already knew exactly what he was about to say.

"So, what's happened to Sandy? This will be the third lawyer that's come off this case now."

"It's not as straightforward as that and you know it. Clearly, he has got to her and there's nothing either of us can do about it!" Daniels quickly became animated; Macpherson poured him a glass of whiskey and passed it to him.

"I know it's not your fault but it's convenient that this has happened less than seventy-two hours before the trial is due to start. I thought we'd prepped her so well. What's actually happened?" Macpherson was now sat down in one of the chairs opposite her partner, legs crossed and drinking her own glass of whiskey.

"She got a letter through the mail this morning with a lot of personal information on it about her children. Their names, their school, DOB and even pictures. It's freaked her. She's dropped the case immediately."

Macpherson rolled her eyes and looked across the room into an empty space and took a large gulp of her drink.

"Son of a bitch. Let me talk to her in the morning. Woman to woman it might convince her to dig in even deeper to beat him."

"I had to convince her not to resign let alone continue with the goddam case!"

"Son of a bitch," Macpherson repeated slowly.

Daniels pinched at his trousers and shuffled off the seat and was now standing over Macpherson after making his way over to a tall wooden drinks cabinet behind her to refill his glass.

"What now, then? If we give this up the press will crucify

us. It'll hit us harder than just this case."

Macpherson twisted to answer Daniel's question turned statement, but he put his hand on her shoulder to keep her seated.

"I have an idea but it's not one that you're going to like at all." The pair locked eyes as Macpherson waited for Daniels to finish his sentence having perched himself back on the arm of his chair. "Ryan?"

"Absolutely not. No way. Not in a million years." Macpherson leapt to her feet and started pacing around the room.

"It makes the most logical sense to give this case to Ryan. He would handle it best in the current circumstances," Daniels responded, trying to reason with his now irate partner.

"You just want to give it to him because you don't like him; you want to see him fail."

"That's partly true, yes, but I do stand by the fact that I think he's the next best suited lawyer at the firm to take this case on. Especially at such short notice."

"If you think I'm going to throw my protégé and arguably the next big name to come out of our firm to DeShawn Arlington then you're sadly mistaken."

Daniels rose to his feet to try and calm his usually ice-cold partner down and bring her round to his thought process.

"This needs to be a decision made jointly and unless you have another proposal then this is all we currently have. The trial starts on Friday."

He was quickly shrugged off and now it was Macpherson's turn to head to the drinks cabinet, shaking her head on the way at her partner's proposal. Standing on tiptoes she reached to the top shelf and pulled down an old bottle, blew off the dust, unscrewed the lid and poured herself a glass to the brim. She took another large gulp.

"I've thought about it and the answer is still no." She returned to the middle of the room to rejoin Daniels who hadn't moved.

"Well, I need a better proposal from you then by the time I walk into the office tomorrow morning, otherwise I'll be asking him myself."

"You'll do no such thing. He doesn't like you and you know he'll come straight to me for advice if you approach him."

Daniels placed his glass on the coffee table next to him and headed for the library door to leave the room.

"There's clearly no reasoning with you about this tonight so I'll leave," he bit back. Daniels walked out of the open door into the hallway and shouted back, "Just remember who you first lost a case to, and you didn't turn out that bad." He knew exactly what seed he was planting and before he could reach the front door Macpherson poked her head out of the library.

"Come back, let's try and talk about this rationally." After a minute or two of awkward silence Macpherson blurted out what had clearly been on her mind since Daniels first brought up the idea. "Knowing what we know I just don't know if I can do it to him. He's not ready for his first loss."

"From the outside it looks like a sure thing though, doesn't it? Even Sandy's PI couldn't dig up what we know or anything shady about the case so—"

"Let's cut the bullshit," Macpherson said bluntly. "It's DeShawn Arlington. With what we both already know, the outcome is he is going to win. It's what he does."

The room fell quiet again. The two partners were both very tense over the subject and still not any closer to an agreement.

"He is going to win, you're right, but we can treat this as a learning curve for Ryan. See how he reacts and bounces back from defeat."

Macpherson raised her hand to her face and rubbed the side of it as she looked towards one of the room's large bookcases.

"It could be too early, though. He'd be jumping straight into the major leagues."

"Do you see yourself in him? You're mentoring him, after all. How far could he go?" Macpherson now stared into the bottom of her empty glass.

"All the way. He could be named partner one day."

"So then, it's sink or swim time. If he sinks, then we know not to invest any more time." Macpherson was getting annoyed because the more they spoke about it, the more Daniels was starting to make a legitimate case to give it to Ryan.

"I just don't want it to be against DeShawn. It took me a while to get over what happened in our case."

Daniels knew that this inevitably would come up after his earlier comment.

"Yet here we are having this discussion with your name on the door."

Macpherson knew deep down that anything she said, he would have an answer for. Daniels had prepared for this and caught her off guard.

The two continued their debate back and forth but Daniels shut Macpherson down at every objection. Any doubt or question she had against his idea he fired a solution back instantly. Very soon she found herself out of objections. She stood up, collected Daniels' glass and refilled them for the last time that evening. As she turned to come back, Daniels stood immediately behind her and she forced his glass into his hand.

"So, it's settled," he said. "Ryan is going to take the case against DeShawn Arlington. He'll lose but it'll be a learning curve and we get to see how he bounces back from it." He took a sip of his drink and as he lowered the glass, he couldn't hide his smugness at getting his own way. It was clearly visible for Macpherson to see. "It's for his future with the firm."

"Wipe that smirk off your face. He might yet say no."

"Are you kidding?" Daniels couldn't conceal it any longer as his smirk widened and was now ear to ear. "The man is completely obsessed with sport; you think he'd turn down the chance to represent three of the city's biggest stars?"

Once again, his answer silenced Macpherson. She knew in her heart he wouldn't turn down the case whether it was sports stars, movie stars or any old regular Joe because that's the type of lawyer Ryan had become. It looked as if Macpherson had finally accepted defeat. Her mouth was slightly open, but nothing was coming out of it. She stuttered, paused, stuttered again and now knew herself that this discussion was over and by tomorrow morning Ryan would be the first chair on this case.

"OK, he takes the case, but I'm the one to brief him tomorrow morning in the office. Without you anywhere in sight."

They both finished whatever was left in their glasses and stood up, and for the second time that night Daniels headed towards the front door.

"I will pop down to your office around noon. Maybe we could brief him together in the afternoon." He opened the door and stepped out back into the rain.

"We could but we probably won't. You've got your way so just let me deal with it from here on in." Macpherson faked a sarcastic smile and closed the door as Daniels headed back down the stairs. His driver jumped out from the car, avoiding large puddles as he opened the car door, and seconds later they were gone into the night heading back towards the Upper East Side.

"Emilia, I'm home," Ryan called out as he shut the door, took off his shoes and started walking down the hall. He caught a glimpse of himself in the mirror as he walked past and stopped to straighten out his tie and sweep over his usually flawless hair. As he reached the door into the kitchen and living area he flicked on the light.

"Nooooo," Emilia shouted out. "Lights off and close your eyes, please."

Ryan stopped in his tracks, shut his eyes, and back-peddled slowly to turn the lights off. He waited by the door.

"Is everything OK?" he asked. "You do know if you're not wearing any clothes, I have seen it all before."

Emilia walked over to join her husband at the door.

"Don't be so crude, it's just a surprise." She took him by the hand and led him towards the sofa. "Now sit and wait there. Keep your eyes closed."

"We don't get enough time together as it is, I was kind of hoping for a peaceful night."

As the sound of her footsteps got quieter, Ryan squinted to see if he could make out anything. The room was dark. All he could make out was a dim glow from in front of him. Emilia quickly started making her way back, so he closed his eyes again.

"Are you ready? Three, two, one and open."

Just before he opened his eyes a strong smell of pizza filled his nose and he knew exactly what he was going to see.

"Joey's pizza," he said as he opened his eyes grinning.

"Double pepperoni. Just the way you like it."

Ryan then proceeded to scan the rest of the room. The lights were off and lit candles were scattered throughout the apartment which would have explained the dim glow. As he looked down to the table in front of him a six-pack of Heineken was chilling in an ice bucket next to his favourite large pizza. He looked back up and was met with his wife's cheesy grin.

"Surprise," she squealed as she extended her arms to show everything off.

"What's this in aid of? I mean I'm not complaining about my favourite pizza on a Tuesday night, but I thought we were being healthy again?"

"Well, it's not every Tuesday night that your husband wins his twenty-ninth case in a row, is it?" Her open arms were now draped over his shoulders and she pulled him in for a cuddle.

"How did you hear about the win already?"

She gently pushed him back onto the sofa and sat down next to him.

"You should know by now I hear about everything. I'm very well connected." Laughing she grabbed the TV remote and flicked it on. "Let's scrap the usual TV and watch a film as well."

"*Moneyball*," Ryan said eagerly. "I might just have to win a case every night of the week if this is what it's worth."

Empty bottles of beer lined the table, Emilia's glass of wine had a mouthful left in it and two slices of pizza remained in the box. About fifteen minutes of the film remained as Brad Pitt's character Billy Beane was shown round the Boston Red Sox stadium. The night had got the better of both Ryan and Emilia after they'd discussed the case as they had both fallen asleep on the sofa under a blanket. Ryan sat upright with his feet on the edge of the table and Emilia had her head on Ryan's shoulder and was sprawled across the sofa. All of a sudden, the dim light turned into a bright one as Ryan's phone started to vibrate furiously beside him on the arm of the sofa. He shot up immediately and in doing so woke his wife as well. The pair of them, startled, didn't know what was going on but after quickly coming to his senses Ryan picked up his phone to see Macpherson's name on the screen. He glanced at the time; it was 12.15 a.m. Surely Macpherson wasn't calling at this hour to congratulate him on winning the case.

"Can't the pleasantries wait until the morning? I'll be in the office in eight hours or less," Ryan said as he answered the phone through a yawn.

"Congratulations. Well done. You did your job," Macpherson retorted in an ironic but harsh tone. "Now, are you alone? This is a business call."

Ryan nudged Emilia's head off his shoulder and then shuffled off the sofa. He made his way towards the bedroom so he could take the call in private.

"I am now. What's up?" He shut the door to the bedroom and left a tired Emilia to clear up the food and drink.

"I need to ask you something and I need you to think very carefully about the answer before you reply." With bated breath Ryan waited for his boss to continue talking. "Sandy is off the DeShawn Arlington case. Do yo—"

"Yes, I'll take it." Ryan cut off Macpherson mid-sentence and did exactly the opposite to what she told him to do.

Macpherson sighed. "Ryan, do you ever listen?"

"I knew what you were going to say so I saved you finishing the sentence. Of course, I'll take that case on." Ryan could hear through the phone as Macpherson nervously shuffled some papers around her end.

"Ryan, this isn't your average case against DeShawn. He has a reputation."

"And so do I," Ryan interrupted again.

"Yes, I know, but you're building your reputation, he already ha—"

"Do you think I'm not ready for this?" Ryan was getting a hunch that although Macpherson was offering him the case, she didn't really want him to take it.

"Will you let me finish already before jumping to any more conclusions?" Ryan held back; he could sense how irate

Macpherson was. "You know how highly I think of you, Ryan, but I also want you to know my reservations. DeShawn is a dog. He's where he is for a reason." A rare occasion occurred as Ryan didn't know how to take what he perceived to be a backhanded compliment. Macpherson continued, "Am I on the fence about you taking this? Yes. If you decide to accept the case, will I back you as much as I possibly can? Yes."

"Then it's decided, I will take the case with your backing." That wasn't the answer that Macpherson wanted to hear, she'd hoped to convince Ryan to at least sleep on it so she could hatch some kind of plan to put him off accepting it tomorrow when they met in the office. Ryan's phone started to vibrate in his ear, Daniels was calling. "Hey, Daniels is calling me. I assume it's related to this?" "Let it ring out, he'll just think your asleep. I want to speak to you in my office before Daniels has an input in this."

The decision to answer the call was taken out of his hands as he put the phone to his ear to finish the conversation and his battery died. Annoyed, Ryan plugged his phone in and headed to the bathroom.

"Who was that calling so late?"

Emilia was already changed and in bed by the time Ryan remerged from the bathroom.

"It was…" Ryan remembered that Macpherson had asked for him to be alone when taking the call, "… Macpherson. She just called to say congratulations for winning the case."

Emilia rolled over, yawning in the process and flicked her bedside lamp off.

"That couldn't have waited a few hours until the morning?"

"You know what she's like, Em, she doesn't switch off. Ever." Ryan pulled back the covers and joined his other half in bed. In the last twenty minutes since being awoken by Macpherson's call he had gone from fast asleep to wide awake.

His mind was racing with a million different thoughts so going to sleep wasn't going to happen. The main one being in less than three days' time he would be thrust into the limelight and the biggest case of his career. Emilia seemed to drift back off to sleep fairly quickly which allowed Ryan to lay there staring at the ceiling. His phone came back to life to give his side of the room a white glow. Ryan picked it up immediately to see a message from Macpherson:

*My office first thing in the morning. This is far from agreed.*

## 02

# WEDNESDAY 14TH OCTOBER, 5.55 A.M.

Ryan rolled over and looked at the clock beside his bed. The time read 5.55 a.m. He had got into bed at gone midnight and all in all he couldn't have slept for more than two hours. He had been to the toilet about eight times, been into the kitchen to get a drink about six times and then spent half the night quietly pacing around the bathroom trying not to wake up his other half. Macpherson's doubt in him during their phone call had made him want to prepare as much as he possibly could before they met that morning. Not wanting to look and feel awful, he was prepared to give it one last attempt to sleep before his alarm but failing that he was going to get up and get going with his day. He rolled over and in doing so nudged Emilia in her lower back with his knee. She kicked out at him.

"Will you please go to sleep or just get up and stay out the bedroom." She flipped her pillow over and pulled the covers up over her shoulder. Ryan's decision was made. He got up. Making his way out of the bedroom he slipped into his dressing gown and closed the door behind him. He switched the TV on then muted it before making his way over to the kitchen, picking up the cold slices of pizza that were left over. He sat down in front of the TV; truth be told he wasn't really paying any attention to what was on the screen. As he finished the first slice of pizza it dawned on him that this would be the first case that he would need to use a private investigator. He started to think hard about who he could ask for recommendations and soon his imagination was running wild with who he might hire, what they might find and how he would use it in the case.

With the time edging closer to 7 a.m. now, Ryan had decided to go to work and get into the office as early as possible to set up his day. Not wanting to disturb his wife again, he ironed a shirt that had just been washed and used the same suit from the day before. Which was very unlike him. He got ready in the bathroom in the hallway, avoiding the ensuite, and put on his shoes that were by the front door. As he closed the door, he texted Emilia to let her know that he had already left and didn't want to wake her. Next, he ordered an Uber to take him to the office. Ryan waited patiently downstairs for it to arrive. When it did, he ran down the steps and into the back to avoid getting his suit wet as the rain from last night had continued into the next day. As the car moved quickly down towards the office, Ryan rested his head on the window and watched as the sky began to lighten up. He fell into a deep daydream thinking about multiple ways on how this case could play out but the car stopping abruptly outside the office brought him back to reality. He smiled at the driver and said thank you before getting out and making his way into the Manhattan skyscraper.

As expected for this time of the morning the office was largely still in darkness. A couple of associates looked to have pulled all-nighters by their dishevelled looks and the Chinese takeout boxes by the bin in the reception. Ryan walked past a maintenance person who was fixing a light in one of the meeting rooms and pushed open the glass door to his office. As he flicked the lights on a voice greeted him.

"Morning, Ryan."

"Jesus Christ. You scared the life out of me, what are you doing sitting in the dark in my office?" Daniels was positioned on the sofa towards the right side of the office, his suit jacket next to him, and one foot on the table with an empty whiskey glass in his hand. "What an unpleasant surprise this is first thing," Ryan continued as he put his briefcase on the table and made his way over to his desk. "What can I do for you?"

"It's more about what I can do for you, Mr Jackson, in this instance." Daniels stood up and walked towards Ryan. "I would like you to take on the De—"

"I've already agreed to do it. I spoke with Macpherson late last night." Ryan cut across Daniels as he opened his laptop and started to look at his emails.

"What time? I called you last night as well."

"Yes, I saw. I was already on the phone to Macpherson when you called." Ryan was tapping away at his keyboard, trying not to make eye-contact with his boss.

"So why did you not call me back when you had finished your call?" Ryan continued to tap away at his keyboard whilst Daniels waited impatiently for an answer. "Well?"

"Well, what?" Ryan said now looking up at Daniels. "It was gone midnight after I got off the phone and I went to sleep before things inevitably pick up pace today." He went back to what he was doing which immediately enraged Daniels. He pushed Ryan's laptop closed.

"In future, if your boss rings you and you're awake you either pick up or call him back. OK?"

"I would if it was Macpherson and not you." Ryan stood

up and leaned on his desk and was now virtually nose to nose with his boss, both of them snarling at each other.

"What on earth is going on here?" Macpherson said as she walked into the room. "I told the pair of you not to talk to each other before I was in and here you are looking like you're about to start a goddam boxing fight."

"It's 8 a.m. and he was in my office waiting for me when I arrived – what did you want me to do?"

"What I want you to do right now, is shut up." She looked over at Daniels. "We had a deal last night. What do you think you're doing?" He shuffled back towards the sofa he was sitting on when Ryan first entered the room. "In fact, I don't want you to answer that. I'll talk to you later." Quickly, looking rather sheepish, he made his way out of the office, closing the door on his way out.

Macpherson turned her attention back to Ryan.

"Is this how you really want to start today off? Like this?"

Ryan opened his laptop and turned it round to face Macpherson. Solitaire was on the screen.

"I was just making it look like I was working to try and get rid of him."

"And you just had to give in, didn't you?" Macpherson moaned heading towards the door. "We don't have time for this. I'm supposed to be preparing you for the biggest trial of your life."

"Let's get going then. We're both here now so what's stopping us?"

"My office at 9 a.m. Not a minute later."

"Ryan is now on the case." Macpherson swivelled around on her chair to face the New York skyline. There was a slight pause as the person on the other end of the phone responded. "That's correct, Ryan Jackson. It's certainly going to make the case interesting."

As she scoured the city's buildings she ran out of window and her eyes met the large clock on the far wall of her office. It was 8.59 a.m. "I've got to go," she said hastily. She could see Ryan now only steps away from her office door. "I'll call you back later."

As Ryan walked in, she put the phone down and sat up straight.

"Who was that? Anyone important?"

"No one interesting, just a client moaning about their board." She pointed to where she wanted Ryan to sit and then got up to sit with him. "How much sleep did you get last night?" she asked as she sat down opposite him.

"Not a lot. I thought about a million and one things related to this case."

"Just as I thought you would do," Macpherson chuckled as she leaned forward to the table to pick up the large pile of folders. "Are you sure you want this?"

"I've never been so sure of something in my life."

She passed him the papers. He held the majority of them, but a few fell onto the floor. "These are your case papers. Everything that Sandy had should be in there."

Ryan bent down to scoop up what was on the floor.

"I thought you wanted to prepare me for this?"

"My preparation was me telling you about it last night on the phone; you've had nine hours." Macpherson started to walk back towards her desk. "So, unless you want me to win the case for you as well, I suggest you get to work. Welcome to the major leagues."

Wanting to show initiative, Ryan ensured he had all he needed and headed towards the door. He still had the niggling thought in the back of his mind about using a private investigator. He left the room but after two or three steps changed his mind and turned back.

"I assume I'm going to need to hire a PI?"

Macpherson was caught slightly off guard by Ryan's question so ushered him back inside the room and told him to shut the door behind him.

"Why would you need a PI?"

"To look into the case and make sure everything is in order so there won't be any surprises?"

"Do you not think Sandy would have already done that?" Macpherson raised her finger to point at what Ryan was holding. "I've just told you. Everything you need is in there."

"Do you know who she used?"

Macpherson rapidly started to become irritated that Ryan was pressing ahead with his questioning.

"I don't, Ryan," she replied firmly. "She reports into Daniels. Just like you report more into me. So, I assume it would have been someone he recommended." Macpherson, thinking her answer would have satisfied Ryan, turned her laptop on and started to type in her password.

"I shouldn't get my own one to look into the case then?"

"Do you even have a PI, Ryan? One you can really trust and that would deliver you what you wanted on two days' notice?"

"No, I was going to ask you to rec—"

"Well, then in this instance I suggest you review what you have, get up to speed with everything and start to prepare yourself accordingly."

If you got close enough the only noise coming from Ryan's office was either him frantically flicking through the case briefs or him groaning at all the information he was having to digest. He had skipped lunch as he tried to consume as much of the material as he possibly could and with time ticking on towards the end of the day, he was starting to flag a little bit. He pulled open his draw to see if there were any protein bars in there, but he was met with empty wrappers. He really didn't want to leave the office. He turned his personal phone off from airplane mode and before he could load a food delivery app, he was met with an abundance of missed calls, emails, and text messages. Most of them were from Emilia. It dawned on Ryan that he had left this morning without as much as a goodbye and had been uncontactable throughout the day. He sent her a text message telling her he would explain everything that evening when he was home and went back to ordering food. Within fifteen minutes he had sushi on the way and his head buried back in the mountain of papers laid out in front of him. It wasn't long before a new noise occurred in the form of a knock on his office door. Daniels was standing there holding out what smelt like Ryan's sushi. Ryan reluctantly ushered him in knowing he would otherwise have to get up for his food.

"I bumped into this guy coming out the elevator," Daniels said as he placed it on the desk. Ryan peered into the bag to make sure everything was there. "I also wanted to apologize for earlier." Daniels extended his hand out to Ryan. "I know this must be a crazy day for you and I acted inappropriately."

Ryan waited a few seconds before half-heartedly shaking his hand because an idea had presented itself in which Daniels was needed.

"Sit down." Ryan gestured towards the chair next to where he was sitting. "If you're really sorry then you might be able to help." Ryan screwed one of the pieces of paper up and threw it into the trash can by the side of his desk. "This guy has never been on the losing side in a case, right?" He puffed out his cheeks and pushed himself back in his chair.

"Never," replied Daniels. "He always finds a win no matter how much it looks as if he's in the wrong."

Ryan wandered aimlessly around his office, deep in thought.

"So, what makes this case any different then? Why is this

one billed as a sure thing?" He continued over to the far side of his office and stopped with his back to Daniels. He waited for an answer.

"I don't know. Maybe his time is up; is that not clear in the briefing?"

"I think it's not as clear cut as people think and he will have a trick or two up his sleeve." He turned around and picked up a folder and threw it towards Daniels.

"What's this?" he asked as he opened it and looked at what's inside.

"Nothing important," Ryan laughed. "But I distracted you for a split second with something that looked important but was completely irrelevant."

"Do you think that's what he is doing to us then?" Daniels stood up, placing the folder back on Ryan's desk.

"Well, you said it yourself, he's never been beaten so what do you think about the case now you're involved?"

"Maybe he got old? Sloppy? Maybe this is even a step too far for him?"

"Maybe that's what he wants you to think." Ryan quickly returned to his desk and flicked through the folders until he found what he was looking for. He turned around and placed the papers into Daniel's hand. "However, these are really relevant. Take a look." Daniels unclipped the sheets of paper and skimmed through the contents. There were five pages in total. "Sum this up for me quickly?"

"This is the report from the PI Sandy used for the case. He reported nothing out of the ordinary after an extensive search on DeShawn and the plaintiffs. She showed me this when it came through. Don't you believe him?"

"I'm only a couple of hours into this and my gut is telling me to hire a new PI." Ryan could see that something was on the tip of Daniels' tongue. "Thoughts?"

"I think that whatever Macpherson told you when you broached the same topic with her is what you should do."

Ryan's PA knocked on the door and ushered Daniels outside. After he exited Ryan picked up one of the lighter folders and flung it across the room sending sheets of paper in all directions. He slumped into his chair; his primary thought was that he didn't agree with Macpherson & Daniels regarding the use of a new PI before the case started.

The night sky was now the backdrop to Ryan's office as he continued to go back and forth over information he had already read at least three times over. Half-lit buildings occupied his eyeline upon every glance up. The day had felt like a week which was largely down to the lack of sleep, food and a constant flow of whiskey which started at around 4 p.m. A steady stream of personal calls, messages and fantasy basketball updates ensured Ryan's distractions were more frequent than he would have liked as his day came to a close. As he silenced another call from a friend, Ryan's PA called out from outside his office.

"Ryan, Emilia is on the line. She wants to know if you have left."

Ryan responded with a thumbs up and then opened his palms to show the number ten. He closed what he was reading and heard his PA tell his wife he had left the office ten minutes ago. He put everything case related into his briefcase, with some folders too big to fit in, and before exiting the office checked to make sure he hadn't forgotten anything.

"Thank you," he said as he walked past his PA. "I owe you. The usual?"

She laughed and nodded at Ryan as he swiftly made his way through the office towards the elevator.

As he stepped out onto the sidewalk it was the first time in over twenty-four hours that there wasn't rain falling. He looked around for a yellow cab to hail down to get home quickly but as he spun round, he collided with someone. Ryan dropped the case files and a number of them fell onto the sidewalk. As he bent down to collect them, he noticed that the person he collided with wasn't helping but remained in the same place. Unexpectedly, Ryan then felt someone very close to his face. A rough, disgruntled voice filled his ear.

"Do yourself a favour and leave those documents on the floor or put them in the bin behind you."

Ryan looked up at the person. Nothing out of the ordinary: American, unshaven, tanned skin, probably late thirties or early forties.

"Sorry, what did you say?" Ryan responded as he stood back up.

"You heard me. Lose the files."

Ryan's face was covered with a puzzled expression. He didn't really know what to say or who the person was.

"This isn't the minor leagues anymore, *kid*. DeShawn Arlington sends his best wishes and says to get lost before Friday morning." The man barged past Ryan and seconds later he was just another New Yorker, gone into the crowds. In a temporary daze over what had just happened Ryan found himself almost stuck to the concrete under his feet. Torn between continuing his journey home and wanting to explore what had just happened, he stood like a statue as life around him continued.

"Excuse me, sir, does this belong to you?" A young girl wearing an NYU sweatshirt was holding two pieces of paper just below his eyeline. "Excuse me, sir?" She repeated herself as Ryan didn't acknowledge or respond to her original question.

"Yes, yes, they're mine. Thank you." Ryan took the papers and shoved them back into his bag. He put his arm out and flagged down a cab driving towards him and got in. Emilia had messaged to say dinner was in the oven. Determined not to let this case take over his night, he zipped the bag up and switched off the notifications to his work emails. He opened his text messages to reply:

*Terrible traffic on 5th, I'll be home ASAP.*

## 03

# WEDNESDAY 14TH OCTOBER, 8.39 P.M.

Ryan slammed the cab door as he rushed to the entrance of his apartment. He stopped just short as he fumbled around searching for the fob to gain entry into the building. Whilst trying to juggle his briefcase, case papers and mobile he patted down his jacket and trouser pockets trying to work out where it was. Not being able to reach his inside pocket, he put his briefcase on the floor and reached in to retrieve the fob knowing it was there as it was the only pocket he hadn't been able to reach. He hovered it over the pad and the green lights appeared for him to enter. As he picked everything back up to go in, before he could push the door, he heard a faint sound behind him.

"Pssst."

Ryan turned around but initially couldn't see anyone. As he turned back to the door the noise came again, but slightly louder.

"Psst, Ryan."

This time around he looked beyond the sidewalk towards

the park trees that lined the opposite side. He could make out a figure dressed in dark clothes nestled between two thick trunks. He put his briefcase and case papers inside the building and approached with caution. After what had just happened outside the office this person could be anyone. As Ryan got closer, he recognized the person's face.

"Sandy, is that you?"

She beckoned Ryan into the park with her hand. There was a gate to enter around 150 yards up so Ryan walked towards it whilst Sandy walked the same route on the opposite side. As he entered, she embraced him, squeezing him tightly for around thirty seconds or so before letting him go. Her hand gently brushed his cheek before the two went back to standing opposite each other.

"Is everything OK? Why are you dressed like this lurking around my apartment?" Ryan was confused to see his colleague in this setting because he was used to seeing her dressed pristinely in the office on a daily basis. She took his hand and led him away from the gate of the park towards somewhere a little quieter.

"I just wanted to make sure you were OK?"

"I'm fine, why wouldn't I be?" The longer this chance encounter went on the more and more confused Ryan was starting to become.

"I heard from Daniels that you were taking on the DeShawn Arlington case. I came to the office to talk to you and saw what happened outside."

"You saw that?" Ryan's tone became heightened.

"Yes, I had just got out of a cab on the opposite corner. Without hearing what was said I knew exactly what was going on." Sandy grabbed Ryan's hand once again. "They didn't tell you why I came off the case, did they?" Her tone had now also changed to a more urgent one.

"No, they didn't, but I didn't exactly ask either."

Sandy scanned the park as if she was expecting someone to be watching or listening to them.

"So naive, so blinded. Follow me." She picked up the pace and headed towards the opposite side of the park.

"Where are we going? I really need to get back and see Emilia." Ryan trailed Sandy by about five paces as they exited the park onto the Upper East.

"You need to know what you're getting yourself into because they won't tell you." She looked left and right upon reaching the road and then headed towards a parked cab. Ryan glanced but stepped out and continued to follow her. "Pelham Bay Park, please, and hurry." Ryan fell back onto the seat and shut the door. The cab U-turned and headed north.

"Did you say Pelham Bay Park? Why are we going to the Bronx at this time of night?" Sandy leaned forward to close the hatch so the driver couldn't hear their conversation.

"There's someone I need you to meet, and it had to be somewhere remote."

"So, you chose the Bronx at what will likely be gone 10 p.m. at night. Are you insane?"

They hurtled towards the Robert Kennedy Bridge, which via Randalls Island would take them into the Bronx and out west towards Pelham Bay.

"I told you there's someone you need to meet, and it couldn't be in Manhattan, or even Brooklyn for that matter." Sandy's reluctance to reveal too many details as to who they were meeting or where they were exactly going made Ryan start to become concerned for his colleague's state of mind.

"Sandy, let's get out of here and maybe we could grab a drink or a coffee, whatever you'd prefer."

"No, I need to do this. You need to hear it."

The cab slowed down as it exited the Hutchinson River Parkway and towards the park.

"Is there somewhere specific you'd like to go," the driver said re-opening the hatch to the back of his cab.

"Yes please, Glover's Rock."

After a few hundred yards the driver pulled over and flicked on his light.

"That'll be $225, please." Sandy handed over four $100 bills and didn't want for any change, instead telling the driver to wait for their return.

Around twenty minutes passed as the pair stood outside. Sandy had continued to be evasive and had barely strung a sentence together since they arrived. Ryan took his phone out of his pocket to check the time; it was 10.14 p.m.

"Sandy, what are we doing here? I'm absolutely freezing, and Emilia is going to kill me when I eventually get home." Ryan had not contacted his wife since he left the office and told her he was on 5th Avenue – over two hours ago.

"One more minute and it will all become clear."

His breath now visible in the cold night air, he frustratingly turned round to see a tall figure approaching them both, from the beach and promenade area.

"Erm, Sandy, is this who or what we're waiting for?"

Sandy turned to stand next to Ryan and then walked towards the figure, ushering Ryan to follow her.

"Thank you, thank you, thank you for coming. You don't know how much we both appreciate this."

Ryan offered out a hand to shake.

"Ryan Jackson, nice to meet you."

He was met with a firm shake.

"Nice to meet you too, Ryan." The mystery man didn't reveal his identity. Ryan looked in Sandy's direction for an answer.

"This is my PI, Ryan."

The trio walked back in the direction Sandy's PI had originally come from, heading down towards Orchard Beach. Silence ensued as they walked past the bus terminal and finally reached their destination. They stood still, placed like three points of a triangle as the waves crashed into the sand.

"We had to meet here, out in the open. Away from everything so I know that no one is watching or listening."

The PI took another glance over his shoulders then looked beyond those in his presence, just as Sandy did in the park.

"Start from the top," she said as she cut across him. "It's best if Ryan knows what we know if he's going to go ahead with representing the firm in this case."

"If this is going to jeopardize me and this case then I'm not sure I want to know." Ryan took a couple of steps back and looked to distance himself from whatever was about to happen. "If I win this case then my reputation is going into the stratosphere."

"You're not going to win this case, that's the issue," the PI muttered.

"I'm not sure if you know who I am, but I'm Ryan Jackson. I'm 29-0 and on face value, what I've spent all day reading isn't about to change that."

Sandy sheepishly edged closer to where Ryan was now standing.

"That's because he couldn't put in the report what he knows." She beckoned him to join the pair of them a little further along the beach. "If he would have put down what he knew in writing then he would've been looking over his shoulder for the rest of his life."

Ryan was trying to process what Sandy had just said. How serious was this? The case papers that he had just spent nye on a whole day going through, what were they? Fake? Incomplete? Untrue? The trial started in under forty-eight hours and his cocksure persona for the first time in his career was starting to wither.

"What do I need to know, then? What's missing from my case papers?"

The PI reached into his pocket and showed him a bus ticket to Kansas.

"The information I know has got me a one-way ticket to Kansas until further notice. Are you sure you want to know?"

"Yes, I do, get on with it already." Ryan was becoming impatient with the whole situation he found himself in. He was cold, tired and on top of everything knew he was going to get an earful from his wife whenever he managed to get home.

"Before he starts, Ryan, just to let you know, I'm also leaving the firm because of this." Sandy took a tissue from her pocket and dabbed at the corner of her eye as a tear rolled down her cheek. "All I've worked for since leaving Harvard and this case has ruined decades worth of work in a month."

Ryan extended his arms to console his upset colleague, the tears rolling down her cheeks now marking his suit. All this time his eyes hadn't left the PI.

"I'm sure I want to know. As Sandy said, start from the top."

Before he could begin, the three found themselves blinded by headlights from several SUVs that screeched to a deafening halt at the end of Park Drive. With the engines still running, twelve doors flung open, and chaos ensued. A number of rather large people made a beeline for them. One could be heard shouting.

"You didn't listen, did you, Victor?"

"I told you this wouldn't end well and they would find out. They always do."

The man who Ryan now knew to be Victor turned and fled north towards Two Tree. As the men got closer to Ryan and Sandy neither of them moved, rooted to the spot. They all ran straight past the pair of them in pursuit of Victor who had a handy head start. As the men's footsteps and voices became a distant sound, the surreal encounter had left the pair of them almost unable to function. Finally, Ryan looked at Sandy.

"You have a lot of explaining to do now he is gone."

Before Sandy could muster a response, a long shadow passed through them and disappeared into the midnight ocean. Ryan squinted, raising his arm to block the headlights to try and work out what it was. The person, who was nowhere near as tall or wide as the previous ones, slowly made his way down the beach. Ryan heard Sandy loudly gulp as he got nearer.

"It looks as if my letter you received yesterday hasn't had the effect I wanted it to, my dear." Ryan still couldn't quite make out the face of this person, but his voice sounded familiar. "If I had wanted you and Victor to meet with Mr Jackson here then I would have orchestrated it." No more than half a meter apart, Ryan looked over at Sandy who had turned ghost white, her bottom lip trembling with fear. "Where are my manners, Mr Jackson? Nice to meet you, I'm DeShawn Arlington."

"Sandy, why don't you go and wait in the cab?" Ryan put a firm hand on her shoulder and then the bottom of her back to guide her back towards Glover's Rock. She shuffled her feet quickly and kept her eyes glued to the sand under them. Not once did she look up as she moved past DeShawn. He moved ever so slightly so she didn't bump into him. Just before she was out of his reach, DeShawn grabbed her right arm.

"I hope this is the last time I see you, Sandy. I don't want to have to attend little Miley's Christmas recital." He let go of her arm, she burst into tears and the shuffle became a run. He turned to focus his attentions on Ryan. "Well, it seems as if you and I will be seeing a lot of each other over the next couple of weeks. Shall we get acquainted?"

Ryan couldn't quite believe what was happening. In the last ninety minutes, he had been dragged by Sandy from his apartment to Pelham Bay Park, had met with her mysterious PI and was now standing opposite DeShawn Arlington – the man he was due to face in court come Friday morning.

"I must say this isn't the usual introduction I have with my opposing numbers," Ryan said hesitantly. "I'm usually in a courtroom and speaking to another lawyer."
"I don't do usual, Mr Jackson, I thought you should know that first and foremost." He gestured to shake Ryan's hand.

"I'm OK, thank you. I don't think that's appropriate right now."

"Appropriate? It's just a handshake between two men or is that another tradition that's died with the younger generation?"

Ryan turned around and looked into the direction Victor ran. Nothing. He then tiptoed to look over DeShawn's shoulder in the direction Sandy ran. Nothing.

"Am I being punk'd right now?"

"Are you being what? Punk'd? What's that?" DeShawn replied, still waiting for his hand to be shaken. Ryan had taken all that he could and walked almost through DeShawn heading back towards the cab. "I wouldn't do that if I was you, Ryan," he snarled as he grabbed his hand and pulled him closer.

They were just a few centimeters apart now. Ryan pushed off.

"I've just seen your henchman chase after a PI, watched you intimidate Sandy and now you want to shake my hand?" Ryan headed for the road once again. "Intimidation will not work against me. All it shows me is you're scared that you're about to lose for the first time."

This time DeShawn didn't pull him back but as he reached the road, one of his henchmen, as Ryan called them, stepped out from an SUV and blocked his path. DeShawn walked up behind him.

"Ten minutes, that's all I ask."

Knowing that he wasn't going to be allowed to leave until this conversation had taken place, Ryan reluctantly climbed into the back of the SUV as DeShawn got in the other side.

"I've heard a lot of positive things about you, Ryan. You don't mind if I call you Ryan, do you?" DeShawn signaled for the car to start moving. "Your representation of Brittany Fornals in the case against Chamberlain Real Estate was very astute. I can't believe you won that."

The car had done a U-turn and was heading back towards Hutchinson River Parkway. As they drove past Glover's Rock, Ryan noticed that the cab and Sandy were now gone.

"Erm, thanks, I suppose."

"No problem. Drink?" DeShawn opened a side cabinet in the back and pulled out two glasses.
"I'm OK, thank you. Where are we going, DeShawn?"

"You're going home, Ryan," he replied with a small smirk on his face. "We're just making sure you get there OK."
"I'm going home," Ryan repeated sounding rather bewildered. "You know where I live?"

"I know where you live, where you work, who you're married to, how many siblings you have, where they live and who they're married to." DeShawn poured himself a glass of what Ryan thought was bourbon.

"I was only appointed to the case officially this morning. How is that even possible?"

"Imagine what else I could find out if you gave me time to do so?"

"You're not going to intimidate me; I've already told you that."

The smirk appeared back on DeShawn's face.

"Ryan, my dear boy, I'm not trying to intimidate you. I just want to get to know my latest dance partner." They sped back over the bridge into Manhattan, past Marcus Garvey Park towards Columbia University. "I need you to know that I am a winner. I need you to know that no matter what you think you know, you will not win."

Ryan didn't respond immediately. He thought about his answer.

"Victor has something on you that you didn't want me to know, and I will find out what that is because when all is said and done – I'm also a winner."

"Not from Victor you won't," DeShawn said, now visibly chuckling to himself.

The car slowly rolled outside Ryan's apartment, park side, where he had met with Sandy just a couple of hours before.

"So, this is you, Ryan." The henchman had got out to open the door for Ryan. "I'm looking forward to seeing you in a few days and do say hello to that lovely wife of yours for me. Emilia, isn't it?"

As Ryan got out, he turned to look back in the car to see if he had left anything behind. DeShawn once again extended his hand and gestured Ryan to shake it.

"See you Friday, DeShawn." Ryan banged the door and in doing so once again rejected the handshake.

"He's a tough one this one; I like him," DeShawn said to his driver as he got back into the front of the car.

"What do you want me to do, boss? Say the word and it's done."

"Nothing tonight, let's see how the first couple of days of the trial go first."

By the time Ryan had reached the door to his apartment the car was gone. Reaching into his jacket pocket once again he opened the door and to his surprise his briefcase and case papers were still there, untouched. He picked them up and closed the door, opting to stay outside rather than going in. He opened his phone and sent an email to his PA asking her to set up meetings with the sports stars first thing in the morning and marked it urgent. The night's events had cast doubt into his mind that wasn't previously there. He knew DeShawn was shady but for Victor to run and Sandy to act the way she did, something was up. He looked up and he knew that going home wasn't going to help him win the case. As another occupant of the building emerged from a cab, Ryan nodded to the driver. He threw his belongings into the back and once the door was shut, opened his phone to text Emilia:

*Bumped into Sandy on the way home. Going back to the office to continue case prep.*

## 04

# THURSDAY 15TH OCTOBER, 6.17 P.M.

Ryan had not long been back in the office. He had spent most of the day back and forth racing around Manhattan between clients' houses and their teams' training facilities. His meeting with DeShawn Arlington last night was constantly at the forefront of his mind as he ticked them off one by one. He had thoroughly been through each of their accounts, the questions they would face in court and asked them point blank if there was anything he didn't know. Each of them confirmed he knew everything he needed to. As he approached the door to leave his office, he could see both Macpherson's and Daniels' office lights were on. He placed his hand on the handle to exit but paused. A day and half into his first major case, he couldn't go to them asking for help, could he? That would only reinforce Macpherson's original phone call that she didn't think he was ready to take this on. Something just didn't feel right about his case files but it was something that he would have to figure out on his own. He listened to his office voicemails, skimmed over the notes that his PA had left on his desk but nothing he saw and heard was case related. Glancing over at the clock on the far side of his office, Ryan noticed that it had just gone seven o'clock. Although he still had 101 questions in his mind to answer, if he didn't leave the office soon, he wouldn't be able to conduct his usual pre-trial ritual and actually make it home this evening to see Emilia, who hadn't properly seen her husband since late on Tuesday night. Standing up from his large glass desk, Ryan loosened his sea-blue tie and unbuttoned his creased navy-blue suit jacket. He headed for the door, finishing his double whiskey on the walk and placing the glass on a table just before he exited the room. There was no way he could possibly take on board any more information relating to the trial after the events of the last forty-eight hours. The office was virtually empty at this time barring the same couple of associates he'd seen days before who were working late again on a big case. After a couple of awkward glances which resulted in even more awkward smiles with the juniors that he wasn't yet familiar with, Ryan headed into the elevator pressing the button for the ground floor and ending his thirteen-hour working day. He watched the elevator numbers count down from 23 to 1, his stomach churning at the fact he was leaving unprepared ahead of tomorrow. A sharp ping brought him back round and he exited the elevator and made his way out of the building.

The sun was setting as he made his way onto the crowded avenue and over the corner of 44th and 7th with a pace to his walk to ensure that he made his night's first destination in plenty of time. The famous millennial saying that *Thursday is the new Friday* was very much in full effect as he strode past Madison Square Garden, Macys, and Bryant Park attempting to make reality a distant thought for a few hours. The bars and cafes he passed that served alcohol were packed full of city workers both male and female clearly winding down after a stressful week; in Ryan's mind they didn't know what a stressful week was. He continued his quick walk north towards Central

Park. Hitting the park and heading west just past 59th he could now see the sign that he was longing for, Mulligans Irish Bar. However, it was barely readable because the light above it was half broken and the sun had now set on the city.

Almost skipping over the last crossing before the bar, he made it through the double doors just after 7.30 p.m. which meant, national anthem aside, he would be seated with a beer before tip-off. Although this was a pre-trial night ritual it was almost always accompanied by a basketball game. This evening was extra special though as Ryan's beloved Brooklyn Nets were facing off against borough rivals New York Knicks at the famous arena he had passed just moments beforehand. As he headed towards the busy bar area that was filled with recently qualified lawyers dressed a lot cheaper than he was, one of the regular bartenders had noticed his arrival and had already popped the cap off a Heineken bottle and presented it to him as he reached the liquor-soaked, solid oak top.

"Put that on my tab will you, Joe, because I'll no doubt be having a few more as this game goes on. I'll square you up Sunday with a hefty tip as usual."

Ryan grabbed the ice-cold bottle and headed towards an empty table that had a clear view of the rival match he was eager to watch. As he sat on the wooden bar stool, he reached over to his coat and pulled out his work phone flicking it on airplane mode. He found himself listening to the people surrounding his table talk about both current cases on which they were juniors and their predictions for the game, which was now underway. The Nets' centre, Nic Claxton, had just got the game's first basket.

As the night and game wore on, the Nets looked likely to be heading for a routine victory over their once great neighbors, so twenty-two points clear and the buzzer sounding for the end of the third quarter, Ryan swallowed what was left of his fifth beer, picked up everything he came with and slung his jacket back over his creased white shirt. Making his way towards the exit he glanced in the direction of the bar and caught Joe's eye as he took an order from another regular. They both acknowledged Ryan leaving and he subtly slipped out onto the now dark street, lit only by the street's lamp posts – the time was fast approaching 9.30 p.m.

Not quite as quickly as he walked from the office to the bar but quicker than usual, Ryan made his way up the barely lit blocks and headed for his Upper West Side penthouse pondering the imminent case, but more importantly how it was going to change his life either for better or worse. Truth be told, he was also excited to spend a full weekend with his wife. The PA to a major real estate tycoon who owned a global company, Emilia was largely able to work where and when she wanted to but more often than not, she found herself flying from major city to major city to ensure the company's stakeholders were kept happy. In turn this continued to make her boss more money than an average worker's wildest imagination. It was simple; the richer her boss got then the easier her job was on a day-to-day basis. Since becoming one of Manhattan's most highly regarded and in-demand lawyers after his move to Macpherson & Daniels, Ryan and Emilia's quality time had dwindled and had not quite put a strain on their relationship, as of yet, but things could easily head that way with his twelve to fifteen-hour days and her usually spending weekends away on business. He always saw Emilia working as unnecessary because of the large sums of money he made. As he approached the main door to their building, he stopped off at the independent convenience store the block before and bought his wife's favorite bunch of flowers and a vintage bottle of Château Beychevelle.

He slowly entered his key into the front door of the penthouse and maneuvered his way in trying to make as little noise as possible to try and surprise his wife, but she had the game on in the background while cooking dinner and knew he'd be home before the final buzzer with the Nets holding such a commanding lead. Making his way down the long, dark hallway towards the kitchen, a strong smell of freshly prepared Mexican food filled his nose and just before he got in sight of Emilia she quipped, "I'm glad you actually made it home this evening considering the stunt you pulled last night. Any later this evening and your dinner would have been in the bin." She knew that Ryan had his pre-trial ritual but thought after the eventful night he had yesterday he would have come straight home to spend some time together. "Also, don't for one moment think a cheap bunch of flowers and an expensive bottle of wine is going to make a single bit of difference!"

Now questioning his choice of firstly going to Mulligans and then buying both the items she had just mentioned, he threw the flowers down the hallway and gently placed the bottle of wine on the floor before entering the room.

"Honestly, you'd never believe the day I've had. I've been to Midtown, to Westchester, to Brooklyn and the office on four separate occasions. Then I had to help Jordan with his case against the Prospect Park Murderer."

Emilia knew the last part wasn't true but couldn't be bothered to challenge him on it. Ryan made his way towards his wife with a big cheesy grin on his face, arms open for an embrace but as he leant in to kiss her on the cheek, she smelt the beer immediately which confirmed where he'd been, and that wasn't the office working with Jordan. Deciding not to act on her instincts knowing her husband's imminent big case she turned to the oven to take out the chicken enchiladas and Ryan headed towards the sofa to catch the remaining minutes of the basketball game.

"Dinner's ready, Ry. Can we at least eat without the distractions of TV tonight?" Emilia asked what many would see as a simple request but when it came to the Nets and Ryan it was like trying to prize candy away from a baby. He slowly made his way over to the kitchen table and finally made eye contact with his wife as the buzzer sounded and the game finished.

"So, when is the next trip to Denver?" he said taking his first mouthful of steaming hot food.

"I assume you mean Dallas, and it's the end of next week. Before you ask, yes, there'll be very little work and lots of keeping Steve's wealthy friends entertained to keep him happy."

The conversation flowed between the pair as they flicked between both of their jobs, general news and some of their mutual friends' problems. After around twenty minutes Ryan smirked.

"Shall I go and get the expensive bottle of red you didn't want?"

Reappearing with the bottle he had previously left outside, Ryan poured two large glasses and returned to the table to finish off dinner and resume the conversation. Although it had now turned to general chit chat, neither of them wanted to stop for fear Ryan's mind would start to wander. Both of them, Ryan in particular, knew that tomorrow he started the biggest court case of his legal career so far which would also see him put his perfect case record on the line against a man he'd already found to be incredibly shady. However, Ryan being the newcomer amongst the big boys, the self-proclaimed hotshot and the up-and-coming star that he was, he couldn't wait to open his eyes the next morning. He would be representing three of the city's most well-known and respected athletes in the NBA: star point guard Luke Best; two-time Superbowl MVP quarterback Henry Craig and the most decorated NHL player in the last decade, Matt Woodman, as they sued their now former super-agent and NYC sports management icon, DeShawn Arlington, for financial mismanagement in a case worth millions of dollars to not only the defendants but also to Macpherson & Daniels. DeShawn was someone the general public had grew fond of as he was born and raised in Brooklyn to a working-class family, and his rags to riches story was widely covered by the city's media after his company signed some of the country's most talked about athletes.

"Are you ready for tomorrow?" Emilia said nervously, not wanting to entice any last-minute jitters Ryan may have had about the case.

"Of course I'm ready, Em. I met with Luke, Henry and Matt throughout today as well as doing all the due diligence I possibly could after running into Sandy last night – I'm going to be fine. I can already picture the headlines in the *New York Journal* when I go 30-0."

Ryan meant what he said but it was also half an act to cover up the doubts he had. They'd finished dinner by now so collected both bowls, stood up and headed towards the dishwasher to tidy up what had been dirtied from preparing the dinner. A very short silence ensured between the pair before Emilia continued to voice her concerns for her husband.

"I've heard and read a lot of the stories about this man, Ryan, and they don't fill me with a lot of confidence. He seems like a bit of a scumbag, and *he always seems to win.*"

Having finished loading the dishwasher, Ryan now made his way back to the kitchen table and cuddled his clearly concerned wife from behind. He didn't get to see this side of

Emilia very often as she had a hard outer shell despite being a very gentle and caring person.

"I honestly can't see this going any other way than a resounding win for the firm and me," said Ryan as he looked to reassure his wife that this case was just like any other of the previous twenty-nine on which he'd led. Knowing that she was already booked in for another business trip at the back end of the following week Ryan wanted to try and settle the nerves which Emilia always got around the start of a new case for him. He gazed lovingly into her eyes and taking both her hands he added, "Listen, by the time you fly to Denver next week this will all be done and dusted, and I might even take a few days' holiday and fly out with you – how does that sound?"

"That actually sounds great. I'd love that," Emilia replied, not bothering to correct him again.

Now with the elephant in the room temporarily squashed and her concerns for him in the open she ushered him towards the L-shaped sofa that overlooked Central Park to the east and flicked on the TV, switching it from NBA highlights to a DVD which she had seemingly prepared beforehand.

"You owe me this from after last night," she whispered, curling up on the sofa underneath a fluffy grey blanket with another bottle of red wine.

Emilia snuggled into Ryan as he reluctantly settled for the romantic film they'd both seen a hundred times, but it was easy viewing and didn't require too much attention considering it was gone 11 p.m. No words were spoken by either of them and as the film's plotline developed, Ryan glanced his tired eyes at the clock. He realized it was now under nine hours until the biggest case of his career got underway. For the first time in his career, he'd be thrust into the limelight for the entire country's media to scrutinize his every move.

He picked up his phone to see multiple notifications from his work emails, social media, messages and missed calls; the eve of a trial was always like this. He tried his hardest to skim through them quickly to see if anything was important but the light from his screen alerted Emilia to what he was doing so she nudged her head into him as a reminder it was their very limited time alone. He put his phone face down on the arm of the sofa and continued to watch the film, but truth be told he wasn't watching at all as his mind was fully focused on tomorrow. His phone buzzed once again so he lifted it slightly to try not to alert Emilia. It was a text message from Macpherson:

*Good luck tomorrow, Ryan, you're going to kill it.*

## 05

# FRIDAY 16TH OCTOBER, 5.55 A.M.

The alarm clock on the bedside table hit 5.55 a.m. and with that a mellow tone radiated throughout the bedroom and the electronic blinds on the far side of the bedroom slowly opened themselves to reveal the green treetops of the borough's most famous park. Having only been in bed for five hours, Ryan slowly pulled back the covers, planted his bare feet on the cold wooden floor then turned to the alarm clock to switch it off. Rising from the bed and looking out the floor to ceiling window over Central Park the tiredness quickly disappeared as it sunk in that today wasn't just any old Friday, it was day number one of a new trial; not just any old trial but it was the DeShawn Arlington case and it started in three hours' time. Today was his Superbowl.

Trying to make as little noise as possible Ryan made his way out of the bedroom and back into the kitchen living area. Like most mornings, he unloaded the contents of last night's dishwasher cycle, made himself a coffee and flicked on the morning news. As expected, before the kettle could even boil the water, his face was plastered across Channel 7's morning news show as they ran a segment on the case that now started in around two and a half hours' time. With Emilia still in bed he chose not to turn the TV up and listen to what they were saying, instead choosing to watch as they flicked between pictures of DeShawn, Luke, Henry and Matt. With a strong coffee now in his hands he made his way towards the hallway bathroom, stepping over the bunch of flowers he quickly disposed of last night. By the time he was done in the shower Emilia was up and pottering around the apartment with breakfast cooking. His lucky suit was hanging on the bedroom door and his shoes had been polished. It was nice having his wife around for the first day of a new trial, but she always made it feel like it was day number one at elementary school. Leaning on one of the kitchen units with nothing but a towel on, Ryan consumed the small breakfast before Emilia had a chance to give him a good morning kiss, and leaving a trail of wet footprints on the floor he made his way to the bedroom to get ready with the clock just gone 7a.m.

He headed towards the front door wearing a suave three-piece navy-blue checkered suit accompanied by brown brogue shoes and his hair looking pristine. Ryan carried his briefcase in his right hand. It contained everything he needed to recap on before entering the courthouse. The conversation this morning had been minimal and unimportant, but it was enough for the pair of them to engage and ensure Ryan didn't start to overthink and lose focus on what was important, which would have been hard because today and this case was all he'd thought about for the last two and a bit days. Emilia had picked the flowers up and put them in a vase, trying to save them from a night and morning without water on the floor. She now occupied the bathroom so as Ryan passed by, he stopped and gave her a gentle kiss on the forehead and turned to leave.

"Please be careful today. I know you sa—" Emilia tried to blurt out a sentence quickly so that she wasn't interrupted but it was no good and Ryan cut her short.

"We went through this last night, didn't we? I'm going to be fine. I'll be home normal time. Love you." Not waiting for an answer because his response was more a statement to ease her concerns, he was gone from the doorway and penthouse within seconds and all that was left behind was the uneasy feeling his wife had had since he arrived home last night.

With the case having the glamour of not only being covered by the country's media but also being held at the New York Supreme Court, it was a little too far downtown for Ryan to retrace his route from the office yesterday evening so he had to head north up Park Avenue and enter the subway station on 86th to catch the A route train down to the financial district. The journey all in all was around forty minutes south to Chambers Street so he had time to take out his notes for the first day of the case and recap, prepare and ensure that he hadn't missed anything. Anything that he knew about, anyway. Today was mainly about confirming who was who in the case, opening statements and they might get to touch briefly on Luke Best's part of the case. Ryan wasn't expecting fireworks immediately, but he was expecting them to come early next week because DeShawn clearly wasn't going to go down without a fight, especially after Wednesday's run-in and millions of pounds at stake. The train had made its way through the first couple of stations so as it fast approached 42nd Street which would then be followed by Penn he knew that the sparsely populated carriage would soon be full of New Yorkers on their morning commute. Wary of who was around him he shuffled his papers, put them back in his briefcase, choosing instead to lean his head back onto the warm glass, close his eyes and go through the opening statement in his head which would set the scene for the forthcoming trial.

Battling his way through the busy carriage as the train rolled into Chambers Street, Ryan stepped onto the crowded platform, looking left and right before heading up towards the exit and making his way to the courthouse. Striding through the tunnels before hitting the stairs, a rather large man sporting a New York Yankees jersey recognized him from the morning news and acknowledged him as they passed by with a slight nod of the head. Ryan's brain started to process that the general public were behind him in this case because of the borough's sports stars involved – if he was to win then maybe he would become a recognizable face himself in NYC. Reaching out with his right hand he pushed the waist-high steel turnstile forwards and with a spring in his step he bounded up the set of stairs leading north to find himself engulfed in the shadows of the courthouse. The buildings seemed to merge into one as he blurred into the background on the opposite side of the road from the entrance. Taking a deep breath, Ryan immersed himself in everything that was going on at that exact moment in the morning as he stood halfway between Lower Manhattan and Wall Street. The sidewalks were a little busier, the traffic a little heavier, the street vendors a little louder but they had to be as across the road from where he stood apart from normal life, stood around two-dozen photographers and a handful of reporters. Gameday was about to start.

Making his way through the thirty or so people with cameras flashing and microphones being thrust in his direction, Ryan lowered his head and focused on the floor as he didn't want to give any comment or be caught with any awkward questions before the trial had started. He wanted to save any media interaction for after he had won. Successfully navigating himself through the crowd and onto the steep steps leading to the court doors Ryan slowed his walk right down now as he was past the madness and wanted to make sure it didn't seem as if he was rushing to get inside. Left foot, right foot, left foot, right foot, left foot.

Now standing at the top of the stairs he lifted his head and made a beeline towards a door already being held open by a security guard. Just as he got to the door the deafening sound of flashing cameras and reporters' shouting filled his ears once again but this time it seemed a hell of a lot louder despite being further away from them. Curiosity got the better of him so he stopped and turned thinking that he would be joined on the walk into the building by his first client involved in the case, NBA point guard Luke Best, but instead what he saw was a shiny black SUV half-parked on the sidewalk with the driver scuttling round to open the door. Ryan already knew it wouldn't be Luke getting out but instead, DeShawn Arlington. Before he could even finish his thought trail there now stood the almighty, or disreputable, depending on who you spoke to, sports agent who represented some of the highest paid and well-known athletes in American sport. Dressed in what the country was now accustomed to seeing him in and not for the occasion, he breezed through the media tightly lipped wearing a baggy white T-shirt tucked into a pair of denim jeans covered by a leather jacket. Dark sunglasses covered his ageing eyes but anyone in the vicinity could see he was fixated on Ryan and by the time he had reached the top of the stairs, they were only a few feet apart and the usually calm lawyer now resembled the charging bull statue just a few blocks from them. DeShawn made it his job to enter the building through the same door that was virtually blocked off by a combination of the security guard and Ryan, and as he squeezed through so close to the other two that you could smell the excessive amount of aftershave he was wearing, he didn't break his stride and certainly didn't mutter a word to

Ryan as he entered the building and then stopped for security checks. The psychological battle had begun, it was 1-0 to DeShawn as Ryan walked in after him perplexed by what he had just witnessed.

After being shown to one of the side rooms of the court to prepare, Ryan took off his jacket to hang it over the back of the chair, unpacked his briefcase and found the notes to go over with Luke upon his arrival. He then headed back over to exit the door once more. He wanted to catch up with Judge Sullivan before DeShawn's representation arrived.

"Knock knock," Ryan said sarcastically as he opened the door to Judge Sullivan's office without waiting for an invitation in. As he peered his head inside the half-open door, his eyes saw the judge already standing and with a big smile on his face.

"Come in, Ryan, how you doing? How's that lovely wife of yours?" he quipped before the door was even shut.

"I'm great, thanks, and she's even better despite still married to me for all her sins. Let's cut the small talk and get right down to the business that we're here for – did you see that game last night?" Ryan knew that Judge Sullivan was a huge New York Knicks fan; he could even have been a season ticket holder at The Garden.

"Don't talk to me about that pile of garbage," was the short and simple answer that came back. "Have you ever seen a shooting guard score seven points all night off eleven three-point attempts?" the judge said angrily as he turned and headed back to the chair that was under his desk. Before Ryan could even look to make a sarcastic comment or joke regarding the Knicks the judge continued his rant without pausing for breath. "Another thing is we need Luke back ASAP because this kid we drafted from Duke last year isn't doing it at all for me."

Being involved in the case coupled with it starting that day, the team's star player hadn't been involved in any of the last four games which subsequently ended in four defeats with three of them being ten points or more.

"Don't worry, Your Honor, we will have this case wrapped up in no time and you'll have your point guard back. It's a very straightforward case of financial mismanagement, there has been no push back from Mr Arlington's team, so I hope to have this wrapped up by this time next week."

A slight pause ensued between the pair but was ended by a timid knock on the door, so it looked as if the basketball chat was going to have to take a back seat. A loud "Come in" from the judge was all it needed for the room's occupancy to move from two to three people. In walked a small man with glasses, scruffy hair as if he hadn't combed it that morning and his suit looking slightly baggy on the bottom. Was this who Ryan would really be squaring off against?

"Good morning, Your Honor, my name is Willia..."

Before the clearly nervous new entry to the room could even finish his first sentence he had finished it for him by his opposing number.

"William O'Neill."

Ryan looked absolutely bewildered that in a case of this magnitude he would be going up against William O'Neill. This was the same William O'Neill that he had shared a classroom with at Yale University and watched as he struggled to get through his degree, graduating by the skin of his teeth with a 2.2 that almost ended any hope of working at a top firm. The last time Ryan had even heard this guy's name, a mutual friend said they thought he was working for a small firm based out in New Jersey dealing with mainly social housing cases and doing a lot more pro bono work than he should have been at that stage of his career.

"As you two are already familiar with each other, which makes my life a hell of a lot easier, I can skip the pleasantries," the judge said standing back up from the chair he'd only been sitting in for a matter of minutes. "Ryan, you're familiar with how I rule my courtroom, William not so much, so let me be very clear: I am tough but fair when it comes to being the man on the bench so as long as you two play by the rules then we will all get along just fine – OK?"

The door was now being held open by Judge Sullivan because he wasn't waiting for an answer, he just wanted an understanding from both lawyers and them out of his chambers as the trial was due to commence in twenty-five minutes so needed to prepare as much as they did. Both lawyers nodded as they walked out of the room.

"Good luck, Ryan, may the best man win," William said with a slight stutter which no doubt didn't help improve Ryan's opinion of him one bit.

"Luck doesn't come into this, Will, it's all about preparation and who's in the right and who's in the wrong and unfortunately for you in this case I'm in the right," Ryan shot back sharply as he turned to walk towards the stairs that would lead him back to the room where his belongings were and hopefully his client for a briefing.

A burly man dressed in all black now covered almost all of the door which confirmed that Luke would be inside the room, and they could have a quick chat to go over everything one last time before the case got underway. Ryan thought about opening the door with a comment about last night's game but immediately changed his mind and wanted to keep the short time they had together strictly business to ensure things went as smoothly as possible.

"Luke, how you doing? Are you nervous at all?" Ryan said

as he walked into the room and tried to make his presence known immediately.

"Nervous? Man, I play in front of 20,000-odd people every other night in one of the world's most well-known arenas. Why would I be nervous now?"

The smiles were mutual as they shook hands and Ryan took a seat, searching for a specific piece of paper to show to his client.

"So just to be clear one final time before we head in and there's no turning back, you believe that DeShawn Arlington stole, or withheld, part of your final year's salary with the Celtics before you signed with the Knicks to the sum of $7.3 million dollars?" The question from Ryan was as blunt as they come but he needed to hear it come out of Luke's mouth one more time to make sure.

"Yes, that's correct, $7.3 million dollars he has of mine." His client confirmed what he already knew but hearing it one more time didn't hurt anybody and that was the reason he was seen as one of the best lawyers in the city; he was thorough and tried his upmost to ensure no stone was left unturned. With time running out before they had to make their way down the corridor and enter the courtroom Ryan had one more question for his client before he fought tooth and nail for him.

"The final thing from me and I know we spoke about this yesterday, but I need you to think long and hard before you answer because there's no turning back after this point. You are positive that there is absolutely no reason why DeShawn has stolen this money from you? There's nothing that he's going to say in there that's going to surprise me?"

By the time Ryan had asked the question their eyes were fixated onto each other's; you could cut the tension in the room with a knife. Then as if he'd just been given some good news or hit the game-winning shot at The Garden, the smile reappeared on Luke's face and he said with a grin from side to side, "I have no idea why he's kept that money. There's no reason behind it as far as I'm concerned. Can we please go get my money back now?"

The clock read 8.55 a.m., and slowly nodding his head, Ryan put his papers into his briefcase and put his jacket back on. As he followed Luke out, he sent a message to Macpherson:

*This is it. It's time.*

## 06

# FRIDAY 16TH OCTOBER, 9.04 A.M.

"Your Honor, members of the jury, it is my job over the coming weeks to prove to you that Mr DeShawn Arlington knowingly stole millions of dollars of his clients' money for his own benefit." As direct and to the point as an opening line could get, Ryan wanted to hammer home the truth into the jury's mind from the offset. "He gained their trust with his rags-to-riches story and his charming persona whilst all the time he was stealing money out of their pockets that they'd rightfully earned." The second part of the statement he wanted to reinforce the crime but also to make the jury aware that the accused could be deceivingly charming when he wanted to be before he called him to the stand later on and they fell for his act. "The final thing from me before I hand over is that I want you all to know how ashamed I am to be a New Yorker today. When this man who is held in such high regard by the great people of this city is a liar and a thief then I cannot be proud of where I come from – hopefully by the end of this case I will have my sense of pride back."

Unbuttoning his blazer as he walked back to his chair, Ryan had nailed the final part of the opening statement in his mind as he appealed to the jury's subconscious feelings about New York and how they perceived it. As Ryan reached his chair it was now the turn of his old classmate William to start his statement.

"Your Honor, ladies and gentlemen of the jury, Mr Arlington would like to strongly deny all claims brought against him by his former clients and go on record to say this is a huge waste of everyone's time. We would go as far as to say this was an abuse of process – thank you."

To everyone's surprise William then turned from facing the jury and the judge and headed back towards his desk where the defendant was uncontrollably grinning.

Ryan's mind was back to racing a thousand thoughts both good and bad at what had just taken place! How on earth could the defense lawyer deliver an opening statement that consisted of about thirty words and lasted under ninety seconds? Was the defendant that much in the wrong that they were going to nod and agree throughout the trial? If that was the case, then why didn't they settle out of court and make this ten times easier and cheaper? Was it the fact that William was so far out of his depth in this case that those words were all he could muster? Had his former college classmate bitten off more than he could chew, and he had only realized that when it came to start the trial? DeShawn was known as a shrewd businessman from Brooklyn who had come from nothing to everything so surely, he would have done his background research when hiring a lawyer in a case that could cost him millions of dollars. By the time all these questions and thoughts had been processed, both lawyers, the plaintiff and the defendant were all sat down facing the judge waiting for further instruction.

'Mr O'Neill, is there anything else you would like to add before we move swiftly onto witness testimonies and cross-examinations? This is your one chance to set the scene for your defense of Mr Arlington," the astounded judge added.

William glanced at DeShawn who gave nothing away before he returned to face the judge.

"Thank you, Your Honor, but that is all we would like to say at this time."

There wasn't a single person in the courtroom who wasn't shocked at what they had just heard from the opening statements and then the chance to add that was declined. Still, it seemed as if both sides had put forward their *arguments* so without further ado it was time to press on.

"Well, in that case I would like to thank both lawyers for their contributions to open the case and we shall proceed."

Standing to become the only man in the room to do so, Ryan called his first witness for the trial.

"We'd like to call Miss Isobel Hayes to the stand."

A tall, slim brunette walked through the room and made her way to the witness stand to start the proceedings. After swearing herself in, Ryan got right down to the nitty gritty straight away.

"Miss Hayes, could you please tell the jury how you know DeShawn Arlington," he asked as he meandered around the empty floor space that separated all involved.

"I was his personal assistant for just under a year. He hired me because a mutual friend introduced us at an event," replied the striking brunette who was looking at the jury whilst answering.

"So, you spent just under a year working with the defendant – how would you describe him?" Ryan wanted to reinforce the comment he had made earlier about how DeShawn could be charming when he wanted to. Isobel took the bait before he'd even finished his sentence.

"How would you describe him?" Still focused on the twelve

jurors and almost avoiding any kind of eye contact with her former boss, the perfect response ensued. "It was like working for Jekyll and Hyde." She took a short pause before continuing, "One moment he'd be very charming, polite and courteous, almost like a father figure to people around the office. Then the next moment he'd be full of anger and hatred, swearing, shouting, raising his voice and this whole other person would appear."

Using the word charming was imperative as it was what Ryan had used earlier; he was only just getting started on tearing down his character.

"What about the type of people he had around him? Clients? Employees? Friends? As his personal assistant, surely you must have seen a lot of people, managed both his work and personal diaries?" The questions were going to be short and simple because he didn't want her to trip herself up by saying the wrong thing but on the other hand Ryan needed to paint the picture he wanted to.

"I only managed his work diary. I never arranged his personal diary; his calendar would just be blocked out. I couldn't see any detail."

"So, you never knew what he was doing when he wasn't in the office?"

'No, I wouldn't – that was either handled by him or Tiffany but never me." Her attention had now finally switched from the jury to her former employer and her piercing green eyes looked like they were trying to burn a hole in him.

"Tiffany? Who was Tiffany?" Ryan knew of her role, but the jury didn't and neither did a lot of other people to be quite honest – including Isobel.

"No one really knew who Tiffany was, she would just show up as and when she pleased, handle DeShawn's personal diary and always dealt with the people unrelated to the business."

Her voice was now stained with a tint of anger, or jealousy, you couldn't quite tell, but she looked as if she was going to launch into a full-scale rant. "It was always about her and nothing I did was ever good enough to be let into DeShawn's world. It was always *Tiff this and Tiff that*."

Feeling his witness starting to lose focus of why she was up there Ryan quickly cut her off before she could continue.

"Finally, from me, Miss Hayes, do you know who handled Mr Arlington's finances? Was there a team or a department in the office that did this?" Character and his personal affairs having already been covered Ryan finally wanted the people in the room to know how shady things really were.

"In the year I worked there I never met anyone or heard anyone talk about someone from finance or accounting, which I thought was weird for such a big company."

His work here was done from the defense's side so now it was down to how his opposite number was going to cross-examine.

"No further questions from me, Your Honor."

Again, it was almost as if he was awaiting instructions from his master as it took a slight nod of DeShawn's head before William stood up and started his questioning.

"Thanks for your answers so far, Miss Hayes, I just have a handful, maybe six, questions that I would like to ask you," he started with. "You worked for Mr Arlington for around a year which has already been confirmed, but why did you leave?"

The piercing green eyes were now nervously flicking from Ryan to DeShawn and then to the jury.

"I left because I found another job which was closer to where I was living." The answer was short just like they had prepared them to be. Glancing over his shoulder at the man he was representing another nod of the head came so he pushed on.

"The real reason why you left my client's company, please, Miss Hayes, and remember you're under oath."

The real reason? The real reason as far as Ryan was concerned was what she'd just said; that's the reason she told him half a dozen times when they'd met just a few days before.

"I, erm, well it was, basically…" – her eyes were now looking at no one in the room but the floor as she hesitated before finishing her answer – "… I had an affair with one of the company's top agents and his wife found out." Ryan gulped and slumped a little into his chair before she continued to dig deeper hole. "His wife gave him an ultimatum that either I left or he did, which he presented to DeShawn and DeShawn chose him because he makes him more money." She turned to Ryan and tried to squeeze out an additional few words. "I couldn't tell you because he made me sign an ND…" Cut off before she could finish William continued to grind away.

"So, when my client relieved you of your duties was it a simple goodbye?"

"Yes, it was. We parted ways and he wished me well," she replied still not knowing where to look.

"There was no financial sum of money exchanged between the pair of you?" The question was asked because the answer was a closed one and would portray DeShawn in a good light.

"He paid me a year's salary so just over $62,000."

"On top of the year's salary he paid you did Mr Arlington also give you an outstanding reference that allowed you to secure your next job, which is the one you're currently in?"

Again, the answer was going to be something that Ryan didn't want the jury to hear.

"Yes, he did."

The response was soft almost as if the witness didn't want to say it and just wanted this to end. It was getting worse and worse by the second, for the case being built against the defendant was being torn down at the first opportunity.

"One final question from me, Your Honor. Miss Hayes, you said DeShawn could get angry and swear and shout at his employees – did he ever lose his temper directly with you or was he more of a father figure like you described earlier?"

"He never shouted at me once, it was always the agents or whoever was calling him."

The damage was done. Ryan thought he had a solid first witness to open with and start to paint the picture that he wanted but she crumbled, instantly. Why didn't she say about the NDA? Making his way back to his chair, back turned on a disheveled witness, William finally finished, "No further questions, Your Honor."

With witness one being more of a hinderance than she was a help Ryan needed to make sure that he nailed the second witness to the cross otherwise the first part of this case was going to fall apart quicker than the Knicks did the previous night.

"Your Honor, we would like to call our second witness to the stand, please." He turned to look at the defendant. "Mr DeShawn Arlington." He slowly rose from his chair and ambled over to the witness box smiling at the jury as he went by. "Remember, Mr Arlington, you're about to be sworn in so no telling lies." You could sense the sarcasm in Ryan's voice. After being sworn in Ryan pressed ahead. "Could you please confirm your full name for the court, so we know you can tell the truth?"

Out the corner of his eye he noticed the judge glaring at him so decided in his mind that the digs he had already taken would be his last. After clearing his throat, DeShawn spoke.

"My full name is DeShawn Marlon Arlington." Question number one answered.

"And are you the former sports agent of Luke Best, Henry Craig and Matt Woodman?" The nods that he used to engage his lawyer he was now using to engage Ryan. Nodding to the question he eventually confirmed he was. "So, let me ask you why you are no longer the agent of the three people I just mentioned?"

"I suppose that is a question that you would have to ask them?"

Answering a question with another question drove Ryan insane as it felt to him that the question he was asking in the first place clearly wasn't good enough.

"But I am asking you, Mr Arlington, why you're not their agent anymore, because I know their answer already."

"Well, if you know already, why don't you tell the court so I can save my breath?"

Ryan was getting absolutely nowhere with this questioning and instead DeShawn was doing to him what he wanted Isobel to do to them.

"You're not their agent because you knowingly stole millions of pounds from them for your own financial gain." He quickly walked towards the witness box as if he was squaring up to someone in the street for a fight. "These men trusted you so much with their finances, their careers, their well-being, that you thought they wouldn't notice if a *little money* went missing?" Without pointing a finger or slamming his hands on the edge of the box there wasn't any more Ryan could do in the heat of the moment.

"See, that's the funny thing right there, how different people see different things." He turned from looking over the courtroom to looking and scanning the jury one by one. "You see, what you've been told is from one man's perspective, but what if I told you that the money, this $7.3 million dollars that you're repeating, was for a service?"

Another question to answer a question, just what Ryan wanted. Trying to reassume his foothold on the questioning he resorted to the sarcasm he had opened with.

"It must have been a pretty high-class service for that amount of money, Mr Arlington – what did you do? Dispose of a murder weapon?" He finished his question chuckling. You couldn't tell if it was a nervous chuckle or a funny one. DeShawn pondered the question, raising his hand to his chin and stroking it a few times. He was of course wondering how best to answer the question, but the lengthy pause put Ryan slightly on edge that he may have unearthed something that he didn't want to.

"You're a big basketball fan, aren't you, Mr Jackson? I mean, I've seen you courtside at plenty of games before."

Not quite the answer that Ryan was expecting but he went with it to see where it led him. "Yes, you're correct, I like basketball and I support the Brooklyn Nets."

You could see a few of the jurors acknowledge his answer which meant they either now stood with him as Nets fans or hated him because they were Knicks fans.

"So, you'd be familiar with last season when the Celtics beat the Mavericks on the last game of the season to clinch the number one spot in the Eastern conference rankings?"

One question intrigued him but now he was absolutely bemused about the second question regarding basketball. Did DeShawn think he was talking to one of his employees back in the office, all of a sudden?

"Yes, I'm aware of that game, thank you, but I don't see the link between your two questions and why you stole money from my clients," Ryan responded trying to navigate his way back to the case and also reaffirm his position as the one asking the questions here.

"Well, you asked me what service I provided your client,

and I was getting to that, I just wanted to give you some background before doing so."

"I'm sure we're all going to be thrilled to hear about this service so please continue." Ryan had fully lost control of the process, but this story could link to the information that Victor knew. He could flip it later on or even counter with other questions now if DeShawn willingly tripped himself up.

"Do you know how hard those Celtics players partied that night?" Had Luke murdered someone? The sarcastic question that triggered this whole basketball-based conversation was now looking more and more likely to become a reality. "Let me tell you a piece of information for free about that night those players partied lik–"

"OBJECTION!"

DeShawn's monologue grinded to an instant halt as the word rang loud around the court for everyone to hear – but it didn't come from Ryan. Turning to his opposite number for an answer, he was sitting, almost daydreaming, at his desk and shared Ryan's puzzled expression. They both turned and there was Luke Best standing behind the desk, leaning forward staring through Ryan at DeShawn.

"Objection overruled, Mr Best, you do not have the grounds in my courtroom to appeal. Please sit down.!" Ryan turned and walked back towards his client looking for a clue as to why he'd just done what he did, but before he could reach him Judge Sullivan continued. "As for you, Mr Jackson, please keep all of you clients under control moving forward."

By the end of the sentence, Ryan was now back at the desk and leant in closely to Luke, so their conversation remained between the pair of them.

"Do you know what he's about to say?"

The expression on the plaintiff's face said it all but he

answered anyway, "I do, and I didn't think he'd go there but here we are."

As if it wasn't bad enough that his first witness had withheld information, he was now being blindsided by one of the men he was representing.

"I assume he was about to reveal why $7.3 million of your money never made it to your bank account?"

"He was indeed."

"And what's the reason you didn't tell me the truth?" Ryan's voice became a little louder and you could hear the anger in it if you were sitting in the first row of the bench.

"Well, two reasons, the first being we all signed confidentiality agreements after the incident and the second being I didn't think it was going to cost me *that much money.*"

The second person in as many hours whose judgment had been clouded by agreements that didn't stand up when it related to a crime. Ryan had to think fast.

He spun round, pulled on his jacket a little tighter and walked back to the center of the room.

"No further questions from us, Your Honor." This was the world's worst possible start to the case; he needed a way to salvage it and further questioning of DeShawn wasn't it. "In fact, Your Honor, can we finish for the day?"

Ryan couldn't work out the look on the judge's face; whether it was anger, disappointment or whether he was outright stunned at the request.

"If opposing council agree then we shall reconvene Monday morning at 9 a.m."

William looked up at DeShawn who was halfway through walking back and the accustomed nod came.

"That's fine with us, Your Honor."

"Fantastic, then, in that case, court adjourned until Monday."

Down came the gavel on proceedings and the judge left the bench being the first to exit the court. Following him was a mixture of jurors and people in attendance watching the trial, then went William and DeShawn who were both whispering to each other as they walked past Ryan and Luke. Both still seated, Ryan looked disheveled after day one of the trial. The courtroom was empty before Ryan collected his papers, put them into his briefcase and slammed it shut. Buttoning his blazer, he turned to leave and as he did Luke stuttered, "Listen, man, I was going to tell yo—"

Then just like when Luke had cut DeShawn off moments earlier Ryan returned the favor.

"You screwed me, Luke. You screwed me, the start of the case, EVERYTHING! The doubt already in the jurors' minds now will be hard to change." Ryan had launched into a tirade at a man who was a national icon, worth millions and millions of dollars. "My office tomorrow morning, 10 a.m. I don't care if it's a Saturday – be there."

Ryan unlocked his phone and found the joint conversation that contained him, Macpherson and Daniels:

*We couldn't have started the trial worse.*

## 07

# SATURDAY 17TH OCTOBER, 8.07 A.M.

It seemed eerily quiet as Ryan exited the ground floor of his apartment block at just gone 8 a.m. the next morning. New York was a city that was always vibrant and busy with something going on but being out that early on a weekend and especially heading to the office it was quieter than usual. Expecting none of his fellow colleagues to be in that day, even the associates, Ryan was dressed in a casual grey tracksuit with box-fresh white trainers on as he plodded down Central Park West towards the city. Reaching his favorite spot in Mulligans, he debated whether or not going inside and starting early would be a good idea. He knew it'd be open for breakfast but in hindsight he needed to keep himself sharp for what was about to take place. He couldn't allow any more screw-ups to happen in this case or he could kiss goodbye to winning it. As the sun got higher it started to light the vast skyscrapers and in doing so showed how empty they really were on weekends. It reaffirmed the eeriness Ryan first felt leaving his apartment. A couple of blocks before the office he stopped at a coffee shop and picked up a pastry and an espresso and continued to plod on. The whole walk in and even more so now as he was in sight of his destination, Ryan played out in his mind different scenarios as to why DeShawn had charged Luke $7.3 million for a service. What on earth could his client have done that warranted paying out that sum of money?

As he reached the front of his building, he let himself in through one of the side doors not to alert the receptionist and security guard and headed over to the elevator and up to his office. With ideas still rattling around in his head which were getting more and more absurd as he jumped from one to the other, Ryan walked out onto a virtually empty floor all bar two contractors who were tucked away in the far right corner doing a moves and changes task on one of the conference rooms. The time had just gone 9 a.m. after the walk in and pit-stop for breakfast, so Ryan had just under an hour to prepare himself for the conversation with Luke. He didn't quite know what he had to prepare but he'd thought to himself he better have some kind of plan as to how they were going to combat yesterday's abysmal showing in court, otherwise the case would be dismissed very quickly and his reputation in tatters. He paced up and down his corner office whilst bouncing one of the many signed basketballs that littered the room. As he pondered how to open, his office phone buzzed, and it was Luke to say he was coming up to the office now – how had nearly as hour passed already? Placing the ball back on its stand next to the table, his eyes found the empty whiskey glass from Thursday night. All of a sudden Mulligans didn't seem like a bad idea, so he grabbed a decanter and poured himself a small glass of whiskey which he downed in one. Although completely unnecessary this early in the morning Ryan thought it was needed for whatever was about to come.

As he made his way into the main boardroom, he was left absolutely shell-shocked at what he saw sitting in front of him. Luke was there accompanied by DeShawn Arlington.

"What the fuck is he doing here?" Ryan could only muster the most obvious words and response that sprung into his mind. He slowly started to make his way towards the large conference-room table and stopped three or four seats from them and sat down. He was still lost for words. He didn't know how to follow up his opening question but eventually Luke started to speak.

"Listen, I know this doesn't look legit right now and I know you know I lied to you, but I thought if the three of us got together in a room we may be able to sort all this out?" said Luke very hesitantly.

The naivety of this young man was almost astonishing that during a high-profile court case he would bring together his own lawyer and the man he was suing, as if they could all meet up for a beer. DeShawn went to open his mouth to say something, but Ryan wasn't in the mood to listen right now because what was happening was wrong on so many levels.

"I don't care what you've got to say. This whole court case is partly driven by you and it's against you, so why are you even here?" The amazement of the situation he found himself in was slowly turning into aggression sprinkled with a little bit of panic as he didn't want this to jeopardize everything. DeShawn hadn't quite responded to Ryan's question yet but from experience on questioning him in court he knew he took his time to answer. "Come on, man, SPEAK!"

"Luke reached out to me last night and thought it would be best if we did this together. To see if we could come to some kind of *arrangement*." The reply finally came accompanied by the smirk that he sported both on Wednesday night and the previous day during the trial. Ryan looked over at Luke who had been pretty silent in all of this. For someone who Ryan thought very highly of, he didn't look like positively contributing anytime soon.

Ryan continued to look at his client, then back to his opposition and then back again, scanning between the two of them as he made the executive decision that this *meeting*, or whatever you wanted to refer to it as, needed to end.

"Listen, DeShawn, I'm going to have to ask you to leave, I need to talk to Luke alone."

First and foremost, Ryan needed to find out about this service DeShawn had provided Luke with. Why on earth Luke thought it was a good idea bringing DeShawn to Macpherson & Daniels' office and potentially jeopardizing everything was something that they could talk about later. Finally, Luke found his voice.

"I brought him here so we could cut a deal. I know why he kept the $7.3 million but maybe we could agree for him to give some back."

"Oh, so now you want to talk? Now you want to contribute to the conversation?" Ryan said sarcastically because if it wasn't sarcasm it was going to be anger. "DeShawn, I've already asked you once and I don't want to have to do it again: please leave."

Ignoring his client's only input to the conversation so far Ryan pressed ahead with making the meeting just the pair of them. Reluctantly DeShawn stood up from his chair and headed towards the door.

"Just so you know, I would have given you back $2 million if Ryan would have listened." It echoed around the empty office as he headed towards the reception area as he walked out of the boardroom. He knew the parting gift would drive a wedge between Ryan and Luke and start their conversation off on the wrong foot.

"I just need you to know none of this was done to deceive you. If I'd known I could have told you about the NDA then I would have, man, but you don't want to break contract with a man like DeShawn." Starting to open up now it was just the two of them in the room, Ryan could sense that he was finally going to learn about what happened and if he could actually help in any way.

"I just need you to start from the top, Luke, and leave nothing out. I will help you to the best of my ability, but I need to know everything. I need to know it before you leave this office."

Luke stood up, took a deep breath and wandered over towards the window.

"Alright, I'll tell you everything."

Before they got started Ryan went back to his office and returned with the decanter of whiskey but with two glasses instead of one. He poured two large drinks, or large enough for just gone 10.45 a.m. on a Saturday morning, slid one over to Luke who drank the entire glass in one go, before he got started.

"So, what happened from the moment after you left the court that night?"

Luke thought he was just going to explain the incident to Ryan, but he really did want him to start from the top.

"So, we were all celebrating in the locker room, we'd won the Eastern Conference title and with it being the end of the regular season we get a break before the play-offs. Coach said we could party because we weren't leaving until the morning." Luke was still standing up at this point, but he was pacing up and down the boardroom and still looking over the city as it started to come alive. "So, we had a few beers in the locker room whilst we got changed, did media duty, etc., and then one of the vets who used to play for Dallas called in a favor and got us a table at one of the city's nightclubs."

"I'm assuming you cleared it with coach and then went?"

"Incorrect." Luke turned to face Ryan and he lowered his

head and started shaking it. "Coach said we could celebrate but he meant together at the hotel, drinking, laughing, behind closed doors where the media couldn't see." Another deep breath came just like it did when he agreed to tell all and it was obvious how much he regretted this fateful night. "We went back to the hotel and had a few drinks with the coaching team then five or six of us pretended to go to bed but when we left the hotel bar, we slipped out a fire exit and got a cab to the club where the table was." So far Ryan didn't see much wrong with the story. Coach had given them the all-clear to drink and plenty of sports stars went to nightclubs mid-season, off-season, even pre-season so everything was all good so far in his mind. "So, we're in the club having a good time, the drinks are flowing, the music is good and there's plenty of girls in there."

"He's covering up an affair?" Ryan interrupted Luke mid-sentence with his assumption.

"Hell no, man, I would never cheat on my wife. What do you take me for?" Luke snapped back quickly. How Ryan could even come to that assumption having got to know him.

"Sorry, I just assumed with the drinks and the girls that that's where it was heading."

"Anyway, we were all having a good time and then the guy who organized the table rounded the boys up and said come on, we're bouncing to a strip joint he knew." This was the part where it was probably going to go downhill. Luke went on to explain that he had his reservations about going to wherever this strip club was and that he even contemplated going back to the team's hotel. "In the end, man, I had to go with them because if I had got caught returning on my own then I would have blown it for the rest of the guys and I didn't want to be that guy." Ryan hadn't spoken for a while, but he was trying to process every piece of information he was being told and how he could use it. "So, we get into the second club and they know we're coming so we have pick of the dancers, a private room, basically we're completely hidden from the general public." Luke paused and stopped walking to retreat back to the chair that wasn't far from where Ryan was completely focused on every word that came out of his mouth. He took the last gulp of whiskey from his glass before continuing. "We were in there for about thirty minutes and Kyle Rayner, my ex-Celtics teammate, disappeared and came back with a large white rock and just threw it in the middle of the table."

"Large white rock as in cocaine?" Ryan bluntly asked back.

"Yes, a large white rock as in cocaine, correct." You could still hear the regret in his voice as he continued to replay the night. He almost didn't want to finish the story. "He threw it in the middle of us all and said it was a present for making #1 seed, that he was going to retire regardless of how the play-offs went so he wanted to treat his boys. I didn't do any, though, because I don't take drugs."

Things started to fall into place in Ryan's mind. Kyle Rayner missed the ECF matches because he was banned by the NBA for a positive drug test, not because of the injury the Celtics reported.

"So, Kyle failed a drug test from the cocaine from that night?" Luke nodded slowly as he took another gulp of whiskey from the glass that Ryan had refilled – how could a professional athlete have been so careless!? "OK, so you went to a strip club, there was illegal class A drugs there and one of your teammates failed a test, but I don't see how that cost you a substantial amount of money?" Ryan continued to poke and prod because it didn't add up to him.

"I wasn't finished," was the reply he got as Luke's attention switched back up from the glass. "Probably ten days or so after that night, DeShawn called me to the office and said he had something urgent that he needed to talk to me about."

"He covered up your involvement in that evening, didn't he?"

"He did. He made me completely disappear from the whole debacle." Luke's response made Ryan think for a slight second that maybe there was some good in DeShawn before he remembered he charged Luke over $7 million to make this happen. "One of the barmaids from the club that night, a blonde girl who was bringing in the drinks, had been recording us and taking photos all night and she had some very compromising pictures of me with alcohol, strippers and sitting near the drugs. We were negotiating my deal with the Knicks at the time, and I couldn't afford the bad publicity." Finally, it was out in the open. What had happened. Why it happened. How it happened. Ryan had a clear picture on everything. "He basically said to me that he could make it go away, I could go on as normal and that this would never come to light. I just had to pay him, which I agreed, but I didn't think it would cost that amount of money."

Ryan enthusiastically nodded to conclude the story but also to agree that it was a rather large sum of money to make someone like a barmaid go away.

"Nothing more since? No more extra money? No whispers about a leak?"

"Nothing."

It had been clear sailing for Luke since DeShawn promised it would disappear.

Ryan didn't reply. Instead, he stood up and took Luke's place in pacing up and down the room looking out and trying to figure out his next move. Technically, he was between a rock and a hard place because he couldn't use what he'd just heard in court. Luke's image would be damaged and potentially unrepairable with the New York media, but he also couldn't let

DeShawn walk away with the money because it would mean he'd lose his first case. Although there were another two clients to represent, they hadn't got onto Henry and Matt yet in the case, so all focus was still on Luke.

"Let me think until tomorrow and then I'll come to you with a plan in the evening," Ryan eventually said. "Let me process all the information, taking into account the NDA signed and see if there's a way that I can swing it. There should be but I need to think hard."

It was Ryan's turn to finish the remainder of his whiskey as he took a large gulp. If he had known all of this from the start then they could have come up with a strategy from day one to combat it but being on the back foot now he didn't quite know in his mind how he was going to play it.

Ryan realized that it was Saturday and Luke probably now had other things to be doing and other people to see. He joined Ryan in standing and made his way towards the conference-room door. It was nearly midday.

"Wait for my call to recap and I'll see you at the courthouse first thing Monday morning."

Ryan exited south of the room and headed back towards his office whilst Luke went out the nearest door and headed towards the elevator. Reaching his office and nestling into his chair, he leaned back staring up at the ceiling and for the first time probably in his career he really had no idea how he was going to flip this for his benefit. He hadn't gained the reputation he had for nothing, but he didn't want to win the case at someone else's expense. He picked up his office phone and internally dialed Macpherson's number and it took a few seconds for him to remember that it was Saturday and she wouldn't be working. Collecting his tracksuit top, he made his way towards the elevator to leave the office and, deep in thought, he walked straight past one of the few people in the office and completely ignored the associate as he said goodbye. As he waited to go down, his phone buzzed in his pocket. It was a text from Emilia reminding him that they had afternoon plans and were meeting her parents for a late lunch in Greenwich Village – which truthfully, he had completely forgotten about. Ryan decided that it was too late to go home and change and that his casual tracksuit would have to suffice for the get-together and hoped Emilia's snooty parents wouldn't hold it against him. Exiting the building and onto the street he headed south-west towards Greenwich Village on a walk that would no doubt mold his next move in the case. He replied to his wife:

*Just finished with Luke, Greenwich bound as I type.*

## 08

# SUNDAY 18TH OCTOBER, 10.11 A.M.

Left foot, right foot, left foot, right foot, left foot. Ryan wasn't making his way back into the Supreme Court but instead pounding his way through Central Park on his weekly run that happened every Sunday morning. He used to be able to go to the gym daily but as he moved up in his work and the cases became bigger, the hours became longer so he found himself having to find new ways to keep fit, which was now two laps of Central Park, around twelve and a half miles. Usually when he made his way around it would be accompanied by a podcast or two, but he left his headphones at home this morning as he wanted to try and think clearly how to tackle yesterday's news. All throughout the lunch with Emilia's parents, the drinks after and even their rare alone time in the evening, Ryan had countless ideas rattling around in his head, but they all ultimately led back to either DeShawn getting away with it or him having to convince Luke to tarnish his reputation to get his money back. As he finished his first lap, he was still none the wiser as to what to do and he wished he had brought his headphones as a distraction for the final six miles as the warm autumn sun was making the run tougher. As he turned the corner, he noticed a small cart up ahead selling drinks and confectionery, so he decided to pick up the pace initially and then stop for a quick water break before completing the course.

"Just a small bottle of water, please."

The guy working opened his cart and handed him the drink which he consumed immediately before paying and putting the rubbish in the recycling bin next to him.

"Are you Ryan Jackson?" Just as he was about to set off on his run again, a lady standing behind him asked a question, which at first startled him but he regained composure to confirm who he was.

"That's correct, I am but sorry, do I know you?"

The lady reached into her bag and pulled out a small black cellphone that looked like it was from the nineties.

"This is for you." She handed him the phone then proceeded to walk towards an exit east of the park. Very confused at this point, Ryan took a few moments to look at the phone before he could hear a voice coming from the speaker.

"Ryan speaking," he said hesitantly putting the phone to his ear.

"So how did your little chat with Luke go yesterday? Did he tell you the truth and that I didn't steal that money you're saying I did?" DeShawn Arlington's voice rang through Ryan's ears; it was like he couldn't escape this man the past couple of days.

"He did tell me what happened, and I still think you've stolen from him. There's no way it cost that amount of money to pay off a barmaid, so you took some kind of cut."

"Of course I took a cut, Ryan, what do you take me for? I'm a businessman."

"But why would you take more money from someone who you're already earning money off?"

"You ever wondered why you work for someone, Ryan, and I don't?"

Another merry-go-round was taking place with questions being answered with questions and Ryan really wasn't in the mood for this as he needed to finish his run and work on his non-existent plan for the case.

"What do you really want, DeShawn? I'm busy running at the moment. If you want anything then we'll do it properly tomorrow morning at the courthouse." Ryan threw the phone in the recycling bin but could still vaguely hear DeShawn's voice as he set back off to finish his run. The last time he cut him short it cost Luke a $2 million refund so he wondered how much today's debacle would cost one of them.

Coming to the end of his run he didn't know whether to go home, to go back out or just head straight to Mulligans to pay off his weekly tab. With Emilia away working next weekend he knew they wouldn't have much more time together especially with him in the middle of the trial, so he decided to plod on a little further and make the right choice in spending the afternoon and evening with his wife. Walking the last couple of blocks from the park to the bar and using it as a cool-down, he withdrew $150 from a nearby cash machine and headed into what would be a pretty empty Mulligans at this time of the day. Barring a couple of tourists eating brunch and a regular propping up the bar, the large space was occupied with empty tables and chairs but there was a familiar face working. As Ryan got to the bar there was already an open Heineken waiting for him which probably wasn't the best remedy after a twelve-mile run.

"No thanks, man, I'm just here to settle up my weekly tab and I'll be off. I need to eat and see Emilia." With that, his phone buzzed. It was a message from Emilia to say she had to pop into the city to buy some things and she'd be back mid to late afternoon. The bartender had returned by the time Ryan had replied to Emilia.

"Bill this week is a small one, pal, just the $89."

Ryan looked back up from his phone and pulling the money out of his pocket replied, "Here's $150. I'll have the Heineken, three more and a chicken salad, please," as he settled in to watch the sports news on the big screen above the bar.

Several hours passed and the three beers became more like six as he watched the same sports headlines repeat themselves over and over again. Despite having already debated them with Joe, he started again with the new bartender when he started his shift. His mind had temporarily forgotten about what was going on with work and he seemed to be escaping everything through passionately talking sport to people he didn't really know. This went on until someone walked in wearing a NY Knicks jersey with Luke Best on the back and all of a sudden, he was back to square one thinking about the case. He opened his phone to see a missed call from Emilia, a missed call from Luke and a couple of messages from friends in one of their group chats. He debated replying but ultimately decided to ignore all and order another beer. Emilia said when she'd be back and in Ryan's mind that time hadn't arrived yet, so as the bar started to fill up Ryan made his way over to a back corner and sat by himself having a one-man debate on his final decision. His phone buzzed again. Emilia was calling this time, so he decided to pick it up.

"Hey, Em, what's up?"

"Don't what's up me. I expected you to be home when I got back and you're not – where are you? Mulligans?"

He was thinking to himself that it had been five hours so he couldn't say he was still running.

"I came home, showered and popped down to settle the bill. I'll be home shortly." Ryan was lying but he didn't think it through still being in his running clothes.

"No, you didn't, because your running clothes aren't in the washing, Ryan. I'm not in the mood; I've had a weird afternoon. Can you come home, please?" Emilia's voice cracked towards the back end of her response, and you could hear she was ready to burst into tears. It made for uncomfortable listening. Ryan got up almost immediately and proceeded to the doors to head home.

"I'll be home in ten to fifteen minutes. Whatever is wrong, sit tight and I'll be home shortly." He hadn't even put the phone down before he was racing back up to their apartment to comfort his wife.

The front door was locked when Ryan arrived home and fumbling for his keys in a hurry, it only took longer before he could open it. He was greeted by every light in the apartment being on and Emilia was on the sofa, her long brown hair tied in a ponytail. She had been crying as her make-up was smudged and there were some crumpled tissues beside her.

"What's up? What's happened?" Ryan rushed over to his wife's side and cuddled her as she nestled her head into his shoulder.

"I popped over to the East Village because I needed to buy some clothes and I wanted to grab a coffee and I noticed these two men; they followed me for most of my afternoon." Ryan hesitated for a second and thought to himself that there were plenty of weird characters in New York City and if one had taken a liking to his wife it was probably more flattering than sinister. "They followed me into almost every shop: clothes, coffee, even the bakery. At one point I'm sure I caught one of them taking pictures of me, Ryan."

"With your family's background and now me taking on a case against DeShawn Arlington it was probably just the media or some local bloggers."

"They weren't either of those types, they were wearing suits and got into a blacked-out SUV!"

"Suits? So, they were grown men? What else did they look like?" Ryan started to panic now. He slipped his phone out of his pocket discreetly to send a text to Macpherson.

"They were big guys, Ryan, suited, far enough in the background for a normal person not to notice but growing up with Dad and now you, I did." She lifted her head from his shoulder and looked him square in the eyes and he could see fear he hadn't seen before. Whoever it was, how could they be so brazen and follow Emilia in broad daylight? Suddenly it clicked.

"Wait here, I'll be back in a minute." Ryan stood up and walked towards the bedroom, pulling his phone out and dialing one of the last numbers. Over the course of the last few days his anger had topped out at different stages – being embarrassed in court, DeShawn in his office but right now he was absolutely raging. As he shut the door a voice came from the other end of the phone.

"I've been trying to reach you all day, Ryan. Where you been?" It was Luke he had called.

"Tell DeShawn to call me now." Ryan put the phone down and launched it onto the bed, filled with frustration.

The minutes after the call to Luke passed by slowly and Ryan couldn't work out if it was the numerous bottles of beer wearing off or the frustration and aggression building up waiting for DeShawn to call him. He still hadn't been back out to see Emilia and how she was coping. He needed to speak to DeShawn to rule out that it wasn't him that had his wife followed. Ryan could handle him being followed in the park earlier, but he didn't want his family brought into his line of work; it wasn't fair. A few more minutes passed which tipped Ryan over the edge. He grabbed his phone and went to redial

Luke and as he did, it started to ring with an incoming call from an unknown number. He took a deep breath and answered.

"Now I have your attention, don't I?" Before Ryan could even get out one of the hundreds of ways he had thought about starting this conversation, DeShawn was straight in confirming Ryan's hunch.

"You had my wife followed around the city and for WHAT REASON?" Ryan started calmly but finished his sentence shouting down the phone before the conversation had even really begun.

"My question first and then I'll answer yours. Do I have your attention now?" Unlike DeShawn to be answering a question with another question. Ryan was already running out of nerves for him to get on and he'd only been in his life for three days.

"Yes, you have my attention. Now why the fuck were you following my wife this afternoon?"

"I can be a very big problem for people who aren't on my side, Ryan. I have built a multi-million-pound empire from nothing; do you think I want to lose it?" DeShawn didn't answer Ryan's question but what he did do was give Ryan an insight into the fact that he had done something that could come back to haunt him. Brushing over the comment as he wanted to think more about it and see how he could use it in the courtroom, Ryan circled back to the question he'd asked multiple times around and finally got an answer. "I wanted your attention, and I got what I wanted. I don't want this case to proceed. I don't like people digging into me and so far, you seem undeterred. As much as I admire that quality, I don't when it's against me."

DeShawn was starting to show a new side to Ryan which gave the situation a bit of a silver lining, but Ryan was still super angry at the fact his wife was followed.

"If you ever follow my wife again, then…"

"Then you'll do what? Absolutely nothing, I'll tell you that for free." DeShawn spoke over Ryan and didn't take his threat lightly. "Despite your paper threats, I've done your job for you. Call Luke and he'll fill you in." DeShawn hung up and Ryan's silver lining to the situation looked to have quickly disappeared. He scrambled to call Luke and find out what he had agreed. After a couple of questionable choices in the past seventy-two hours he was fearful as to what his client had done.

He popped his head out of the bedroom and signaled with his hands to Emilia that all was well and that he'd be five minutes. Ryan still had a call or two to make but he didn't want to leave his wife outside still scared. As he shut the door, he dialed Luke to find out how another conversation with DeShawn without him present had led to the situation being resolved.

"Luke, did you talk to DeShawn again?" Luke was in a joyous mood when he picked up the phone, not that Ryan would have known because he barely let him speak as he continued rambling. "I'll answer that for you: yes, you did. You're talking to him again without me knowing or being present. Was there much point in hiring me at all?"

"Listen, Ryan, we all live in DeShawn's world. He does things how and when he wants." Ryan was slowly starting to learn this, and he wasn't too impressed. Was he in over his head? "Anyway, you did your job and got me some of the money back so I'm happy."

"What have you agreed to, Luke? We need to talk this through properly."

"No, we don't. It's signed, sealed and delivered; he's going to give me back $3.25 million."

You couldn't get two polar opposite people at the moment Luke revealed the settlement. Luke seemed happy to be getting nearly half his money back, but Ryan was deflated and let down. At least he was over the anger he felt earlier on.

"You never take the first offer, Luke, never. They always try and low-ball you. We could have driven up if you'd let me do my job!"

It was a win for Ryan in the fact they settled on a number, but it wasn't the type of win that he wanted; he wanted to nail the opposition to the cross in court and have the glory that came with it.

"That wasn't his first offer. His first offer was $2 million yesterday at your office and then he upped it, so I agreed to take it. Man, it's nearly fifty per cent back."

"Do you not wonder why he's willing to give back fifty per cent? What is he hiding?" He was losing the battle to convince his client that they should continue the war in court. Going in tomorrow with only two of his three plaintiffs left wouldn't impress Judge Sullivan.

"Ryan, you're not listening, I'm taking the money and Tiffany is going to sort the rest. Speak to his lawyer and get it tied up, but I'm done. I want back on the court."

Dealing with a sports star Ryan wanted to launch into a full-blown, coach-esque type monologue about what it meant to win. Was this really a win when they could win so much more? On the other hand, it was Sunday afternoon, and he knew he was fighting a losing battle. Explaining the whole situation and comforting Emilia was still his top priority. He wanted her to be right again.

"OK, Luke, you win, we'll settle for the $3.25 million but I still need you in court tomorrow to tie some things up – 8 a.m.?"

"See you tomorrow, Ryan."

As they hung up the phone on each other Ryan breathed a sigh of relief after the last hour that he'd had. Part one of the court case seemed tied up but he had learned more in the last seventy-two hours than the last twenty-nine cases he'd won put together. Plenty had warned him about DeShawn Arlington and the type of man he could be but now Ryan was really starting to see all this for himself. He laid back on the bed and stared at the ceiling momentarily before remembering his wife and making his way back to the living room.

Upon entering the room, he noticed his wife had got up and was in the kitchen keeping herself busy. He moved towards her with a smile on his face to continue the reassurance that he had everything under control.

"It was him, wasn't it? DeShawn had me followed because of your case against him." Ryan couldn't believe Emilia had figured it out from him making two calls, but in all honesty she had heard him shouting through the walls and put two and two together. "Ryan, I told you before this case started that I had heard things. I've read things, too. This man really isn't someone I like the sound of."

How could he possibly reassure her everything was going to be OK? He had already been followed, as had she, and the trial was barely twenty-four hours in.

"I've got this under control, you know I have. When have you seen me worried?"

"It doesn't matter if you're not worried, *I am*," Emilia replied.

Ryan opened the fridge, pulled out a bottle of wine and turned to put his arm around his wife, the smile still very much firmly on his face as it had been their whole conversation.

"What did I tell you when you first raised those concerns? I'm going to win and it's going to be fine." Pouring a couple of glasses of wine he led Emilia towards the sofa, picking up the TV remote off the kitchen worktop on the way. "Now how about the finale of that show we've been watching? I need a good distraction."

Reluctantly Emilia smiled back, following her husband to the sofa as he flicked through looking for the right TV channel. As they nestled down to have a rare lazy Sunday together Ryan opened his phone to check the NFL scores but instead saw an unread message in the chat with Macpherson & Daniels from Daniels:

*What's the latest with Luke? Ryan, please provide an update on the case.*

## 09

## MONDAY 19TH OCTOBER, 7.27 A.M.

*The next stop will be Chambers Street.*

As Ryan sat waiting for the train to depart Canal Street Station, he unlocked his phone and connected to the station's Wi-Fi. Opening his email he sent a quick one-liner to William O'Neill to meet him in the judge's chambers before the day's proceedings started. Ryan was almost certain that what had happened at the weekend between him, Luke and DeShawn his opposite number would have no clue about. He had already been up several hours as he had to go to the office to draw up and process paperwork on the agreement that had taken place the afternoon before. As he exited the station, he chose not to head in through the front entrance this time where the media was but instead, he slipped through a side door to start his working day fairly low key. After passing the security checks and being led to the same room as Friday, Ryan set himself up to deal with Luke first, then Henry afterwards. He withdrew the document Luke needed to sign to 'settle' his part of the case against DeShawn, but Ryan was still planning one last assault on Luke to get him to change his mind and proceed with the case as planned.

The clock was just about to strike 8 a.m. when Luke walked in on time as planned yesterday. Ryan was impressed at his client's timekeeping this early on a Monday morning especially after the stories he had been told on Saturday. He slumped himself in the chair opposite Ryan, took a deep breath, exhaled and said joyfully, "Let's get this shit over and done, shall we? I've got practice at 9.30 a.m. and I need to get up to Westchester yet."

It seemed as if Ryan's last-ditch attempt was going to be in vain, but he thought he didn't have anything to lose so he might as well try.

"Luke, I know $3.5 million seems like a win, right, but—"

"Let me sign the papers, Ryan, and I'm out of here." Luke's voice was raised, and he pre-empted Ryan would try to convince him against the deal again. "I came from a broken home, Ryan, I never met my father, I have five brothers and sisters, so I know what's a win and what's not."

"But I'm just—"

"Don't say anything. Basketball is a short career so I know all the money I can get will ensure MY family is set up for LIFE. So, I'm going to ask you again, where do I sign?"

Knowing that all his efforts from here on in would be in vain and that he was very clearly losing the battle, Ryan handed Luke two pieces of paper that outlined DeShawn Arlington's willingness to pay him $3.5 million and settle this case.

"The first document is the outline of the deal which was agreed by you both and the second document is *another* NDA so that no one can talk about that night, this case, this settlement or anything to do with this again." Luke's eyes skimmed over the pages as he looked for any red flags but ultimately all he took in was the number of dollars that would be going back into his back account now this had been settled. "You'll see that I even took the liberty of charging my fees to DeShawn so the money you get back from him will be in full."

Luke grinned from ear to ear as he leaned back, and the chair tipped with him. Looking like a schoolkid, he withdrew a pen from his jacket pocket.

"This is the pen I used to sign my Celtics and Knicks deal. This is my lucky pen; man, I love this pen." His chair came crashing back down with a bang as he signed both documents and flipped them back round the table to Ryan. "So we're done here now?"

Ryan nodded his head reluctantly. The battle on paper was won but it felt like a loss to him. Standing up from his chair one of Luke's security guards behind him opened the door back to the hallway.

"Listen, Ryan, you're a good man, I can see that and even through the shit that happened this weekend you still tried to help me."

"It's my job, Luke, that's what I am paid to do."

"I know that, but sometimes people go above and beyond in their jobs, and I just wanted to let you know that I appreciate you. Just be careful of DeShawn. There's a lot you and other people don't know. I just don't want to see you get hurt."

A response wasn't needed as the two mutually knew this was the end of Luke's involvement in the trial. He exited the room and after pondering a few what ifs for a moment, Ryan headed up to Judge Sullivan to let him know what had happened and how they were moving forward.

As he approached the judge's chambers he could see the door was open and could hear that Judge Sullivan was on the phone. Making his presence known visually so it didn't seem like he was listening in, Ryan poked his head through the door and waved to get his attention. He beckoned Ryan in and pointed at one of the empty chairs across from him and quickly finished his call.

"This is becoming far too frequent, you being in here, Ryan. People might start to question it." They both chuckled but Ryan's was significantly shorter than the judge's as he was delivering news that he didn't want to, and that became apparent to the judge quite clearly.

"DeShawn Arlington and Luke Best made a deal on the weekend to settle the case outside of the trial. I tried to convince him not to, but he didn't listen to me. The figure was good enough for him, so he took it."

You could sense the disappointment Judge Sullivan was feeling at what he'd just been told; after Friday's opening statements and early finish, this wasn't going the way he thought the case would either.

"You said DeShawn and Luke settled the case; were you not involved in the deal?"

Immediately Ryan knew this was going to make for an uncomfortable few minutes, but he had to ride them out to come out with any kind of credibility.

"Yes, they made a deal. Having worked together previously DeShawn reached out to Luke on Sunday afternoon and made the deal, I was informed Sunday evening and I have the signed documents."

"I must say, this isn't going the way that I thought it would, Ryan." The judge stood up, turning his back on Ryan to look elsewhere within the room. "You know you're held in very high regard by the senior judges in New York, don't you?"

"I didn't… I mean I did, well, I didn't know that, Your Honor. Thank you." Ryan seemed taken aback by what he'd just been told. Maybe this was the light at the end of the tunnel that he needed.

"Let's not have that change from this trial, please?" The judge followed up his previous statement and all of a sudden Ryan came crashing back down to earth again.

"I'm doing all I can with this, Your Honor, but if they cooperate without me there's not much I can do about it." Arguing with a judge wasn't how he intended to start this week in court, but Ryan thought that he needed to defend himself otherwise this so-called reputation he had wouldn't exist by the time this case was finished. "The rest of the case will run smoothly; you have my word on that, I promise."

He was hoping that he could swing the judge back around because the last thing he needed after all this was a judge that sided against him as well.

William still hadn't arrived yet despite Ryan telling him where he would be and that he was needed as part of the case, but time was ticking on, and he needed to speak with Henry before today's session began. As he got up to leave, the judge sat down, not opposite him, but now behind his desk.

"Ryan, do you know how big this case is to *everyone* involved?" In his head Ryan was trying to work out how many people could be affected as he didn't want to undermine Judge Sullivan's question. "Well, let me tell you before you figure out the wrong answer. Many lawyers, many judges, even the Attorney General of the state of New York has tried and failed to bring down DeShawn Arlington so this will not only be the jewel in your crown, but this will also define my career and benefit this great state."

You could have heard a pin drop down the hallway in a room with a closed door. The judge's eyes were burning a hole in the side of Ryan's head, and he didn't know where to look.

"Do I make myself clear how important this case is now?"

"Yes, Your Honor, everything is crystal clear to me now," Ryan replied as he stood up and brushed himself off and walked towards the still open door. As he reached it, he was met with William almost running into the room, hair messy as usual and his crumpled suit was sporting a coffee stain from his commute that morning.

"Sorry I'm late, Your Honor, there was a delay on my train but I'm here now."

The judge looked him up and down and didn't know whether to respond accordingly or sarcastically but either-or Ryan beat him to punch. Squeezing past him at the door to make sure they didn't touch, Ryan said, "DeShawn and Luke settled for $3.5 million, the judge knows about it all and we're moving on with the case. See you in court in twenty minutes."

Ryan buttoned up his blazer as he sprung down the stairs and prepped himself accordingly to start fresh with Henry Craig's part in the trial. The NFL star quarterback had had his final parachute wages payment from the NY Giants in DeShawn's bank account for the past two seasons and Ryan hoped that unlike Luke there was no hidden agenda with Henry and that he could start to turn the screw against William and DeShawn.

Assuming the room was empty because there were no security guards guarding the door, Ryan wasn't subtle about entering. Bursting through the closed door Ryan was met by a startled client who, holding his hands up, looked like he was about to be interrogated by the FBI. Henry Craig was smartly dressed, clutching a team-branded water bottle and sweating profusely.

"Sorry to startle you like that, Henry, I just assumed no one was in here. You came by yourself today?"

"Yeah, man, my driver is in the car waiting as per coach's request but apart from that it's just me." Henry's response was prompt but there was a slight stutter in it which caught Ryan's attention and he now noticed how sweaty his client looked already.

"Everything alright with you today? You look really hot.

Want me to turn up the AC?" Ryan made a gesture towards the thermostat which was just behind Henry to the right, but he shook his head and politely declined his offer, instead unbuttoning the top button of his shirt trying not to mess up his tie.

"I just don't like courts, Ryan. I've only ever been in one before and that was when I was sixteen when I got caught shoplifting, and since then I've lived an exemplary life." He wasn't joking when he said that, either; Henry Craig was the darling of the American public's eye. He married his childhood sweetheart and had two children with her, he led his local college to a state championship, founded his own charity and had never been caught in any scandal to date which is why Ryan had a good feeling that today was the start of the trial moving back in his favor.

Ryan opened his briefcase and put the signed papers from Luke and Judge Sullivan into a wallet at the back to ensure they didn't become crushed and took out the file that he had made from his previous preparation meetings with Henry. He flicked over the first two or three pages and then looked up to start confirming.

"I know we have done this a couple of times already, but I just need to make sure I have everything correct."

"Yeah, sure, it's fine, whatever makes this go quicker and smoother I'm happy for." Henry wasn't looking any better by this point, so Ryan got up and flicked the AC on himself. Looking at his client he was now nervous about putting him on the stand; if he was like this privately, what would he be like publicly?

"So just to recap with you, DeShawn Arlington currently has your last wages payment from your final season with the Giants?"

The discrepancy was from a few years ago and Henry was late to the case against DeShawn, but seeing other athletes come forward had prompted him to reach out to the team at Macpherson & Daniels for help.

"That's right, I never saw a penny of that, which hurt considering the injury I got in the Superbowl match."

"Which was? Can you please confirm the amount which he kept from you?"

"$5.1 million," Henry responded shuddering at the answer.

These guys had mega contracts with bonuses for everything you could imagine but all throughout his short preparation for this case, Ryan couldn't get his head around how these guys could just take losing millions and millions of dollars.

"So, just to confirm, one final time, DeShawn Arlington stole $5.1 million of your money for his own gain, and you have no idea why he did it?"

"None at all. He kept promising that it was coming and it never did."

"And there was no reason why he would hold it back? Did you break a clause in your contract? Did he provide any services on top of what he should have?" Henry was a bit taken aback by the last question regarding services and he looked at Ryan with a puzzled look on his face and didn't really know how to answer the question.

"A service? What do you mean?" Ryan didn't even know how to answer his own question let alone expect Henry to give him a worthy response. The only way that question would mean anything was if he was to break attorney-client privilege with Luke and explain what he knew. He sat pondering how to come back as the pair sat awkwardly in the room looking at each other.

Ryan's phone buzzed while he was still thinking of how to word this to Henry. He looked at it to see Macpherson's name. He sent an automatic reply to his boss and finally came back with an answer to Henry's question.

"A service outside of your contract. I'm not saying you're

a shady man, but this trial has already thrown up things that I didn't know, about other plaintiffs."

"Man, it's hot in here, isn't it?" Henry stood up from his chair yanking his tie off and opening another button. "It's hot in here, isn't it? It's not just me."

The moment Ryan burst into the room Henry had looked uncomfortable which in turn wasn't making Ryan feel any better. The question remained unanswered as Henry tried to cool himself down standing under the AC unit.

"As I said, this wasn't intended to offend you or make you feel uncomfortable, I've just learned that DeShawn can be a shady character and I wanted to make sure everything was covered before we go in."

At this point Henry had his back to Ryan and his shirt was basically off as he tried to cool down. The unit was making noises, but it wasn't loud enough for him not to have heard what Ryan just said. Getting impatient with the fact he was getting nowhere trying to skirt around what he needed to say, Ryan just blurted it out.

"Has he ever made you sign an NDA? Has he taken money from you to make something *go away*?" Without mentioning Luke's name and impeaching himself Ryan couldn't have been any more to the point but the look on Henry's face when he had turned around without actually saying anything, told Ryan everything that he needed to know.

"You've got to be fucking kidding me! What's he got you on? Smuggling illegal immigrants? Bribery of a police officer?" Ryan was usually a calm character in his line of work but all he seemed to be doing so far was getting angry and losing his rag on this case – why was everyone lying to him? "Before you answer, I'm going to tell you so it's very clear in your mind. NDAs do not hold up in a court of law so whatever he has done for you will come out."

He glanced up at the clock which read 8.45 a.m. so they only had about ten, maybe fifteen minutes at a push before they went in. Ryan now feared for another shambolic day in court where DeShawn came out smelling of roses and the case slipped further away from him.

Macpherson rang his phone again so Ryan thought it must be important.

"Wait here, I need to take this." Ryan stood up and exited the room.

"I just wanted to wish you good luck, Ryan. I know we didn't get off to the best start with Luke Best but Henry's a sure-fire thing. Go kill it today."

"If you say so. I've just found out he's another one who didn't disclose an NDA. America's sweetheart has skeletons in his closet that are about to become public." Ryan's tone of voice was hushed but you could tell on the inside he was screaming from the rooftops as he made his way down the corridor to a quieter and less crowded part of the building.

"What's he done?"

"I don't know yet, we haven't quite got to that, but I'm sure I'll find out when I go back in." Ryan had even less time now to listen to Henry's story, think how to counter it and then use it in court. He had a whole day of witnesses lined up, but Henry's integrity, public image and character were the driving forces behind it all.

"Get back in there, find out and do what you can. Come back to the office after you're dismissed. Daniels and I will be waiting."

Ryan locked the phone and made his way back to the room – nine minutes until they were due in court.

"We've got under ten minutes so talk fast."

Ryan entered the room wanting Henry's explanation to be

quick and simple but he wasn't quite prepared for what he was met with: an empty room. It was a small enough room that there wasn't anywhere to hide so Ryan thought maybe he had gone to the toilet before the trial started. As he collected the pieces of paper from on the desk, he noticed one of them was turned over with something scribbled on the back of it. Ryan picked it up for a closer inspection.

> *I can't do this, I'm sorry, my family mean more than money. Henry.*

## 10

# MONDAY 19TH OCTOBER, 4.45 P.M.

"Henry, it's Ryan, this is the fourth time I've called and left a message now, so I hope that when I get back to my office in around forty-five minutes you're going to be there to explain what the hell went down today."

Ryan trudged down the courthouse steps towards the subway station with the early evening rain pelting his suit and soaking him through. It was apt that the weather matched his mood after he took another battering in court today with witnesses pulled apart and William using high-profile athletes to build DeShawn's credibility. Henry going AWOL a matter of minutes before they were due to start the week's proceedings, focusing on his part of the case further dented his chances of actually winning. To make matters worse you could tell how furious Judge Sullivan was with everything that had happened. Ryan waited on the platform, rain dripped from the cuffs of his suit jacket, and he knew that he was going back to the office to give his two bosses more bad news and to think of *another* plan that was no doubt going to become pointless by the start of Matt's involvement. He boarded the crowded train and zoned out temporarily as a couple of street performers danced their way through the carriage to a loud hip-hop song. He contemplated going home to regroup and see Emilia but deep down Ryan knew this wasn't the best thing to do as much as he wanted to, so he sighed and waited for his stop.

As he walked up the steps to exit the station the rain got a lot worse. It was torrential, soaking Ryan through by the time he had taken a couple of steps on the sidewalk. He thought about jogging to the office, but he was wet enough now and knew he had spare clothes in his office to change into when he got there. He also didn't want to start the meeting with Macpherson and Daniels anytime sooner than he had to because it wasn't going to be one of his most enjoyable meetings with them. Entering the building he removed his suit jacket and shook his body as if he was a dog after getting out of a river. His white shirt stuck to him and was now completely see-through, and he left wet footprints as he made his way to the elevator. He let a couple of people exit before entering and pressing for his floor, unbuttoning his shirt on the way up as it didn't make much difference if it was on or off. Making his way through the sparsely occupied office he could see that his superiors were already in the boardroom waiting for him. Catching Daniels' eye as he walked past, he smiled and signaled he'd be two minutes as he headed to his office to change. Checking his emails and office phone voicemails quickly there was no communication at all from Henry as he slipped into a fresh shirt and trousers. It was time to go and face the music. He quickly unlocked his phone and sent a text to Emilia telling her he'd be home late and not to make him dinner, but she'd preempted this already as she was used to him coming home all hours of the night during a trial if something wasn't going his way. He lumbered down the office and entered the boardroom.

"Evening, both, how are you?" Ryan asked the question through gritted teeth and a false smile as he tried to hide his horrid day and start the conversation off on a positive note. Macpherson responded first.

"We are both fine thanks, Ryan, but it's more you that we're worried about after today's showing in court." How did they know already? The day had finished not even an hour ago for the people involved so news travelled fast if they really knew. "Let's just say Judge Sullivan and I go back a long way," she followed up. "We're both members of the same country and golf club and have been for over twenty years."

Sometimes this game was all about who you knew not what you knew and ever since moving to such a prestigious firm as Macpherson & Daniels Ryan was learning that day by day.

"So, come on then, what happened? Tell us and we will see if we can help," Daniels added as he slid over a large glass of whiskey from across the desk.

"Henry left before the trial. Macpherson rang so I answered out in the corridor and when I got back, he had gone. Left a note saying he couldn't do this to his family."

"Couldn't do what exactly? Recoup millions of pounds for them to spend?"

"He's hiding something, similar to Luke, there's something he's not telling me." Ryan took a large swig of the whiskey and continued, "I mentioned about *a service* and *NDA* without mentioning Luke's name and he went as white as a ghost."

Macpherson and Daniels looked at each other in disbelief before both turning their focus back on Ryan.

"Ryan, do you know why we hired you? Why you have a corner office at one of largest firms in the city?"

Ryan couldn't figure out whether it was a rhetorical question or not so he made it look as if he was deep in thought and hoped they would answer it for him.

"You're undoubtedly one of the best young lawyers we've seen in a long time but the shoddiness you've shown so far on this case proves you have a lot to learn in this game."

The tone a dull one, Ryan couldn't quite work out who said it because he daydreamed whilst still trying to look like he was thinking of an answer. Was now a good time for sarcasm as opposed to beforehand?

"I honestly don't know what it is with these guys and what DeShawn Arlington does to them. I did my due diligence as well as I could on short notice, Sandy used a PI and still things are coming up daily that I don't know about." Now was probably the best time if there ever was one to explain about the incident last week with Victor and Sandy. Ryan finished his glass of whiskey and poured himself another large glass before continuing, "This guy is so shady, yet he's never lost a case before – why?"

"Because he is shady, you said it yourself; he stops at nothing to win and usually does." Daniels kicked back and put his feet up on the desk. "Remember the time that he beat you?" he said looking sideways at Macpherson.

"You've gone up against DeShawn before?" Ryan tucked his chair and himself in a little tighter with his full attention now on his boss.

"I knew you'd bring that up tonight. I'm going to get sushi and some more drink before we start this story. Either of you two want anything?" Macpherson exited the room whilst the other two checked their phones.

As she unscrewed the lid from a bottle of wine and gorged on sushi from the shop across the street you could tell Macpherson was delaying the inevitable whilst trying to find the best way to come across in the story. Ryan prompted her by restarting the conversation.

"So what happened with you and DeShawn in a previous case?"

"It was nothing, we went head to head on a case and I lost fair and square."

"Was it fair and square, though? What was it about?"

Daniels' phone buzzed and he was distracted temporarily whilst Ryan fired quick questions. He got up from his chair and headed towards the exit.

"I have dinner waiting for me – I've done what I came to do. Listen carefully, Ryan, and buck your ideas up – I'll call you later, Mac."

Within moments it was just the two of them left in the room and Ryan repeated the same question.

"So what happened?"

"It was years ago in a trivial case that I thought I could win; DeShawn had signed some young college kids from Austin who then turned pro years later and he tried to hold them to it." Macpherson had already finished her first glass of wine and poured another as Ryan waited with bated breath for her story to continue. "He signed them from all sports – NBA, NHL, NFL, MLS and just tried to cling onto them when they were drafted."

"What was a Brooklyn native doing out in Austin? Tip-off, you think?"

"I have no idea, it looked like a clean-cut case, though, when I got it, but DeShawn just did everything to throw me off my game and eventually it worked, and the case was dismissed."

Ryan leaned back on his chair, deep in thought about what to ask next as the information he was getting was very short and sweet. He could tell his boss didn't want to talk about it but he was trying to educate himself.

"How did he throw you off? He's been doing that to me the past few days but I didn't want to mention it."

"He just kept chipping away at little things and then when I got close to what I thought was winning he threatened my family." Macpherson was holding her glass of wine swishing it around as she rotated her wrist, completely lost in the moment.

"What did you do? Walk away?" The sound of Ryan's voice snapped her back into the room and she looked up at Ryan.

"I threw the case out. It was the only way; it's what he wanted."

Ryan was stunned. Macpherson was one of, if not the most respected and feared legal women in New York and had been for decades.

"I can see what you want to say, Ryan. It's OK, you can say it. Everyone loses cases; it's part of the game."

Ryan still didn't know what to say back to her; his mouth was open but there was no response.

"I need something stronger than wine." Daniels had taken his decanter of whiskey with him so Macpherson got up to get a bottle from her office. Ryan didn't move.

She reemerged moments later with liquor under her arm but no glass in hand so it seemed as if Ryan was going to be drinking the bottled beer for the rest of this conversation. She sat down and placed the bottle on the table. Ryan drank from the half-full bottle. He had just about regained his composure and was ready to ask questions again.

"How do I beat him?"

"Now that is the golden question and that is why we gave you the case, Ryan."

It was slowly starting to make sense in his head, why a case of this magnitude had landed in his lap over the rest of the lawyers at the firm. He thought that either one of his bosses would have taken it once Sandy bailed but with Macpherson already trying and losing and Daniels knowing what happened, it made sense why they handed it down to him.

"He's not quite threatened my family yet but he did have Emilia followed yesterday around the city."

The wandering eyes of his mentor quickly came back to focus on him.

"That means he's worried about you – if he's already trying to strongarm you then he sees you as a threat."

Ryan found himself content with the compliment he'd just received. So far in his mind he had spent two days in court with this man and he had convincingly lost both days.

"Ryan, do you want me to be truthful with you? Do you mind?"

"Do I have much of a choice in the matter?" They both chuckled slightly at Ryan's response but you could tell that neither party was here for jokes.

"We knew you were going to lose this case, that's why we gave it to you. We both know you're extremely good at what you do but we wanted to see how you reacted in defeat – so that one day we could put your name on that wall."

Her eyes looked through Ryan to the wall that separated the two elevators. Ryan turned around and slowly said, "Macpherson, Daniels and Jackson."

Both caught in the moment, silence followed, whilst Ryan looked at the wall imagining his name up there. The moment passed and he turned back around.

"What if I don't lose to DeShawn? What if I beat him? Then what?"

"I like the enthusiasm but you won't do – many have tried and many have failed; there's no shame in that, Ryan. Like we said it's what you do after which is key for us."

Ryan pushed himself away from the desk and stood up to leave the room. He didn't need to hear any more. As he got to the door he turned and looked at his boss.

"Thanks for setting me up to fail. For your information I'm

going to beat DeShawn Arlington and now when I do I want my name on that wall." He walked out of the boardroom and headed for his office.

Macpherson picked up her phone and sent a text to Daniels:

*It's done. He knows what we know. It's all or nothing…*

Furiously Ryan grabbed an old coat that was hanging up in the office and headed to leave. As he got to the lobby, he could still see Macpherson sitting in the boardroom drinking but decided not to go in and continue venting as it'd get him nowhere. The few moments between getting in and out of the elevator Ryan briefly tried to get his head around the fact he had been set up by his bosses to lose a case. Were Luke, Henry and Matt in on it? Did Judge Sullivan know he would lose? Did DeShawn give Luke the settlement so he felt a small win? The rain had stopped by now but Ryan put his coat on just in case on the off chance it started up again. He had decided to walk home and although he could jump on the subway at any given point, he wanted the walk so he could clear his mind and think and not take all this home to Emilia. She would absolutely hit the roof if she found out what Ryan just did. As Ryan stamped the wet sidewalk, zoned out, he stepped in a rather large puddle that splashed up his trouser leg and soaked his shoe through – was this day ever going to end? The bright lights blurred into one as he passed by Macys and continued to head north. He pulled his phone from his pocket but the battery had died so he didn't know if Henry had tried calling him or if Emilia had messaged at all. He usually avoided walking through Times Square because it was so busy but today, he thought it might help. As he got there, he looked up at the Mega Screen to see the news rolling past the bottom and noticed Luke had had a career-high game that afternoon as the Knicks had beaten Wizards on kids' day at The Garden. At least someone had a positive outcome from the day. The remaining blocks went quickly and as Ryan hit the park, he made the decision to veer west; Mulligans it was. His head was still all over the place and if he went back now it would just cause an argument with Emilia that he didn't want to have.

By the time Ryan got into the bar it was around 8.45 p.m. and the rain had started again so he was slightly wet but the coat had saved him from a similar fate to earlier. The bar was mildly busy but the weather drove the tourists away as it always did, so there was space at the bar to perch himself. One of the regular barmen was working so like clockwork by the time Ryan got to the bar stool there was an uncapped Heineken waiting for him.

"You look like how I feel about working this 164-hour shift, buddy," said the barman as Ryan swiped the beer and guzzled it down. Mixing whiskey and beer on a Tuesday night in the middle of a trial wasn't one of his usual habits but then this was no ordinary trial.

"Don't even get me started, man. Have you got an iPhone charger that I can borrow?"

The guy turned round to unplug his phone and handed Ryan one of the extra-long chargers that you buy online.

"Here, this should do the trick and your phone will be next to you."

He disappeared to continue serving other customers further down the bar and Ryan waited for it to charge up. As he waited, he looked up at the screen and with the Knicks having played and Nets having a night off the TV was showing just a generic sports news channel recapping every team that populated the New York tri-state area. It flicked to soccer which he didn't really have an interest in, so he impatiently looked down at his phone as if it was the phone's fault that it had run out of battery and was taking so long to charge. As his iPhone eventually lit up, he signaled for another beer and as his phone began to wildly buzz, ding and beep, his eyes tried to capture every piece of information that appeared. Unknown number, Emilia, email, email, Emilia, Macpherson, email, social media, email – nothing from Henry. Slamming the phone back onto the bar, the noise echoed around and everyone turned to look. He held his hand up to apologize but he wasn't sorry because his bad day wasn't getting any better. He downed the entire bottle of the second beer and signaled again this time for another two, ending any hope he would make it home to Emilia anytime soon. He opened the text messages from her to make sure she was OK after yesterday but in hindsight they were more text messages to make sure that he was OK after the day. He started to type a response:

*In Mulligans, awful day. Don't wait up, I love you x x x*

## 11

# TUESDAY 20TH OCTOBER, 3.42 A.M.

Ryan's phone shook on the bedside table next to his head and the bright light lit up the pitch-black room. He slept through the first couple of vibrations but a heel to the shin from Emilia, who had clearly been woken by it, quickly brought him to his senses and he fumbled for his phone. As he looked at the screen his eyes adjusted to see it was Henry Craig's name and number. Ryan answered sounding half asleep because he was in fact half asleep, but it wasn't a call that he could afford to miss.

"Meet me outside the MetLife Stadium in forty-five minutes. I'll be waiting underneath the MetLife Central sign." Henry cut the phone off and left Ryan a little bewildered, still lying in bed and now back in the dark. He heaved himself up and looked at his alarm clock, 3.45 a.m. He had only been in bed for a couple of hours after coming home from Mulligans and then drinking half a bottle of red wine in the flat and watching the end of a terrible movie. He knew he had to go and meet Henry as it was imperative to the case.

"Who the hell was that?" Emilia fumed as she rolled over and was greeted by the now cold side of the bed as Ryan wasn't there.

"It was Henry. He wants to meet me now so I need to get dressed and go." Standing up, he flicked the flashlight on his phone to guide him out of the room. "Go back to sleep, Em, it's still the middle of the night and I'll be back before I go to work anyway."

He collected a tracksuit he had draped over the back of Emilia's make-up chair and made his way into the living room to get dressed. A mixture of heavy drinking and lack of sleep made Ryan feel groggy and lethargic, but he knew whatever was about to happen with Henry he needed to be at the top of his game. He flicked on the kettle for a coffee and opened his phone to order an Uber over to New Jersey.

He opened the door at the bottom of his flats and made his way down the stairs and into the cab waiting for him.

"MetLife Stadium please, bud, by the sign."

"At this hour? Boy, you must be a dedicated fan. What tickets are going on sale?"

Ryan chuckled as the car pulled away and headed towards the George Washington Bridge and into New Jersey. As they crossed the bridge Ryan looked south towards the skyline of Manhattan and he got caught in the moment thinking how life would change if he became a named partner. He spent a couple of minutes away with the fairies before they took the exit on the bridge and headed towards the MetLife via I-95 Express.

Because of the time, the cab driver was able to drop Ryan basically where he had asked. He got out and promised a tip. Turning to head towards the meeting point, he glanced down at his watch and saw he was around five or six minutes early for the meet time suggested by Henry. As he walked down towards the MetLife Central area Ryan noticed there was someone already there dressed in an all-black tracksuit, hood up and black trainers. He was hoping that it would be Henry but whoever it was clearly didn't want to be seen there in that attire. As he got a little closer the person turned to face him and it was indeed Henry. He rushed towards Ryan to meet him halfway.

"Let's walk and talk; we can't stay here too long," he said ushering Ryan back towards the way that he came from.

"I appreciate you finally reaching out after yesterday's debacle, I really do, but did it have to be at 4.30 a.m. in the morning and in New Jersey?"

"I'm sorry about earlier, I just… I just froze and I couldn't have been put on the stand."

"It's fine, well it's not, but I'd rather it happened how it did rather than the case be made any worse."

The two of them started to walk and talk around the complex – Henry had complete access as he still used the physio and rehab section at the club and they wouldn't be disturbed at this time of the morning.

"I still don't get the 4.30 a.m. meeting, Henry. Couldn't we have done this at a more normal hour? Or at least inside somewhere?" Ryan now pulled his hood up to cover his head as the night temperature sent shivers down the back of his neck.

"I needed to talk to you about why I left earlier and I needed to know it was just me and you and no one else. Pass me your phone." Starved of sleep and not wanting to delay, Ryan handed over his phone which Henry switched off and placed in his pocket. "It's not that I don't trust you, I just don't trust other people. You've been nothing but honest with me," he continued as he now switched his own phone off as well.

With what happened with Luke and the real reason behind his missing money Ryan knew whatever he was about to hear wasn't going to help the case but at least he'd finally know the truth and just maybe he could think of yet another way to spin this.

"So come on then, what *service* did DeShawn provide you with that cost you over $5 million?"

"Firstly, I want to know how you know about DeShawn's services?"

"Let's just say whatever you're about to tell me, it seems as if DeShawn has done it to others and will likely do it again." Henry stopped in his steps and looked at Ryan as if he wanted more explanation from his lawyer. "I can't say any more, you know that, but you can, so what happened?"

"The image the general public has, the image the media has, basically the image that everyone in this country has of me was saved by DeShawn a few years ago." Henry removed the hood from his head but didn't turn to look at Ryan, instead continuing to face forward, almost as if he was talking to himself to get this weight off his shoulders. "Three years ago, the season before the injury in the Superbowl, do you remember the Giants losing to the Cowboys in the NFC Championship game?"

Ryan wasn't into NFL as much as other sports but he knew enough to hold a conversation and he'd usually watch the NY games if he had the time to.

"Yes, I remember that game. Isn't that the one where you—"

"Don't say it, but yes, it was *that* game you're thinking of." The disappointment was still clear to hear in Henry's voice as he continued his story, "Well, basically, after the game, coach gave a rousing speech, consoled us all, etc., but he had to fly to Tampa for his daughter's wedding so we were left on our own in Dallas before we came home." Straight away in Ryan's mind he flicked back to Luke's story about going out after winning a game, but it couldn't have been the same story because they lost. "Well, we got changed, spoke to the media and then headed back to the team hotel, as you would."

Ryan was about to interrupt Henry to finish his story for him to see if it mirrored Luke's and they had both been caught in strip clubs.

"Let me guess, you then went out to—"

"No, let me finish please, Ryan, I need to get this off my chest finally."

It was the second time one of them had interrupted the conversation so Ryan decided that maybe it was best if he just let Henry say what he needed to.

"Everyone kind of did their own thing when we got back. Some went to their rooms, some went to the bar, some went to the sauna but generally, we were spread across the hotel." Henry paused, his mind elsewhere; the words just didn't seem to want to come out. "Only me and DeShawn know about this. You swear you won't tell anyone?"

"Attorney-client privilege; I couldn't even if I wanted to."

It looked as if Henry was finally about to tell all. So far having a few beers after losing a championship game wasn't worth paying your agent millions of dollars to cover up.

"I was in the bar with maybe seven or eight of the guys, a few of them players and a few coaches. Anyway, behind the bar serving us there was this gorgeous blonde who spent literally the whole night looking at me."

"So, you had an affair with this blonde woman and that's what DeShawn covered up?" Ryan couldn't help but interrupt him again to try and finish a story that looked to be heading only one way.

"Well, kind of, yes, I don't actually know if I did or I didn't."

Now it was Ryan's turn to slow down as he was slightly perplexed about the situation. "How can you not know if you had sex with another woman?"

"Can I finish my story and then you can ask your questions?"

"That's fine but can we please get a hot drink or something, I am officially frozen."

After they'd been inside to warm up and get a drink the pair exited one of the park's many buildings and continued their walk. The sun was starting to rise and covered some of the facility in a tinge of orange. The time was fast approaching 6 a.m. now and Ryan was conscious that he was due in court in three hours and still had to get back from New Jersey and change into his suit.

"So go on, how did it all unfold with this mystery blonde?"

"Well, basically, as the numbers started to dwindle in our group, I started looking at her more and she was looking back and we exchanged a few smiles. I don't know what got into me; I'm a happily married man." They were starting to cross paths with more people now as the staff started to appear to set up the day for when the players arrived to train. Henry's voice dropped to a whisper even with no one within earshot. "Well, when I was the only one left, I ordered another drink and headed over to the side of the bar to chat to her and that's all I intended to do."

"Good intentions from a man in your position – so what went wrong?"

"I don't know, that's where it all goes a little bit hazy. I remember drinking my drink and having a laugh with her. She was funny, she was originally from New York and supported the Jets so there was a bit of back and forth but then that's where my memory finishes."

"I assume that's because of the drink you'd consumed all night, if I was to take a guess?"

"Well again, no, because I felt completely fine, like I had only had six or seven maybe, and then all of a sudden the next thing I'm waking up in her room, with her gone and me naked."

"OK – so you've made a drunken mistake. How does

DeShawn come into all this?" Ryan was trying to piece together how DeShawn got involved in Henry's mistake, unless Henry was the one who told him.

"He knew because the woman tried to blackmail me."

Luke had put himself at risk by being an NBA point guard in a strip club and now Henry had put himself at risk by being an NFL quarterback and having an affair. Would these elite athletes ever learn that they were more than recognizable to the general public?

"You slept with a woman who you already knew liked the NFL and knew who you were? How could you be so stupid?" Ryan's response was his first thought but somewhere in between thinking it and saying it the question became a rhetorical one. "You've won the Superbowl, been in magazine photoshoots and part of commercial campaigns for the biggest of companies – how did you really think this was going to end?"

"I don't know, I clearly wasn't thinking straight after that game, was I?"

"Hold up, you said she was gone when you woke up so how did she try and blackmail you?"

"Well, opposite the bed was a mirror and she had stuck three polaroid pictures to it of me and her, not doing anything but it would have been hard to convince someone otherwise."

*Why on earth would a woman in this day and age be carrying round a polaroid camera* Ryan thought? Unless she was a photographer, he found it a little bit weird she would have had that piece of equipment on her.

"On the back of one of the photos she had written:

*Mr Craig, thanks for last night but what would your wife think? If I were you, I would contact me ASAP so we can sort this out.*

She left her number on a different polaroid and the last one just had a lipstick kiss on it. I panicked and called DeShawn to help."

Ryan rolled his eyes hearing that DeShawn had *helped* the whole situation go away. Apart from a slightly different scenario, the situation Henry had got himself into seemed all too familiar to Luke's story.

"Let me guess, you called DeShawn and told him what had happened, he said he would sort it, came back with a figure from this blonde lady which you agreed to, and you've heard nothing more since?"

"She vanished and I've never mentioned it to anyone else since that day." Henry's voice was a little louder now the story was over and he looked a lot perkier, almost as if he was free from a massive weight off his shoulders. "DeShawn at the time advised that we both sign NDAs on the matter to protect each other and I agreed."

"So why did you decide you'd now sue him for $5.1 million after all of the above being kept quiet?"

"If I'm honest, Ryan, I need the money. My wife spends money like it's going out of fashion, the kids are at private school and I invested in a real estate project that collapsed and there's not much money left."

It was now a lot busier around the park as practically all of the staff were now there and some of the existing Giants' players were arriving.

"So, you heard about Luke and Matt and thought you'd chance your arm? Not knowing your NDA would be broken?"

"Pretty much. If I knew it would have caused all this, I certainly would've thought twice." Henry stopped walking and sat down on a bench. "So where do we go from here now? Do I withdraw? Do you still want me to testify?"

"I don't know, I haven't figured that out yet. Be at court

at 9 a.m. and let me do some thinking between now and then."

Ryan raised his wrist and looked at his watch. It read 7.15 a.m. and he was up against it now timewise to get to court on time. Henry passed him his phone back and he turned to leave, opening an app to try and book transport back to the city. Something in his mind clicked.

"Henry, did you ever question the amount? The $5.1 million she asked for?"

"No, I didn't. I trusted DeShawn and just wanted this gone so I agreed."

Ryan nodded and pondered the answer. It was such a specific amount.

"Actually, be at court for midday. I've got some bits to sort beforehand." With that he was off down the pathway heading for the exit.

As he reached the front of the stadium the cab was waiting to pick him up and take him back to his apartment. Surprisingly it was the same man who had dropped him off.

"You again?" the man said with a smile appearing. "Did you get those tickets you wanted?"

Ryan laughed at the question but didn't humor him with an answer.

"I need to get back to the Upper West quickly. This journey was $20 earlier so I'll give you $50 if we can get there in under forty-five minutes."

Without saying a word the driver turned around, switched off his sat nav and sped away from the stadium, but this time rather than the bridge, he headed for the Lincoln Tunnel.

The figure of $5.1 million was still rattling around in his head after Henry had explained what really happened. It was so precise – why would the woman have asked for that exact amount? Bearing in mind that the figure matched his last parachute payment from the Giants, it wasn't a coincidence to him that both totals were the same. Was he on to something? He was shooting fish in a barrel at the moment but it was all he could do after having two of his three clients hide NDAs thinking they held up in a court of law. He opened his phone and started writing a text to Macpherson:

*I think I might have something.*

## 12

# TUESDAY 20TH OCTOBER, 7.50 A.M.

The Uber broke hard outside Ryan's apartment and he ran into the building at speed. As instructed, the driver sat waiting outside to take Ryan to his final destination. As he burst through the door panting, Emilia was walking out of the bathroom in nothing but a towel and jumped at the noise.

"Christ, Ryan, I thought you were a burglar for a second there," she snapped.

"What, at 7.55 a.m. in the morning?" He laughed as he squeezed past his wife, lifting and turning her in the process and made his way towards the bedroom. Throwing back the wardrobe doors he picked out the first suit he could see and slung on a sky-blue shirt as a complement, grabbed a tie and headed back out to the lounge.

"Ryan, I know you're in the middle of a trial but am I actually going to see you before I leave on Friday?" Emilia was used to not seeing her husband as much as she'd like during his cases but usually, he didn't spend late nights drinking followed by random early morning meetings.

"I'm sorry, I'm so, so sorry. This case isn't going to plan and I'm just trying to do all I can to win it, you know what I'm like."

Unfortunately for Emilia she did know what he was like so if something wasn't going Ryan's way and he had his back against the wall, likelihood was that she would be pushed aside temporarily.

"You know what next week is, right? Please tell me you haven't forgotten?"

Ryan was trying to put his shoes on, make a coffee to go and he still hadn't done his hair yet but now his brain was in overdrive trying to work out what was happening the next week.

"Of course I haven't forgotten; where are we going and what time again?" He hoped that the generic question would give him a good enough answer so that he could work out what Emilia was talking about as she left the lounge and headed to the bedroom.

As he bent down to splash some water over his face, he was met with the reflection of Emilia now standing behind him and blocking the doorway to the bathroom.

"You've forgotten, haven't you?"

"Em, I haven't got time for this at all this morning. I'm going to be late." He rinsed his hands and shook them dry choosing not to use the towel to the left of him. "I have to leave, like now. Can you move, please?"

She reluctantly moved her arm and he made his way towards the front door.

"Nowhere is booked yet, you can choose the place, time and even the date if you truly remember."

Ryan opened the door and headed out with whatever he replied to his wife lost in between him closing the door and rushing down the hallway.

Momentarily his brain scanned its memory for what could possibly be happening next week that he had completely forgotten about, however the thought didn't even get him out the elevator before his attention was turned back to what it should have been on – the trial. His phone pinged up and it was a reply from Macpherson:

*Don't do anything stupid, I'll meet you at the court.*

Macpherson hadn't been seen anywhere near a court for a good five or six years so the fact she was going to show her face this morning made Ryan feel both nervous and excited at the same time. She was either going to show up to help Ryan or, after their conversation last night, hinder him. Recklessly zigzagging through traffic to make it downtown on time, the cab driver was really trying to earn the extra money Ryan had promised him when they left New Jersey. Skipping a red light three blocks from the courthouse they narrowly avoided a motorbike that was clearly already speeding towards them from the other direction.

"OK, man, I want to get there on time, but I also want to get there alive," Ryan said from the back of the vehicle after the near miss.

They arrived with time to spare which was ideal as Ryan could have a very quick briefing with Macpherson before the trial started for the day. Ryan opened his wallet and gave the guy $110 for the journey which was double what the journey cost and quick as flash he disappeared into the building and headed for the side room that he had occupied so far. As he barged into the room, he was met with the most unsuspecting sight: his opposing number, DeShawn, and Macpherson. William quickly made his way to his feet.

"Err, I'm sorry, Ryan, they must have switched rooms today. You're down the hall in room 3."

Ryan was completely stunned and had his hand glued on

the doorknob. Why was Macpherson in the room with the people he was up against? Ryan thought she was coming to see and speak with him. Removing his hand, barely standing upright he calmly said, "Does someone want to tell me what's going on here?" Silence. "I said, does someone want to tell me what's going on here and why my boss is sitting with my opponent midway through a fucking trial?"

Still, no one replied to Ryan but instead Macpherson stood up and walked over towards him.

"We're done here now so let's continue this conversation between you and me down the hall, shall we?"

Neither of them said a word the whole way down the corridor but as soon as they got into the room Ryan exploded into a fit of rage.

"I've been up since fucking 3.30 this morning for this case and firm, I've been over bridges and through tunnels to New Jersey and back before 9 a.m. and you're in there having a chat with the opposition!"

They did not have much time at all before Ryan had to be in court so Macpherson tried to pour water on his flames.

"Firstly, calm down. Secondly, you need to remember who you now represent, Ryan. We are one of the biggest and most prestigious law firms in the city, not some up and coming shop where you can act however you want." She removed her suit jacket and took a seat on one of four that were in the room. "So are you going to tell me why you were in New Jersey at 4 a.m. this morning?"

Ryan went over and poured himself a cup of water from the machine in the corner, drank the entire cup before refilling it and heading back to the table. Visibly, he was still furious.

"Henry called me at 3.30 a.m. this morning and asked

me to go over to the Giants' complex to meet him after he disappeared yesterday."

A small smile appeared out of the side of Macpherson's mouth.

"Brilliant, so at least you've found him and spoken to him. That's one worry off my mind."

However, no quicker than the smile appeared than it disappeared when Ryan told her that Henry was in the same boat as Luke and had lied about the money. It was time for Ryan to go into court. Macpherson said that she would wait to catch up at the break and lunch but for now Ryan had done all he could.

"I've already been into Judge Sullivan and cleared it with him for you to call DeShawn back to the stand so feel free to," Macpherson said as Ryan walked out.

He still did not have any clarity on what they were doing together but maybe she had not lost her touch after all.

"You may all be seated," Judge Sullivan said as he sat down to begin the morning's proceedings. He scoured the courtroom carefully. "I see that you still have not brought your client Mr Craig with you, Mr Jackson? Are you taking this seriously at all?"

Ryan stood up from his seat and buttoned his jacket before walking towards the judge.

"He will be here for the afternoon, Your Honor. I spoke with him this morning and asked him to be here from midday."

Macpherson entered the courtroom and took a seat towards the back of the room.

"I'm glad he'll be here this afternoon but let's see how this morning plays out first." He held up a piece of paper to read that he had brought with him. "This morning it was agreed that Mr Arlington could be called back to the stand so I assume that is what you're going to do, Mr Jackson?"

Ryan took a quick glance over his shoulder and caught the eye of Macpherson who didn't give any indication that's what he shouldn't do.

"That's correct, Your Honor, I would like to call DeShawn Arlington back to the stand."

He turned to face the man he had just called upon and as usual he grinned a slimy smile as he slowly rose to his feet and made his way over to the witness box.

"What could you possibly want with me again, Ryan?" DeShawn said after being sworn back in and making himself comfortable.

Ryan proceeded to a central position but did not once take his eyes off DeShawn when doing so.

"I just think after some recent conversations I have had, that there were some things I missed off from when you were last here. Is that OK?"

"It's completely fine by me, young man, please go on."

Everything about DeShawn irked Ryan and as the days went on, he was getting more and more determined to beat him.

"The amounts of money we've discussed so far, $7.3 million and $5.1 million, are very specific."

"Objection, Your Honor, the $7.3 million is no longer relevant in this case," William shouted.

Without hesitation the judge sustained the objection as the jury knew the first figure related to Luke Best who was no longer part of the case.

"Sorry, Your Honor, I will rephrase that. $5.1 million is a very specific number to go missing, isn't it?"

"Yes, you're right, it is a very specific number, isn't it? Why do you ask?" The smirk was still very prominent on his face as he responded.

"I am just thinking why would you steal $5.1 million

dollars and not $5 million or $5.5 million? The numbers don't add up to me."

"I didn't steal anything from Henry Craig and if you continue to say that, then you'll find a deformation of character suit coming your way once this nonsense is finished."

It was the first time DeShawn had broken his character as he snapped back at Ryan but little did he know it was the answer Ryan wanted.

"That's right, you didn't steal it but Henry paid you that figure to—"

The doors swung open at the back of the courtroom and Henry Craig entered the room.

He wasn't due for another two and a half hours and his arrival had completely thrown Ryan off course as he was about to detonate a bomb that would have helped him, no doubt, but was going to throw Henry under a bus.

"Mr Craig, it's wonderful of you to join us finally. Please take a seat," said Judge Sullivan as a few sniggers broke out.

"Sorry, Your Honor, I had a few urgent family things to tie up before I could be here but I'm here now and I would like to formally withdraw my case against DeShawn Arlington."

Ryan's jaw hit the floor, DeShawn's smile widened even more and Macpherson put her head in her hands. Ryan quickly made his way over to Henry and you couldn't have got a sheet of paper between the pair as he leaned in and started a conversation in a quiet tone. However, he couldn't get more than three or four words out before Henry stopped him.

"Ryan, I know you're going to argue but I need to either settle or drop the case. My family means more to me than money and as much as I'm struggling, I'm sure I could do some punditry or take a job coaching; this isn't the way."

Ryan didn't really know what to say because Henry had

already announced to the judge, jury, and everyone else that he was withdrawing.

"Now listen, Mr Craig, if you want to stand by what you just said then I will have no hesitation in settling your part of this case right now." Judge Sullivan hovered over his gavel to finish the second part of the trial.

DeShawn beckoned William over and whispered in his ear which led him to announce, "Your Honor, Mr Arlington has requested a break so he can speak with Mr Jackson and Mr Craig."

The judge glanced at the clock; they had only been in the morning session for a little over thirty minutes.

"Granted, fifteen minutes recess but when I come back this had better be sorted."

The four of them exited court together and headed back to William and DeShawn's allocated room to discuss Henry's way out. Ryan was visibly furious with Henry, also with himself, but most of all DeShawn as the compassion he showed in the courtroom would look great. It could well be the final nail in the trial's coffin. As the door closed and the four of them cramped in, you could cut the tension with a knife between Ryan and the others. It felt like three versus one. DeShawn was first to speak.

"What happened, Henry? How has it come to this after all we've been through?" His tone was condescending and very *Godfather*-esque towards Henry.

"I'm sorry, DeShawn. I just need the money. I saw Luke and Matt were going through with this and I thought, why not, I might recoup some of the money."

"But you're worth millions and millions of dollars. I've witnessed the contracts you've signed!"

"You know the wife, she spends like crazy," Henry replied

sounding like a broken man. "There's not much left already; I had to try."

DeShawn pondered his reply, leaned into William and they quietly exchanged words and as he pulled away, he was interrupted by a knock at the door.

"Come in," William blurted out, finally making a decision of his own without having to consult DeShawn. Macpherson appeared and promptly shut the door squeezing herself into the crowded room, her back against the now closed door.

"Who's she?"

Henry didn't want anybody else in on this.

"She's fine. Don't worry about her, she can stay," came from DeShawn before Ryan could open his mouth. Macpherson and Ryan made eye contact and you could tell that DeShawn was driving a wedge between them.

"$1.6 million. I'll give you $1.6 million to settle this case against me despite you already confirming you'll drop it."

Henry's eyes lit up at the figure and he outstretched his hand to shake DeShawn's before anyone else could say a word. Ryan rolled his eyes which was a good job because his boss's eyes were burning a hole in the side of his head. Macpherson and Ryan trudged out to the corridor and Henry followed shortly after but not before giving DeShawn a hug and thanking him for the money.

Ryan made his way back to the other room, followed by the other two who were both engrossed in their phones which he assumed was about what had just happened. As Henry reached the room, before he could say anything, Macpherson slammed the door and launched into a tirade.

"You lying piece of shit. How dare you jump on a bandwagon for a financial gain knowing you were the one lying. People like you make me sick."

Henry was taken aback by Macpherson and her words as he wasn't properly introduced to her and didn't really know who she was.

"Don't talk to me like that, you're nothing to do with this case."

By now Macpherson was spitting feathers at Henry and what came next ensured Ryan's client promptly left the room.

"I'm Ryan's boss and one half of Macpherson & Daniels. I know Ryan met you at 4 a.m. this morning to discuss something sensitive and you had better pray tonight when you sleep, I don't accidentally leak it to the press. Now get lost."

With just the two of them left in the room Ryan thought that this would be a time to regroup, to go again with a little guidance from his boss. So far, the trial had been a rocky road for the young lawyer but her being there today showed Ryan she was up for being in the trenches alongside him.

"Thanks, although I could have done that myself," Ryan opened with.

"I'm glad you could do something for yourself because so far you haven't done much."

Ryan raised an eyebrow and stuttered his response, "What?"

"Do not what me! Two of the three clients in this case have lied to you and settled their cases seventy-two hours into the trial. We're going to be the laughing stock of the city come the end of this trial – buck your fucking ideas up." Ryan went to reply to Macpherson but nothing came out and even if it did Macpherson would have spoken over him. "This isn't the minor leagues anymore, Ryan. We dragged you out of that. We see something in you, you know this and you told me the other night you were going to win this." He really couldn't read his boss one bit; firstly she was having a go at him and now she was trying to support him and tell him how good he was?

"Now you need to get back in there and salvage something with whatever witnesses you have left today. Don't focus on the case, focus on DeShawn, OK!?"

"Yes, boss, got it."

Macpherson turned and left the room and Ryan started to regroup.

A faint knock at the door of his room and he realized time was up and he was due back in the courtroom to resume proceedings. He had half an idea about his next move and how to approach the rest of the day but if this trial had taught him anything it was that DeShawn was probably already a step ahead of whatever he was thinking. Had he finally reached a level where he couldn't outsmart and outhustle the opposition? It was even a fellow lawyer who was getting the better of him and that was what was eating at him inside. He made his way over to the door fiddling with his phone on the way. He opened his text messages and started writing one to Emilia's dad:

*Are you in the city today? I need to meet you to talk – Yale Club 8 p.m.?*

## 13

# TUESDAY 20TH OCTOBER, 6.58 P.M.

Ryan had been holed up in a dingy-lit bar since the end of the day's proceedings. It was now fast approaching 7 p.m. already so he had not moved for nearly two hours whilst consuming a lot of whiskey. He didn't fit in in the place he'd chosen to drink as many of the people that surrounded him were aged between twenty-one and twenty-five and clearly on a wage that meant they had to take advantage of the bar's happy-hour offering. He tipped his whiskey glass up and stared through the bottom of it into nothing before downing the small amount of liquor that was left in it. Gesturing to the bartender that he was done, he left a couple of $100 bills under a napkin and headed out. The bill would have come to just over half of that, but he figured someone needed it more than him. As he pulled his beige trench coat on, he headed east towards Brooklyn Bridge as he needed to catch a train back towards Grand Central to meet Emilia's father who had graciously decided to come into the city to meet Ryan after he heard how the case was going. As Ryan got to the station, he glanced up and in the night lights, decided to walk a little further and onto the bridge. Walking towards Brooklyn he stopped about a quarter of the way over the bridge and turned to reveal Manhattan's skyline in all its glory which was the real reason why he decided to go onto the bridge. He paused for a moment, ensuring he wasn't in anyone's way so he wouldn't be disturbed. Ryan breathed deeply and looked at the buildings one by one. A smile temporarily appeared before a tourist tapped him and asked him to take a photo. As he turned back and looked again, the moment had passed but the short trip had served its purpose and he headed back to the station.

Both the Knicks and the Nets must have been at home that night as Ryan found himself in the middle of a sea of jerseys as he waited patiently for the train to arrive. When it arrived, he boarded the train followed by a sea of blue and orange which meant he was heading back towards central Manhattan rather than towards his beloved Brooklyn. As the stations passed, he eavesdropped into various different conversations going on around him which helped distract him from the day he had had and the conversation he was about to have. Ryan had always got on with Emilia's dad but that's really all they did do, just get on. Both very driven by work, Emilia's dad had recently retired in the last few years but that's when Ryan really started to pick up speed, so they'd never really had time to bond as much. The train emptied of basketball fans at 33rd Street so Ryan knew his stop was next. He positioned himself to make a quick exit because the detour to the bridge had left him short on time and he really didn't want to be late.

As he exited the station and ventured onto Vanderbilt Avenue, he knew that he was only moments away from the Yale Club so he started going over in his head what he was going to say when it came to it. Before he knew it, he was at the entrance so he removed his coat and pulled his wallet out to show security his membership card. He barely used this privilege but kept the card on him at all times in case of days like today. He barely had one foot in the door when his phone rang. He took it out and it was Emilia.

"Hey, Em, what's up? I'm a little busy at the moment."

"What's up? Well, it's about three hours after the working day and I still haven't heard from you, that's what is up, Ryan."

Straight away he knew it was going to be one of those phone calls so he tried to kill it instantly.

"Em, listen, I'm sorry but I'm about to meet your dad. I'll call you after, OK?"

"You're meeting my dad? Where? I didn't know he was in town today?" Her tone changed significantly since she knew where and who he was with.

"We're at the Yale Club, I've just arrived and I need to check in so I'll call you after. Love you." Ryan hung up and proceeded into the building.

"Mr Jackson, welcome back to the Yale Club; may I take your coat?"

Ryan emptied the pockets of his coat and evenly distributed them between his suit jacket and trousers whilst holding his phone out in his hand.

"Mr Rodriguez is already here and he asked me to inform you that when you arrive, he will in the cigar room on level 2."

"Thank you very much," Ryan said as he walked over towards the stairs and headed up to the cigar room. As he made his way past the gym and through the library a familiar face reared his head in the shape of one of his old classmates. Ryan smiled and nodded at him but didn't have time to catch up or revisit old memories, he was here for business only. As he made his way into the cigar room, he noticed Emilia's dad over in the far-right corner seated on an armchair close to a window that looked over the courtyard at the back. He made his way over and put a firm hand on his father-in-law's shoulder as he didn't see him coming.

"José, how are you doing?"

He stood up and embraced Ryan with a cuddle, which Ryan found weird because he was sure the only other time they had hugged was at Ryan and Emilia's wedding. As they sat down José beckoned a waiter over and ordered two King of Denmarks.

"You look and smell like you've had a rough day; what's happened?"

As they waited for the cigars to be brought over Ryan brought him up to speed with what had gone on so far in the trial. Mid-explanation, he thought about what he was saying and he couldn't quite believe it was only day three; it seemed like they'd been going back and forth for a month already. Ryan had not finished bringing José up to speed when their cigars arrived and his father-in-law insisted that they start smoking them instantly. Barely lit, a bottle of whiskey followed with two glasses.

"It sounded like it was going to be one of those conversations and nights," José said with a laugh. He leaned forward, screwed the cap off and poured them both a large glass. "So where were we?"

Ryan continued with the little that was left of his story whilst opposite him Emilia's dad listened with intent and thought of how he could help.

"So let me get this straight, your boss gave you the case knowing you'd lose it?"

"Apparently so, yes."

"And two of your three clients lied about their missing money and have already settled?"

"Correct." Ryan sank back into the cozy armchair.

"Day three of the trial?"

"Yep, you've hit the nail on the head with everything so far."

Glass in hand, José turned his attention to looking out the window and slightly tilted his head as if he were thinking. Ryan was quite happy to stay quiet in the moment so the background noise took over their conversation whilst José pondered. His attention turned back to Ryan.

"So why have we met here? What do you want from me?"

In all the years Ryan had been with Emilia they'd never even once spoken on a professional basis. However, now it seemed as if now it was needed, well, it was on Ryan's side.

"I know in your former line of work you would have had dealings with or known someone off the books that could help with *problems*." Ryan's delicate question was met with no verbal response. Instead, José flicked his eyes to the other side of the room, raised his hand and beckoned someone to join them.

"Ryan, this is my private investigator who I have known for over fifteen years now. He's one of the best in the business."

José used to be the district attorney for Nassau which was a position he held for a number of years until he retired. That's how Ryan had met Emilia, at a fundraising event hosted by his now father-in-law and Ryan had attended on behalf of his former firm. When the unknown man reached them, he stood next to José's side. He was fairly small in height, with a bald head, round glasses and a short beard so he didn't exactly scream PI to Ryan.

"How did you know this is what I wanted? I haven't even asked yet."

José laughed again and finished the glass of whiskey he had poured himself.

"You seem to forget that my daughter is your wife."

Ryan didn't know whether to be angry or thankful to his

wife. She shouldn't have been discussing his case with her father but at the same time she had just saved him a day or so in hopefully putting this guy to work.

"I don't know what to say, José. Honestly, your family has a knack for this kind of thing." Now Ryan had an uplift in his voice and he leaned forward to refill José's glass and offered the man one which he politely declined. The man took a chair from a nearby empty table that wasn't being used and positioned himself in the middle of both of them.

"Sorry, I didn't catch your name. I'm Ryan Jackson," he said offering his hand for a handshake. The guy shook his hand but rebuffed his attempt at exchanging names.

"Don't worry, Ryan, all the time I have worked with him he has never known my full name so don't take it personally." The PI pulled out a business card that had nothing but a number on it and handed it to Ryan. "For the time being this is the number you can contact me on if you need me once we're done here." Ryan took it and placed it into the pocket inside his suit jacket. "As for your name I already knew that, I also know who you work for, the case you're on at the moment and who it's against." Ryan put down his cigar and sat up a little straighter. "The real questions are what do you want me to do and what are you trying to uncover?"

José excused himself from the table and wandered out to the corridor to catch up with an old friend who had walked by and called him by a nickname. He said he would circle back to Ryan once he was done but he had made the introduction so his part was finished; it was down to the other two to conduct business now.

"I need you to look into DeShawn Arlington for me. I need something I can use in my case seeing as you already know what I'm doing." The guy didn't move a muscle after the question; he sat as still as can be. "Did you hear me?" Ryan asked as he waited impatiently for an answer.

"I heard you the first time. I was just trying to figure out the best way to respond," he replied as he folded one leg onto the other.

"I haven't got time for it to be dressed up, I just need to know if it's possible at all."

"OK, then in answer to your question no, I can't look into DeShawn Arlington."

Ryan frowned at the answer and didn't really like the answer he'd just got.

"You've worked with José for nearly two decades but can't do this first job I ask?"

"That's because with José I look into other politicians, millionaires with shady backgrounds, police officers with a history before they went straight. Never did he ask me to look into *someone like DeShawn Arlington*."

Ryan knew that DeShawn wasn't exactly a practicing Christian but for a PI to refuse to look into him and describe him as he did, he started to wonder where DeShawn's reputation and reach finished.

"To give you a clearer picture, you have probably got more chance of me digging up something on the POTUS before DeShawn Arlington, or before I go missing for trying to."

Ryan gazed out of the window he was sitting next to and looked at the townhouses beyond the courtyard. He watched as others went about their lives, not knowing he could see them. When he returned to the room, he found himself alone as the PI had vanished. He scanned the room but he was nowhere to be seen and Ryan found himself right back to where he was when he first walked into the club.

After vacating the room and using the restroom Ryan found

Emilia's dad waiting back at the table for him, full glass of whiskey in his hand and puffing on what looked like a new cigar. He half contemplated leaving and going home but the later he got in the less likely Emilia was to be awake and smell what he'd been up to. As he headed back over, he noticed his friend was now at the cigar bar inside the same room so he decided to detour for a brief catch up with him. He pulled up a chair next to him but was beaten to the opening word.

"What are you drinking, Ryan? Seems like you need something strong if you're getting beaten in court by William O'Neill!"

News travelled fast of the case going against him so far but technically the trial wasn't over.

"Word around the office is that you're about to take your first loss, Ryan? Don't worry, it happens to the best of us."

Ryan was now the only graduate from their year that hadn't lost a case yet but it was widely known his opposite number on this case also didn't win many.

"I'm alright thanks, man, I've got a drink over there and don't worry about the case, it's all under control otherwise I wouldn't be here drinking, would I?" Ryan gestured to the waiter to collect his glass from his table so he could finish his conversation at the bar and to tell José he'd be back over shortly.

"Anyways, enough about me as you seem to know everything anyway. How are you getting on now? Where are you working at the moment?"

Ryan thought it would be nice for at least one conversation today not to be based around the case.

"NBC."

"In house?" Ryan snapped back instantly. Working as an in-house lawyer was the end goal, usually once you'd served your time working for a firm.

"Yes, in-house. My uncle became COO for North America so he fast-tracked my application when a position became available a few months back."

"Go on, talk dirty to me. What's it like? High six figures and other benefits?"

"Like you wouldn't believe, mate! Starting salary of $180k plus bonuses, work nine to five, not a minute more, all travel paid and I spend more time on the golf course than I do in the office."

Ryan was almost a little jealous. He knew there was an aura around him for being unbeaten still but what he was describing sounded like a dream job right now.

"Anyway, I've got to shoot off home." His friend stood and removed his jumper from his shoulders and put it on. "I've got a tee time of 8.33 a.m. so I need to be wide-eyed in under ten hours."

The pair shook hands and agreed to not leave it as long next time but they both knew they'd only bump into each other again in the club.

Ryan headed on back to the table that he originally occupied but as he got nearer, he noticed that Emilia's dad, José, was nowhere to be seen. Ryan sat down and assumed that he would be back imminently so poured himself one final glass of whiskey. As he placed the bottle back on the table, he noticed a leather wallet sitting on top of the cigar menu. Reaching over and opening it, Ryan found that José had squared the bill for their evening and added it all to his account. Skimming to the bottom knowing full well how much King of Denmarks cost, he still winced at the fact they'd spent just over $10,000 and José hadn't let him pay anything towards it. Looking over at the clock on the wall to his right it wasn't much before 11 p.m. so Ryan decided to call it a night and head home, downing the glass he'd just poured himself. He pulled his phone out to send a thank you text but as he did, he saw Emilia's dad had beaten him to it.

> *Focus, Ryan. Think outside the box for the remainder of the case.*
> *Also, for your sake, don't forget it's your wedding anniversary next week.*

## 14

# WEDNESDAY 21ST OCTOBER, 12.09 P.M.

"That's all from me right now, Your Honor. No further questions."

Ryan had just finished questioning Matt Woodman's fiancée and former financial advisor who quite frankly didn't have a good word in her vocabulary to say about DeShawn. She met Matt through her line of work but had to step away once the pair became romantically involved to stop a conflict of interest. However, she had been with him through most of his career which was spent with DeShawn's company. William stood from behind his desk and confirmed that they didn't intend to cross-examine her but they did want one further witness to stand before the lunch break. Judge Sullivan's eyes looked up at the clock. It was already 12.15 p.m.

"I suppose considering how stop-start this trial has been so far the jury can wait another hour or so before lunch," he said waving William on as if he was conducting traffic. "Who would you like to call?"

"We would like to see Matt Woodman to the stand please, Your Honor."

Ryan felt an invisible noose suddenly appear round his neck as he had avoided calling Matt up all morning so he could speak with him privately in the lunch break. He wanted to ideally prepare them both this morning but with Matt's fiancée stuck to his side he didn't have a chance to talk candidly with Matt.

"Surely, Your Honor, that will take more than an hour with both of us questioning him," Ryan said frantically as he joined William in standing.

"If it overruns too much then we can break midway through the questioning, Mr Jackson. That's not uncommon, you should know this."

"We only have a handful of questions to ask Mr Woodman so I doubt that he'll be on the stand long, Your Honor," chimed in William from opposite.

Ryan turned and fired a narrow-eyed look back at his opposition and couldn't help but notice DeShawn sporting his usual grin that he did when something was about to go his way.

"I have no problem with him being called at this time. Please, Mr Woodman, step forward."

"Thank you for taking to the stand, Mr Woodman. I promise on our part this won't take any longer than fifteen minutes," William said as he looked to start his questioning. "To ensure you're following with the oath you've just taken can you please confirm your full name?"

"Matthew James Woodman."

"Now your date of birth, please?"

"September 9th, 1988."

"Fantastic, thank you. Finally, can you please confirm that you currently play ice hockey for New York Islanders in the NHL?"

Getting restless with the condescending questions from William, Matt's voice was starting to tinge with frustration.

"I do but I don't see the point in these stupid questions because what you've said everybody knows already."

Ryan was twiddling with his fingers as he sat, helpless, at his desk. He knew what was about to happen, but he couldn't prevent it. He had the tiniest glimmer of hope that Matt didn't have a past like Luke and Henry and the opposition were just fishing for something.

"All in good time, Mr Woodman, please, we only have a few more questions to ask you."

"Please get to the point, Mr O' Neill, I didn't grant you this so you could waste my time." Judge Sullivan seemed to be getting as impatient as Matt.

"Sorry, Your Honor, like I said this won't take long." William turned to DeShawn and almost like clockwork he nodded at his representation – it was the signal Ryan had grown to fear. William turned his attention back to the man he'd just put on the stand. "Do you remember the 2016/17 season fondly, Mr Woodman?"

Matt stuttered in his reply to the question. Ryan started to think back and from what he could remember it was quite a memorable season for his client.

"Would you like me to repeat the question?" William pressed Matt for a quick response.

"I would like to plead the fifth." His response made Ryan sink into his chair.

"That's a simple question, surely, you'd remember only a few years back? Do you not?"

"I would like to plead the fifth." Matt repeated his answer once again.

"But that was the season you made it three Stanley Cup wins in a row! How could you forget?"

Ryan knew that and if he could remember it so could Matt and probably anyone on the jury who was partially interested in New York sports.

"I particularly want to talk about the final game of the regular season when you travelled to face the Stars, do you remember that game? Chance at regular season history?"

"I would like to plead the fifth." Matt hadn't broken his stare at DeShawn since he started his stance of pleading the fifth and Ryan was desperate for some kind of acknowledgment, something to help him or at least give him hope.

"Objection, Your Honor, speculation." Ryan thought he would throw some kind of lifeline to his client to get him to engage with him.

"Mr O'Neill, I won't ask you again, please get to your point." Judge Sullivan's words cut through the room as it waited on the defense's next move.

"Sorry, Your Honor. Mr Woodman, do you remember meeting a blonde-haired journalist from a local blog before the game?"

Ryan was a bit confused at the follow-up question as it seemed very irrelevant especially seeing as he was told to get to the point.

"Objection, Your Honor, irrelevant."

"Mr O'Neill, this is your final warning."

It was a small victory for Ryan and right now he was happy to take them where he could.

"The woman who preceded you on the stand, was that your fiancée, Mr Woodman?"

"Yes, it was but you already know that." Matt finally came back around from giving the same answers to every question.

"So, you can answer a question if you choose to? Thanks, Mr Woodman, no further questions from me, Your Honor."

It seemed as if he'd got exactly what he wanted to without actually having Matt answer any questions. Ryan stood, helplessness written all over his face.

"No further questions from me either, Your Honor."

"Good. Good work from you both. Let's break for lunch."

"Thanks for the protection in there. What am I paying you for if you let him come at me like that?" Matt quickly snapped at Ryan as they arrived back at the room. Ryan had entered first, holding the door open for Matt and his fiancée who followed closely behind. He blocked the entrance to the room preventing her from coming in.

"I need to talk to Matt alone right now so you're going to have to wait outside."

She stumbled a few steps, taken aback by how close Ryan was to her and his tone of voice.

"She can come in, it's fine, we share everything with each other." Matt walked back towards the door to usher her in.

"Not this time you don't. You can spend thirty minutes away from each other whilst we catch up and go through what happened in there." Ryan shut the door then pulled a chair out for Matt to sit on. "I'll be able to help you when you start telling the truth."

"How dare you!" Matt instantly stood up from the chair he'd only just sat down on and moved towards Ryan in a fit of rage. "How dare you accuse me of lying? What have I lied about? *Go On.*"

"What happened that night in Dallas, Matt? What do they know that I don't?"

"Nothing. Nothing happened at all which is why I didn't say anything in there."

"Matt, you pleaded the fifth, for fuck's sake, and answered other questions. Do you know how guilty that makes you look to the jury?" The pair were basically squaring off now as they continued their war of words. "You sports stars are all the same. I've already had two of you fuck me over and now I'm going to have a third!" Ryan threw his briefcase against the wall in a fit of rage and his cup of water followed. "Whatever DeShawn has done for you, whatever dodgy dealings he's covered up in the past he will bring up in court and no NDA or whatever you've agreed will stop that – wake up, Matt!"

There was no comeback this time. There was no shouting in response to what Ryan said. Matt just stood opposite motionless.

Ninety seconds or so had passed and the dialogue between the pair still hadn't resumed but the tension was starting to filter out of the room. Ryan had started to pick his briefcase and loose items off the floor whilst Matt had got himself a glass of water and taken a seat on the chair nearest the door.

"So, he'll use what he has against me to win this case? No matter what we've agreed in the past?" Matt finally stuttered a response.

"Yes. Yes, he will. You're saying he stole millions of dollars from you so he will do whatever he needs to prove his innocence and no NDA will stop that in a court of law."

"It won't? So why do we sign those things?" Matt was starting to raise his voice again.

"They're iron clad unless brought into a court of law and it directly affects the case. Which I assume it does, as it did with Luke and Henry."

"So, what we do from here? Did they settle with him? Can I?" Matt's immediate action was to throw in the towel. Just as Ryan went to answer he remembered Macpherson telling him he'd lose the case and something inside stopped him.

"I need you to tell me exactly what happened with the local journalist you met before the Stars game." Matt nodded in acknowledgment of Ryan's request. "Don't leave a single detail out."

The room was now tidy as Ryan had cleared the floor of what he'd thrown. Matt had poured himself a new cup of water, refilled Ryan's and they both sat down opposite each other. Ryan waited for Matt to start.

"I can't believe I've been so naive in all of this." Matt put his head in his hands. "The whole situation, accepting it, trusting DeShawn and thinking I could get him to hand over the money. What was I thinking!"

Ryan reached over and put a hand on Matt's shoulder to reassure him.

"You're not the first and certainly won't be the last. The quicker you tell me the truth then we can work out where to go from here."

Matt raised his head as Ryan sat back down.

"In a nutshell—"

"No nutshells," Ryan interjected. "From start to finish so there's no more secrets."

Avoiding eye contact with Ryan, Matt started to tell his story and really did start at the very beginning of the day, going through a lot of unnecessary information.

"As much as I want all the information, it needs to be relatable, Matt, we're on a timescale here." Ryan knew they didn't have long before they needed to be back in court. "Just talk about the moment you met the journalist."

Matt gave Ryan a hard stare for interrupting him and then asking him to move halfway up his story.

"We were doing media for the game and of course the play-offs which were starting soon. We were done for the day when this striking blonde woman came in and said she was late." Ryan briefly switched to autopilot as this information seemed fairly normal. "Our guys checked the sheet, couldn't find her. She was only from a local outlet so they went to turn her away."

"I assume you played knight in shining armor and said you'd answer her questions?"

"She was hot, man, I wanted to see what she had to say."

Matt shrugged his shoulders with his reply as if this was a good enough reason to get himself into whatever mess he had. "She asked a few general sports-related questions, then a few more to do with the team and my teammates and then we were told it was time up and I had to go practice."

That clearly wasn't the end to Matt's story because Ryan couldn't think of a single thing he'd done wrong so far. Matt took a large gulp of his drink and kept Ryan hanging on to his story.

"You giving an extra interview didn't cost you $3.6 million so continue." Ryan pushed Matt for more of the story as he looked at the clock and realized he only had twenty-five minutes left of lunch.

"It's more what happened after the interview that got me into trouble." Matt looked around the room nervously but ended up back at Ryan. "She said she had a few more questions to ask me and could we meet somewhere later on to finish them."

"You took her number and told her yes, didn't you?"

"I repeat – she was hot. I was in Dallas and it was the end of the regular season, man. Come on."

Matt's fiancée knocked at the door and asked to come into the room now but he opened the door and told her to wait outside whilst they finished this conversation. They exchanged a few words and she stormed off annoyed at being kept out of the loop but Ryan didn't care right now because she'd already been up on the stand so she was done as far as he was concerned.

Instead of sitting back down he continued the story whilst walking around the small room.

"I finished practice and after our team meal I hit her up and she said she'd come to the hotel for the remaining questions." The story seemed fairly innocent to this point. Ryan was now thinking back to Henry and that Matt had clearly had an affair like he did. "We were talking about my high-school and college career, where I grew up, being drafted, etc. She was actually asking some really good questions."

"Eighteen minutes, Matt, we've got eighteen minutes left."

"I noticed she had a duffel bag with her but didn't really pay much attention to it. I thought it'd have, I don't know, journalist stuff in it."

"And what was in it, Matt?"

"$2 million in cash."

Wait. What? That wasn't what Ryan was expecting. Why would a small-time local journalist be carrying round that kind of money with her?

"Did you ask her what she was doing with that amount of money on her?" Ryan said slowly as he tried to get his head around it.

"It's what she asked me to do for the money that I was more concerned about."

"Throw the game?" Ryan thought back to the specific game and if memory served him right the Islanders lost the game in OT so they didn't make history.

"She didn't ask me to technically throw the game, just let them score a goal and then come off injured."

"You son of a bitch, you fixed a game." That confession was like a red flag to a raging bull and Ryan was fuming. There was only one thing he hated more than liars in the world and it was cheats. If this came out it would literally rock the sporting world.

"We were 2-0 up with three minutes to go. I let their guy go past me, he scored, and I faked an injury. They brought me straight off because of the play-offs. I didn't think they'd score again and go on to win from there!" Matt's words were irrelevant. He instantly knew he had lost Ryan's respect.

"I don't even want to represent you anymore, let alone

help you out of this mess. You're lucky I don't turn you in myself."

"Please don't. You'll never hear from me again after this. Just help me get out of this."

"So, you took a bribe? Islanders lost. I'm confused what's being covered up?" Ryan really didn't care from this point out, he just wanted to make it through to the end of the day. He needed to speak to Macpherson about the bombshell.

"She contacted my agent at the time, which was DeShawn, told him what I'd done and said if I didn't give back the $2 million with $1.6 million on top for her then she'd leak our conversation which she recorded."

"I wish DeShawn had morals then he would have turned you in there and then." Ryan needed a clear head to think about what he was going to do next and how he was going to approach the afternoon. Going tit for tat with Matt wasn't helping either of them. "I've got ten minutes. Go and see your fiancée and tell her whatever lie will make you sleep easier at night. I'll figure out how to get us through the rest of the day."

"You're not going to say anything in there are you?" The desperation in Matt's voice was now evidently clear.

"Guess we'll find out when we go in, won't we?"

Ten minutes was nowhere near long enough for Ryan to think about what he was going to do but he just wanted rid of Matt so he didn't completely flip out at what he'd just found out about his client. The lies he'd faced so far in this case with strippers, drugs and affairs he could stomach as sports stars were often thrown into the limelight with no sense of how to handle it. Fixing a game on the other hand was something completely immoral. Lunch was nearly over so Ryan opened his briefcase and quickly devoured the rest of an open protein bar that was in there. He glanced momentarily at his phone; hundreds of notifications as per usual, so he didn't pay much attention to what he was actually looking at. He noticed Emilia's name and was drawn to a text message from Macpherson just before 9 a.m. Not bothering to read the initial message from his boss, Ryan opened up their chat and begin to type frantically:

*Now we've got a cheat, all three lied! I'm furious. Can we meet this evening?*

## 15

# WEDNESDAY 21ST OCTOBER, 5.02 P.M.

As the judge and the jury exited the courtroom, both teams stood up and began preparing to leave the courtroom.

"Thank you for not saying anything, thank you for—"

"Don't thank me, Matt, it's my job and you're my client. If it was solely up to me then I would have thrown you under a bus the moment I walked back in from lunch."

Ryan had somehow got through the afternoon session without William pushing for the case to be dismissed. The witnesses called upon and the testimonies they gave were completely pointless after Matt's display earlier on in the day. Matt slung his jacket on and was the first to leave without saying a word to Ryan, his fiancée close in tow behind him as usual. After a brief discussion and a pat on the back William was next to leave the courtroom which left just DeShawn and Ryan basically alone barring a couple of security guards towards the back of the room.

"You're a tenacious little bastard, I'll give you that," DeShawn said walking over towards Ryan. "I knew the ins and outs of this whole case from day one, you didn't and you're still here standing. I take my hat off to you." Ryan didn't know how to take what DeShawn said so just continued to get ready to leave without saying a word. DeShawn edged slightly closer, "Many have stood where you have and many have failed. There's no shame in it, look how your boss bounced back from her *lesson*."

Ryan paused. The last word, lesson, didn't stick right with him at all. He looked up towards DeShawn.

"Lesson?"

"Of course, it's a lesson. A lesson not to meddle in my business. A lesson that no matter how much you know the law sometimes it's not enough."

Ryan had now completely stopped what he was doing and was facing DeShawn square on, in the middle of the room.

"The only lesson that'll be learned by the end of this case is that you'll finally realize that you're not immune from being prosecuted for your shady deals."

DeShawn sniggered and turned away heading for the exit. "Boy, I don't know if you have noticed but after four days two of your clients have settled and the other one is about to be found out as a cheat and quite frankly, he can fuck himself."

"So, you won't be offering Matt a settlement like you did the other two?"

"Hell no. I can deal with adultery and I can deal with the other temptations life can throw at you but I am not dealing with someone who fixes games."

"Wow, DeShawn Arlington has boundaries after all," Ryan replied sarcastically.

Now just a few steps away from leaving the room DeShawn had a final parting gift for Ryan.

"Laugh all you can now, Ryan, because come tomorrow I'll be instructing William to finish this."

As he pushed his way through the door Ryan mimicked DeShawn's sentence and after a few minutes headed the same way whilst fumbling for his phone.

After scrolling through a whole bunch of needless emails from either telemarketers or companies offering him discounts on gym clothes, Ryan turned his attention to Macpherson. He had no emails, text messages, missed calls and voicemails from his boss despite the message he'd left her around five hours ago asking to meet tonight. He double checked everything again but he was right the first time round, nothing from Macpherson. He called and got her voicemail, called straight back and got a voicemail again. Deciding not to leave a message, Ryan huffed as he made his way down onto the subway hoping that by the time he was back above ground his boss would have finally reached out. As he waited with a hundred other people who were starting their commute home Ryan pondered what to do if Macpherson didn't call him. It was either Mulligans for the Nets game or go home and see Emilia. After the long hours and the week he was enduring, going home would probably just end up in an argument with his wife which he didn't want with her going away tomorrow. Providing there was no contact from Macpherson Ryan was set on going home as judging on how the trial was going, he wouldn't be going with her as he had suggested he'd be able to do last week.

Ryan decided to get off a few stops earlier than he needed to so he could at least buy a few beers on the route home and probably pick Emilia up something too. More importantly though, he'd also be able to look for a restaurant to book for their anniversary next week. If things turned sour later on for one reason or another at least he would have that in his back pocket to hopefully help him out. Knowing his wife's love for food from Asia he decided to look up restaurants that served that kind of food and settled on a little place in Nolita called Momofuku that was highly rated from its online reviews. As Ryan walked home, he tried his hardest to forget about the past week or so by taking in the scenery around him. For once he wasn't rushing to get to Mulligans or had his head buried in his phone writing an email to someone. He stopped off at a liquor store that he hadn't used before and bought himself some beers and in the process bought his wife her favorite bottle of Château Beychevelle. After a few more blocks he reached his apartment and before going inside checked his phone quickly; there was still nothing from Macpherson. In the middle of a case this size Ryan was shocked that she'd disappeared for over half a day. He slipped his phone back into his jacket and made his way upstairs to surprise his wife. To most normal couples coming home after work wasn't a surprise but being in the middle of an ongoing trial Ryan saw it as one.

Closing the door behind him and throwing his keys onto the side, loud music filled the flat and almost every light was on. As he made his way down the hallway, he noticed multiple pairs of women's shoes that he didn't recognize as Emilia's, so prepared himself to be met by a room of people that he wasn't expecting.

"Knock knock," Ryan said as he popped his head into the room to make sure it was safe to enter. His eyes were met with Emilia in loungewear with a face mask on and about eight of her friends all looking exactly the same. She seemed somewhat shocked to see her husband home.

"Ryan, baby, I didn't think you would be home this early tonight?" Emilia jumped to her feet and rushed over to greet him before he could get much further in. As she cuddled him Ryan lifted one hand off her back to wave at her friends who were all looking over from the other side of the room.

"I don't remember saying I wouldn't be home either but I see you have company."

"With the Nets on and how the case is going I expected you to go to Mulligans, that's all."

Ryan had barely been home enough to talk about how the case was going so he brushed over Emilia's presumptions because he didn't want to make a scene.

"I can ask them to leave. It's not a problem; they'll understand, knowing you're on a case at the moment."

"It's fine, don't worry; I'll grab a pizza and watch the game in the bedroom. You enjoy your girls' night." Ryan awkwardly smiled at the spectators their conversation had drawn as he grabbed the pizza menu from the kitchen drawer and made his way into the bedroom. The Nets were starting a three-game road trip this evening away in Houston so he had around an hour until the game tipped off anyway.

Showered, changed and pizza ordered Ryan settled in to start watching the pre-game show, however the noise from the girls was getting louder and louder. Picking his phone up from the bedside table where it had been charging Ryan once again expected to see Macpherson's name, but there was nothing. By this point he had forgotten the fact he needed to talk to her and was genuinely more concerned with her general wellbeing. He called and for the third time that evening got his boss's voicemail except this time he left a voicemail asking for a call back and to check if everything was OK. Turning the volume up to try and drown out the squeals and screams that had so far filled his evening, the network was just about to pan courtside for a team update and run through the Nets starting five. As Sarah Kustok ran through everything related to the team, the smell of pepperoni filled the bedroom and from the corner of his eye, he could see Emilia holding his food at the door.

"Large pepperoni pizza?" She placed the pizza on the table next to the door and as she turned to leave Ryan noticed the lid on the box slightly lifted.

"Freeze!"

Ryan swung his feet round to the floor and walked over to the box. There was a slice missing. When he looked back up Emilia was gone as was his chance of getting back the missing slice of the pizza he'd ordered.

What Ryan saw next on TV truly shocked him. The panel in the studio was going back to courtside reporter Ally Love to interview a special guest but as the live cameras started to roll it was none other than DeShawn Arlington. Ryan was stunned. The person he had been up against no longer than three and a bit hours ago was now courtside in Houston watching basketball. How could this be possible when they had to be back in court in twelve hours to continue the trial? It was the ultimate slap in the face. Ryan grabbed the remote and doubled the volume, his bedroom now sounding like a cinema. He eagerly waited for the interview to start. He was glued to the TV.

"Welcome back to downtown Houston and the Toyota Centre. I'm now joined by none other than US super-agent DeShawn Arlington. How are you doing, DeShawn?"

"I'm doing good thanks, how are you? Happy to be here for the first time as well, may I add."

As the interview progressed Ryan still hadn't digested what was happening. How could you fly halfway across the country in the middle of a trial to watch a game? Sure as hell he was about to get his answer.

"DeShawn, you're in the middle of a trial that's being covered nationally, you're against some former clients of yours who happen to be huge names in the US sports world. How are you able to fly out to Dallas to take in a basketball game?"

"Well, I had some business to take care of that needed urgent attention so I thought why not take in the game especially as it's the Nets. I'm a native Brooklynite after all."

"But don't you have to be back in court tomorrow morning

to resume trial?" That's exactly the question Ryan was hoping Ally would ask.

"I do, you're right. I'll fly back straight after the game this evening and be back in NY for 1 a.m. I'll be fine. The case is basically finished anyway. You should expect a conclusion tomorrow." "That's great news, DeShawn. You know me, I wouldn't be doing my job properly if I didn't ask. What business do you have going on here at the moment?"

The famous DeShawn smirk that Ryan has become so accustomed to appeared.

"You know me, Ally, I can't say anything until it's done. All in good time, all in good time."

They panned back to the studio and DeShawn disappeared off Ryan's screen.

He snatched his phone from the bedside table and scrolled down to Macpherson's name again and hit call. Like clockwork, he got her voicemail. He went back into his phonebook and called Daniels, which he only did in case of emergencies. Immediately he got his voicemail. Ryan launched his phone across the room and into the wall, for the second time that day in a fit of rage. The TV remote followed soon after. The noise coming from the living room had stopped and as Ryan flipped his pizza box sending slices in every direction, Emilia opened the door. Her concern for what was going on quickly disappeared after seeing the state of the room.

"Ryan, what on earth is going on?"

"Your friends need to leave, Emilia, I'm not in the mood for guests tonight." Ryan's voice was loud but he was full-on shouting by the time he finished. Emilia entered the room and walked over towards her Ryan.

"Baby, what's wrong? What's happened?" She went to wrap her arms around her husband but he shrugged her off.

"Are you deaf? Go and get your friends to leave NOW!"

You could already hear shuffling coming from the living room as some of Emilia's friends were not waiting for her to return.

"Ryan, stop shouting, you're embarrassing me; everyone can hear you."

"That's the whole point, Emilia. GET. THEM. OUT. OF. THE. APARTMENT. Which will be my apartment soon if you don't do what I say."

Emilia had never seen him like this before. His face was red with anger, his eyes, a snow white. She decided not to add fuel to the fire and left the room quickly. Ryan could hear her talking to her friends but it was hushed and he couldn't make out what was being said. Soon after, the opening and closing of doors took place and the apartment was in complete silence barring the bedroom TV. Ryan picked up the remote and lowered the volume as the game was just beginning. He picked up his phone which was face down to see only a small crack on the top left hand of the screen. Emilia was yet to reappear.

Ryan sulked around the bedroom with his phone gripped tightly in his right hand and the TV still showing the game. His focus wasn't anywhere specific at this point. He was trying to digest what DeShawn had said about the trial finishing tomorrow but kept getting distracted when he walked past the TV and watched the game. With Emilia nowhere to be seen, Ryan decided that he'd give it another couple of minutes and then venture out to her. Maybe being in her company without the game on might help him calm down and focus. He went to the toilet and then settled on the edge of the bed to watch a couple of minutes of the game before going into the other room. He wasn't sure what Emilia he was about to face but he hoped she'd be understanding after he explained to her what had happened. Entering the room, he couldn't see her anywhere. It was littered with face-mask packets, half-drunk bottles of wine and random bowls of snacks that the girls had been eating. He walked out to the bathroom and it was empty. He looked out on the balcony and again it was empty. Finally, he checked the room Emilia used as a walk-in wardrobe but once again she was nowhere to be seen. He gathered she must have left with her girlfriends which he had mixed feelings about. Ultimately, she had given him the space to calm down which was wise after what had just happened. He went to the fridge and opened a bottle of Heineken and noticed a note that she had scribbled rather quickly on the side by the sink. As he picked it up, he noticed that it was Emilia's handwriting on it. He went to screw it up but noticed the note started with 'Ryan'. He uncrumpled it and read on:

*Ryan, I've never seen you like that before. It scared me.*
*I'll give you space tonight and I'm away for the weekend*
*so by Sunday it should be ok.*
*Lots of love, Emilia xxx*

All of sudden Ryan's anger turned to pure emotion as he realized what he had just done. He had taken his anger out on the one person who meant the most to him. He instinctively went to call his wife but he knew for a fact she wouldn't pick up. Should he call her dad? Should he try and find her? Multiple questions running through his head Ryan was now not thinking or concentrating on the case but his marriage. He couldn't believe what he had done. He returned to the balcony in the hope that the cold night air would allow him to regather himself as in the last hour it seemed as if everything had imploded. He breathed in a deep breath, with his eyes closed as the cold wind blew gently across him. He took a couple of large gulps of his beer, opened his eyes, and listened as life around him continued to go on. The hustle and bustle of the people, the music from a nearby bar and the sirens from an ambulance filled his ears. It calmed him. It was a quick reminder that in his beautiful city no matter what was going on, whether it was good or bad, life always carried on. He sat down oblivious to his previous thoughts and peacefully continued to take in what was going on around him.

Around an hour passed and Ryan decided to head back into the apartment. He had completely mellowed out and walked inside a different man. He grabbed another beer and headed to the sofa to put the Nets game on which would in the third quarter by now. They were leading by fourteen points which was good on the road in Houston but if the last fixture between the pair was anything to go by then it wasn't over until it was over. Ryan's phone lit up and his eyes looked down and were met with Macpherson's name. She was alive after all. It was an abrupt message from his boss that read:

> *Judge Sullivan has granted continuance.*
> *Boardroom 9 a.m.*

## 16

# THURSDAY 22ND OCTOBER, 7.41 A.M.

The usual spring in Ryan's step wasn't there. He trudged around the empty apartment in a pair of shorts leaving wet footprints having just got out of the shower. He'd barely slept a wink and couldn't work out if he was hungover or still drunk from the amount of alcohol he'd consumed since Macpherson's last text message. As he fumbled through the coffee machine settings to make himself a double espresso, he collected the sea of wasted food that littered the flat. He was finding himself in extremely unfamiliar territory during a trial and he really didn't know exactly how to handle it. He was desperate to find out the reasons behind the trial being granted continuance but at the same time he had a sinking feeling that it was going to be at the detriment to him or the business. The time was coming up to 7.50 a.m. and he hadn't had a phone call, text or email this morning which was very unusual. He slipped into a casual shirt and trousers knowing that a suit wouldn't be needed if it was an office day. His expectations were that they would be locked in the boardroom trying to figure this out for the majority of the day. He drank the double espresso that he had made himself and picked at a few slices of toast but in truth he had no appetite. He knew Emilia would be coming back whilst he was out at work to collect clothes for the weekend so after brushing his teeth, he scribbled a quick note on the back of her original one and set off to start his day.

The sun was creeping out so Ryan decided a walk to work would be better for him, or at least better for how he was feeling. Last night he emerged himself in the city to calm down but this morning he was oblivious to all that was passing him by. As he reached Times Square, he decided to pause and take a seat on the red steps, mainly to gather his final thoughts. It was now finally starting to sink in that in the next couple of hours the biggest case of his life was more than likely going to either be over or taken off him. It hadn't even been a week yet. How could he have been so naive? How could Luke, Henry and Matt have been so naive not to disclose an NDA? His reputation was going to be in tatters once all of this got out into the industry. It was one thing to lose a case but it was something else to be taken off one. Ryan let his imagination run wild. He came around when a tourist asked him to take a photo of her and her daughter and he obliged, standing up and dusting himself off before doing so.

Ryan reached the office a couple of minutes later than he intended to. He made his way in and up fairly swiftly not stopping for any small talk but did take the time to acknowledge the security guard as he always did. In the elevator up to the office Ryan put his headphones in with no intention of listening to any music but again, to cut out the small talk with his colleagues. As he made his way down the floor and towards his office, Ryan did so without making eye contact to not get distracted. Macpherson and Daniels were already in the boardroom and saw Ryan walking through the office. As he reached his office, he shut the door behind him. He felt a little bit better than he had when he first left his apartment but he still wasn't mentally where he'd usually be on a workday. He opened up his laptop but he still had no emails which at 9 a.m. was unheard of. He unlocked his phone and equally he had no missed calls or texts. Confused, Ryan walked over to the window and grabbed one of his prized basketballs and began to bounce it around his office as he so often did. He was trying to get focused. A gentle knock came at the door and it was Macpherson's personal assistant.

"They're ready for you, Ryan." She then nodded her head towards the conference room before closing the door. After a couple more bounces of the ball, Ryan placed it back on its stand and headed towards the boardroom.

Both Macpherson and Daniels stood as he entered the room and made his way to the opposite side of the large glass table. They both outstretched their hands to greet him. As all three of them sat, the assistant who had just fetched Ryan entered the room with a large jug of water and three glasses and placed them in the middle of them. This was it. Ryan waited for one of them to start. His mind was racing and his heart was almost beating out of his chest. Still no words were communicated by his superiors. The silence was unbearable. Macpherson finally mustered up the courage to mutter something.

"We're taking you off the trial."

For once Ryan didn't know how to react or what to say. His usual cool, calm persona in tense situations like this one was nowhere to be seen and instead he just sat there whilst Macpherson and Daniels waited for his reaction. Still nothing came. Daniels prompted Ryan.

"Did you hear us, Ryan? We're taking you off the—"

"Yes, I heard you alright, you don't need to repeat yourself." Ryan interrupted Daniels as he never really had much respect for him anyway so he didn't need to be told again by him. "Is this why I've had no calls, no emails, no texts this morning?"

All of a sudden it started to make sense to Ryan why his phone was so quiet.

"Correct," said Macpherson as she sat back and crossed her legs. "We asked one of the girls on reception to reroute all your communications until we'd spoken to you so we can sort this out and then get back to business."

"What needs sorting out? I'm fine. I'm in the middle of a case, or I was, at least." Ryan pushed himself out from the table and went to stand up.

"Sit down, Ryan, this is far from over. We have a lot to discuss." Daniels was clearly keen to get on with things.

"Don't tell me what to do. Your name may be on the wall, but I only answer to Macpherson and not you in this firm. Let that be clear."

"Now, now, Ryan, calm down and take a seat, please. The quicker we get everything out in the open, the quicker we can start to rectify it."

Out of principle, Ryan didn't sit down but started to slowly walk up and down the space in-between the chairs and the wall.

"So that's how you got Judge Sullivan to grant continuance, wasn't it? You said you were taking me off the case."

Macpherson and Daniels both looked at each other, each one waiting for the other to answer but they both knew Ryan would only accept it if it came from Macpherson.

"Right again, Ryan. We told Judge Sullivan that we were taking you off the trial and we needed time to prepare the new person on the case which is why he allowed us until Tuesday off."

"Who's getting the case?" Ryan shot back immediately.

"We're not sure yet. I might even take it on to try and limit the damage."

"Limit the damage?" Ryan's voice all of sudden started to mirror last night's exchange with Emilia. "What damage? We're a fucking law firm and I'm losing a case – one, may I add, that you both set me up to lose anyway!" Ryan banged his hands on the table and the noise carried out of the boardroom and people started to look in.

"It's the manner, Ryan. It's not just your name on the line, it's ours too. We pulled you out of the middle-tier cases and into the big ones, remember. This reflects badly on our part too," Daniels chimed in when he shouldn't have.

Macpherson knew that any comment from him wouldn't sit well with Ryan.

"Reflects badly on you? I don't think I made myself clear enough a moment ago. This is my career you're about to destroy." Ryan walked over towards the door closest to his office. "I need time to process all this. Macpherson, I'll be in my office when you want to finish this."

Ryan slammed the door to his office and it shook the surrounding rooms. Despite still feeling the effects of the heavy night he'd just had, he marched over to the whiskey and poured a glass as he expected Macpherson to follow him fairly quickly if he knew his boss. He drank his glass instantly and refilled it before heading back to the basketball he was previously bouncing before the meeting. He removed it from the stand but before he could even bounce it once his door opened and in walked Macpherson.

"Put down the whiskey, Ryan, for Christ's sake. You stank of the stuff when you walked in the room earlier on."

Ryan looked into the bottom of his glass and took the advice he was given by placing it down on his desk. He collapsed into his chair.

"The first sign of something not going your way and this is

how you react?" Macpherson sat opposite him. "This isn't the lawyer that we aggressively pursued to hire." Ryan was leaning back and unresponsive to the comment. "Ryan, sit the fuck up and listen." Ryan shot up like a lightning bolt to face his demanding and angry boss who now had his full attention. "Let this be a harsh lesson to you. Harsher than we thought it would be at the start but here we are."

"You set me up to fail!" Ryan reiterated the earlier point from the boardroom.

"We did set you up to fail but I told you before, it wasn't about losing the case, it's how you handled it and bounced back from defeat." Macpherson had taken the ball away from Ryan and was clutching it in both hands rather than bouncing it. "When the famous 90s Bulls were losing and they had a game-winning shot, who would take it?"

"Michael Jordan. Of course."

"What if Jordan had missed the previous game-winning shot?"

"They'd still give it to him because he's Jordan."

"Exactly, Ryan, and there's my point right there." The sports-related analogy triggered something in Ryan's head and he slowly started to get it. "If you had remained dignified in defeat against DeShawn, put up a good argument and lost the case we couldn't have been happier as your managing partners." Ryan nodded in agreement what with Macpherson was saying. "Staying out late, calling witnesses back to the stand with no evidence and coming into work whining and smelling of liquor isn't what we expected."

Ryan didn't answer but visually you could see he understood what she was saying.

"So, you're calling me the firm's Michael Jordan?"

Macpherson rolled her eyes as if to say was that all Ryan had taken from what she'd just said.

"You've missed the point, Ryan," she said as she walked back towards him.

Ryan hadn't missed the point whatsoever but he was starting to return to the person he was known to be.

"Anyway, we've gone off this morning's topic. Can you please gather your case notes, information, evidence, anything you think I'd need to carry this on and run them up to my office when you're done?" Macpherson edged closer back towards the door.

"I'm glad it's you," Ryan blurted out suddenly. "I'm glad it's you taking on the case and not another lawyer or Daniels."

Macpherson opened the door and exited the room without acknowledging what Ryan had said but they both knew she had heard it and that was good enough for Ryan.

Ryan pottered around his office but kept finding himself either glancing up at the clock or down at his wrist to check the time. The day was passing him by so quickly. He had started to come to terms with the news that he had been taken off the case. The numerous alcoholic drinks at lunch were helping but in hindsight what he wanted was to talk to Emilia. He had tried several times to contact her throughout the day but she wasn't returning any calls or texts. Ryan knew everything would be alright in the end but they'd never fought like this before. He gathered a few loose scraps of paper from his desk and put them into one of the two large cardboard boxes that sat on his desk. As he flicked through the contents everything looked in order to hand over to Macpherson. Leaning back and looking down the office floor he could see Macpherson's lights on; usually that was the signal that she was in her office. Ryan stacked the boxes on top of each other and opened his door with his foot and set off towards the other end of the office. Halfway down he realized there were some bits in his briefcase. Deciding he'd go back for them in a minute he continued trying not to drop everything. When he reached Macpherson's office the door was open and she was on the office phone talking to who Ryan assumed to be a client. She noticed Ryan standing in the doorway and beckoned him in and mouthed to him to shut the door behind him.

"Is this everything?" Macpherson asked as she put down the phone and Ryan unstacked the two boxes.

"Almost everything. I've got some bits in my briefcase I need to give to you." Ryan started to head back towards the door.

"Ryan, wait. Sit down for a moment." She gestured her hand towards one of the four chairs that sat on the other side of her desk. As Ryan turned back and sat down, Macpherson stood up to assume power in the conversation that was about to take place. "Firstly, I've got to tell you not to speak to Daniels the way you did earlier."

"You know I only listen to you in this office, though."

"I know but his name is on the wall so he holds equal power when making decisions." Macpherson was now standing behind Ryan and gently put both her hands onto his shoulders.

"I've been thinking and after talking with Daniels, we've decided to give you a week off, fully paid and it won't come off your annual leave allowance." Ryan didn't quite understand where the gesture was coming from. "Take Emilia to the Caribbean or Europe for a week and relax."

"Why? We're going to Cuba in three or four months' time so that's our next holiday." Ryan's answer to Macpherson was to show a little gratitude but also work out her angle. "Anyway, I'd like to be here in New York to see how this case pans out in the end."

"Ryan, you've been here almost eighteen months and never had a holiday. I, for one, respect and admire your work ethic but you need to recharge your batteries." Ryan had shrugged

Macpherson off by now and had joined her in standing up. "Go away, turn your phone off and when you come back, you'll be raring to go again."

Ryan thought to himself that he was long overdue a trip to Europe but how would it look to his rivals and future clients if as well as being taken off a case he then vanished in the aftermath.

"I'll think about it, boss," Ryan said as he outstretched his hand to shake Macpherson's almost as a thank-you gesture. "Let me speak to Emilia and if it works for both of us, I'll take you up on that offer." Emilia was never going to hear of this idea and Ryan was going to go straight to work on the next case immediately, but Macpherson didn't need to know that. "Let me go and grab those papers from my briefcase, then you have all you need and we can do a proper handover of everything."

Ryan exited the room and quickly walked back down towards his office.

Just as he shut his briefcase Macpherson's personal assistant stuck her head into the room and it startled him.

"I was told to take those back up and to tell you to take the rest of the afternoon off."

Ryan reluctantly handed the papers over as if he didn't trust his colleague to carry them a couple of hundred feet across the office.

"Is that what Macpherson said?"

"Yes. She did, Ryan. She's a great judge of character and although you may not agree, she usually knows what's best."

Ryan found himself alone in his office again as she disappeared. He walked over to his desk to grab his keys, phone and wallet and noticed a text message from Emilia. She had finally surfaced.

*We're fine, Ry. Blow some steam off this weekend and I'll see you Sunday xx*

## 17

# THURSDAY 22ND OCTOBER, 2.58 P.M.

The low sun blinded Ryan as he made his way out of the revolving door and onto the street. It was barely 3 p.m. in the afternoon and he couldn't remember the last time he had left the office so early on a Thursday. He paused on the sidewalk to gather his thoughts and ultimately decide what he was going to do next with his day. Emilia was out of town with work, the majority of his friends would still be working and he'd had too many drinks to go for a run. He opened his recent calls list to see if he could think of anyone he could attempt to meet up with, but he quite quickly came to a decision. Mulligans. It was Thursday, after all. He walked over the road and hailed down a cab and was soon off through the afternoon sunshine to his usual watering hole albeit a couple of hours earlier than usual.

As Ryan pushed the door open and stepped into Mulligans, the bartender was shocked to see him at this time. Ryan was equally as shocked at the bar's emptiness as him walking in doubled the current total number of people in there. As usual though and almost like clockwork by the time he had reached the bar there was a cold open bottle of Heineken waiting for him.

"Quiet today?" Ryan grabbed the bottle as he sat down on a bar stool.

"Quiet every day at this time, my man. We thrive on weeknights and weekends really. Apart from the odd passing tourist the days are quiet for us."

Quiet was an understatement. Ryan thought it must cost the bar to open this early if they got no trade.

"Wouldn't you always want to work this shift?"

The bartender laughed and shook his head as he walked away from Ryan and started counting bottles.

"Absolutely not, my man, rather be here when it's busy and there's sport on and make four times as much in tips."

Ryan glanced up at the screen above the bar and for the first time ever there was no sport on the TV but instead what looked like a regular daytime TV quiz show, or it could have been a rerun.

"No sport?" Ryan pointed up to where he'd been looking.

"Not at this time. Not unless you want reruns of last night's Knicks game." Being a regular he knew Ryan was a Nets fan and wouldn't want to watch their games.

The bartender continued to potter around the bar getting everything ready for when it finally came to life in the early evening. Ryan sporadically looked over at him carrying out his duties but spent most of his time shouting answers to the quiz questions that were being asked on the TV. By the time the bartender had finished doing everything he needed to, Ryan was about four bottles of beer down and the quiz show had ended but another one had just begun. As soon as the theme tune started Ryan recognized it straight away and was familiar with the show as one he used to watch with his family when he was younger.

"Finished?" Ryan said to the bartender as he perched himself against the bar and looked up at the TV.

"Yes, boss," he said laughing as he stood up straight and to attention. "The bar is restocked; the lemons are cut and the ice buckets are full. Sir."

Ryan laughed at him but then lifted his beer bottle to reveal the fact it was almost empty.

"My beer is gone though. Sir."

He turned around and placed another beer in front of Ryan and went back to perching himself on the bar.

"You know this show?" Ryan pointed to the TV as he finished the rest of the beer he did have.

"Yeah, sure. It's been running for years. I don't know it well but I know of it, how come?"

"Let's have a little fun and play a game?" Ryan stood and took his wallet out of his back pocket and placed it onto the bar. "We'll go head to head to guess the correct answer. Let's say $20 an answer?"

The bartender instantly shook his head; he was having no part of getting involved in Ryan's suggested game. "There's no way in hell I'm playing $20 a question when there's what, five questions a round? I'm on bartender money not lawyer."

Ryan thought about his original offer and decided to make it a lot more lucrative for the bartender.

"Let's say every answer you get right, I'll give you $20 and every answer I get right you owe me $5 – sound fair?" He extended his hand and after a short pause and a curious look the bartender shook Ryan's hand. They both looked up at the screen and waited for the questions to start.

The bar remained largely just the pair of them for the next forty-five minutes or so. Somebody walked in and asked for directions to a local bakery they couldn't find and a regular popped in for his daily one Bloody Mary but apart from that they were left to their game. The time was around 4.45 p.m.

and the bartender knew that shortly he would have colleagues coming in to start their shift and it would also start getting busier. As it stood, Ryan owed the bartender $160 and he in turn owed Ryan $85 from the questions they'd answered so far.

"That's me out, Ryan," he said as he stood up from the stool next to him. "This place is about to start getting busy so I need to sort a few more things before it does."

"Wait, wait, wait." Ryan grabbed his arm before he could fully get off the stool. "It's the final round and it's sport – just give it another five to ten minutes of your time."

The bartender could see Ryan doing some calculations in his head.

"At the moment I owe you $75. Let's do double or quits on the first couple of questions. You could be $300 up in the first two questions."

The bartender gave Ryan the same look that he gave him when he agreed to play the game. Ryan knew for a fact someone on his wages who mainly relied on tips couldn't turn down the opportunity to earn that kind of money.

"OK, you have a deal. Two questions though, that's it!"

He swung himself back around and both men turned their eyes back up to the screen. The round was about to start.

*"Question 1: Which west coast Soccer club has been home to Zlatan Ibrahimovic and English superstar David Beckham?"*

Ryan had absolutely no idea about soccer and no idea what the answer was to the question.

"LA Galaxy," the bartender answered before the contestant on the show even had deliberated giving their answer.

"You're pretty certain, aren't you?"

"I spent a summer over in Europe and fell in love with football so I know that's right."

Sure enough within a minute they had it confirmed as LA Galaxy was the correct answer.

"So that's $150 you owe me now?" He rubbed his hands together and looked back up.

Ryan was determined to get the next question correct.

"*Question 2: Where was Michael Jordan born?*"

Before he could even get a syllable out of his mouth the bartender shouted "North Carolina" and proceeded to run off around the bar celebrating his answer.

Ryan sat rooted to the spot and didn't even flinch. He kept his eyes fixated on the screen.

"Brooklyn," he muttered.

The bartender didn't hear him through all the cheering and whooping he was doing. Ryan turned around to locate him and make sure this time he heard him.

"The answer is Brooklyn. He was born in Brooklyn but raised in North Carolina from a young age."

The bartender stopped in his tracks. He was so confident a second ago so why was he now starting to doubt himself.

"It's North Carolina, I'm a hundred per cent sure."

Ryan shrugged his shoulders and pointed back to the TV screen.

"Give it thirty seconds and we'll know for sure."

The sports expert within the team on the show huddled his teammates. Whispering ensued before they separated and gave an answer. *Brooklyn.* Ecstasy turned to agony. The bartender looked as if someone had just told him his dog had died.

"I was so sure; everything I know about him refers to North Carolina."

Ryan put a hand on the man's back.

"It's a bit of a shit question but basketball is my sport like soccer is yours."

Ryan knew $300 to this guy was a much bigger deal than it was to him. The guy had already made his way back round to the bar and had started to pour himself a soft drink.

"Hey, man, one more question. $500 if you get it right before me, no financial loss to you if I get it right."

"I'm not a charity case, man, that deal makes me seem desperate." He finished pouring himself the drink, placing it on the back of the bar, and walked towards the door that led to the cellar.

"Listen, I've had a really shitty day today. Probably the worst day I've had in a very long time and you've helped me take my mind off of things." The bartender slowed down, his back still to Ryan at this point. Ryan continued, "You know me, I know you. We're playing a game and if you end up winning a ton of money from it then so be it. It was my idea, wasn't it?"

"$500 if I win and if I lose then nothing to you?" He'd half turned back and looked at Ryan as he asked the question.

"Absolutely, although we've just missed question 3 so it would now be on question 4."

"Deal." He rushed back over and nearly knocked the stool next to Ryan over as he tried to sit on it. He didn't see or hear one of his colleagues as they walked in.

"Doing nothing again, Freddie?"

Not to lose his concentration from the TV he simply flipped a finger as they squeezed past to get behind the bar.

"*Question 4: Which American city links the sports franchises Mavericks, Stars and Cowboys?*"

"DALLLLLLLLAS!" The bartender screamed at the TV as he then proceeded to stand on the bar and jump up and down. "I thought I was sure last time but I'm one million per cent sure this time round. Show me the moneyyyyyy!" Similar to the last time, Ryan didn't move a muscle and was rooted to his chair but this time he looked lost in thought. "$500. Oh, how I love you Dallas Cowboys, Dallas Mavericks and Dallas Stars."

"That's it. They're all in Dallas." Ryan guzzled his beer down and jumped to his feet. "A bet's a bet, Freddie, but I've got somewhere to be. I'll square you up on Sunday."

At almost full pace Ryan sprinted back to his apartment to gather his things. He was hoping he'd see Emilia but realistically he knew she would be long gone by this time. As he burst through the door, he made his way to the bedroom and threw a couple of shirts and jeans into a carry-on bag, added some toiletries on top and as quick as he came in, headed back for the front door. He repeatedly kept muttering the same sentence over and over again about being naive as he hailed a cab to take him back to the office. It was around 5.30 p.m. now so the footfall and traffic were a little heavier than earlier on. He called Macpherson's mobile and got no answer so tried the switchboard and they put him through to her office line which she answered.

"You will answer this phone but not your mobile to me then, right?" Ryan said before Macpherson could even confirm whose phone it was.

"Ryan, is that you? Are you still drinking?"

Ryan was definitely a little worse for wear after the lunchtime drinks and then eight beers he'd had in Mulligans but there was no stopping a man on a mission.

"I've figured something out in the case, I'm coming back to the office. Wait there." Ryan hung up the phone and encouraged the driver to go a little faster.

They got about three blocks from the office and hit a solid wall of traffic. Ryan waited for a couple of minutes but then jumped out, paid the driver and set off on foot for the office. It was busier than usual due to the dry weather but he weaved in and out of workers and tourists to reach the bottom of the office quicker than he should have. Barely letting people out of the elevator that had come down, Ryan jumped in through the open doors and frantically pushed the button a number of times hoping it would make it go quicker. Bursting out of the elevator like a hungry lion chasing his prey, Ryan made a beeline for Macpherson's office. The door was open and he waited for no invitation before entering.

"Dallas."

Macpherson was startled and looked increasingly confused at how Ryan had opened the conversation.

"The connection, somehow, is Dallas." Ryan threw his bag on the floor and took a seat.

"Luke Best had his photo taken in a strip joint with drugs after playing the Dallas Mavericks." Macpherson nodded. "Then Henry Craig had an alleged affair with a woman after playing the Dallas Cowboys." Macpherson sat up a little straighter, Ryan had her attention. "Finally Matt Woodman was bribed to throw a game against the Dallas Stars. The connection is Dallas."

Macpherson stood making her way towards the whiteboard that was across the room from her desk. It was old school, especially in this day and age with technology but it helped her brainstorm on the extremely rare occasion she got involved on a case.

"I like the theory, it works. But how? That could just be pure coincidence."

Ryan stood up and joined her over at the whiteboard taking the pen out of her hand.

"All three sportsmen are represented by the same person

and they all get caught doing something illegal or in a scandal in the same city? There's no way that's a coincidence!"

"OK, let's say it's not, how do we link DeShawn Arlington to strippers, drugs and a local reporter? He didn't make Henry Craig have an affair, did he?" Ryan went to say something but Macpherson continued what she was saying. "More importantly, what links DeShawn Arlington to Dallas? He's born and bred in Brooklyn!"

Ryan pondered what he'd just heard.

"Think back to your case against him. Geographically where was it set?"

A twinkle instantly appeared in Macpherson's eyes and she knew Ryan was truly onto something.

"Austin."

"And where is Austin?" Ryan turned, grabbed his bag before the question could be answered and headed towards the door. "I know what links them all, I don't know how it links to DeShawn but I'm going to Dallas to find out." "Have you forgotten that you've been taken off the case?" Macpherson promptly fired at the back of Ryan's head as he went to leave the room.

"If I go to Dallas and come back with something positive then you'll have to reconsider. What did you tell me earlier? You were looking for how I reacted to this?"

They both knew that wasn't what Macpherson wanted to hear but Ryan's reaction was more like the lawyer she wanted him to be.

"If you go to Dallas and further tarnish either your name or the firm's name then it won't just be this case you'll be off but after this morning with Daniels he will most definitely want you sacked."

"This is my make-or-break case. My first in the so-called majors. Regardless of what this weekend brings I can't tarnish my name any more in the industry than if people find out I've been removed."

Macpherson agreed with what Ryan had just said; he didn't need to know that. As much as going to Dallas seemed the right thing to do, she couldn't have her name associated with this escapade without speaking to others about it first. Especially given the fact she'd already reminded Ryan at least twice that he had been hauled off the case that morning.

Ryan turned back just as he was about to walk out of the door.
"I didn't come here for an argument. I came here out of respect because you're my mentor and I wanted to tell you my plans but regardless of what you say I'm going."

Two steps later he was out onto the main office floor and heading back towards the elevator. There were no further objections from Macpherson both visually and vocally but just as Ryan was about to step in to go down, he caught his boss standing in her office doorway watching him leave.

The encounter with Macpherson was brief as Ryan had always planned it to be. The doorman downstairs had hailed him a cab that was ready and waiting to whisk him off to LaGuardia Airport where he had an 8 p.m. flight to Dallas already booked. He threw his bag in the boot of the cab and settled into the back whilst they battled their way through the same traffic as earlier on. Ryan looked down at his phone and didn't know who to reach out to. Should he call Luke, Matt or Henry and tell them what was going on? Should he call Emilia and let her know he'd be spending the weekend in Dallas? Thinking about it he should probably speak with all four of them but he remembered someone that may be able to help him. He started writing a text message to Emilia's father, José:

*I'm outside the box and on the way to Dallas. Can you have your PI call me on this number when I land at 11.30 p.m. please?*

## 18

# THURSDAY 22ND OCTOBER, 11.25 P.M.

*Welcome to Dallas, Fort Worth Airport and thank you for flying with Delta.*

A three-hour and fifteen-minute flight seemed like a lifetime to Ryan as he let his vivid imagination run wild with how everything pieced together. If it even did at all. He hadn't drunk a drop of alcohol since leaving Mulligans earlier on and by now was starting to sober up. Despite being asked not to by the cabin manager, Ryan switched his phone on and the notifications went crazy, just like he thought they would. He hadn't been able to get through to Emilia before take-off so he left her a voicemail explaining he'd be in Dallas due to the case and he also had several messages from Luke, Henry and Matt as similar to Emilia they didn't pick up his calls. He had no emails because the firm had clearly forgotten to tell them to stop diverting them. Right now that was a relief as it meant he could fully concentrate on the next couple of days. Macpherson made it pretty clear his career at Macpherson & Daniels would be over if this didn't end well. Ryan undid his seat belt and grabbed his bag from the overhead locker. He had only taken four or five steps off the plane when his phone started to ring from an unknown number. Pretty prompt timing from the PI as no one else would be calling at this hour.

"Thanks for reaching out." Ryan answered the phone in a hushed tone with several people around him.

"You're welcome, Ryan. Let me be clear though, I don't do the chasing so let this be your one and only pass with me. How can I help?"

Ryan glanced over his shoulder to make sure there was nobody within earshot of him.

"I need you to look into a couple of places and dates for me. They're very specific."

"OK – shoot. I've got what I need to take down all the details from you."

Ryan unfolded a piece of paper from his pocket and went on to list the exact dates of the games his clients played in before doing whatever they did DeShawn went on to cover up. He listed the strip club name, the team hotel and name of the local blog and repeated that those places were key to uncovering the truth connecting them all.

"You know my fees?" The PI didn't interrupt any of what Ryan had just spent the last ten minutes talking about but wanted to make it evidently clear his price when he was finished.

"I don't but whatever it is, don't worry, if you come good, I'll happily pay it." Ryan was walking towards where he needed to show his ID.

"No problem, I'll call you in twelve to eighteen hours. Leave it with me."

After flashing his driver's license Ryan made his way out of the airport and towards the taxicab rank.

"Hampton Inn & Suites please."

Ryan barely slept a wink. The alarm that he had set for 8 a.m. went off but by then he had already been up for three hours and had turned his small hotel room into something that wouldn't look out of place on CSI. Post-it notes covered the mirror and TV, there were pieces of loose paper that had been scribbled on all over the floor and a takeaway pizza box covered the small table. As much as he was banking on the PI to uncover something his end, Ryan wanted to see what he could find out whilst he waited for his call. As he marched around the room trying to think of something realistic that connected everything, he chewed away at the other end of the marker pen he'd been using. He sat down on the end of the bed and let out a big sigh, falling back onto the rock-hard mattress and paper-thin sheets. He laid there staring at the ceiling hoping for inspiration but got nothing and nowhere quick. He leapt to his feet and headed into the bathroom to take a shower. He had a busy day planned for himself and he thought he better get started.

Ryan walked into the reception of the hotel and asked if they could call him a cab. He looked to make his first stop at the hotel where Henry Craig spent the night with the barmaid. Whilst he waited for it to arrive, he ambled around the decrepit front area of the hotel looking at the paintings and the outdated decor. He was a long way from the city life he knew and loved but if being here helped with the case then it was worth it. Ryan's cab arrived so he got in quickly, his destination being Rosewood Mansions. As they got closer to the city center Ryan started to feel a little easier about his surroundings. The cab driver kept bringing the conversation back to the Dallas Cowboys at every opportunity, which everyone knew was pretty much what people from Dallas did when talking sports. It took a little longer than expected but by 9.30 a.m. they had reached their destination. Ryan stepped out, brushed himself off and headed inside to find the manager for questioning.

"May I speak to the manager, please?" Ryan said politely to the young woman on the front desk after entering reception.

"I can certainly see if he is available, sir. Will he know what it's regarding?" She picked up the phone to her right-hand side and dialed the extension as Ryan shook his head and mouthed the word no to not interrupt her in case her call was answered. After a brief pause her manager answered the call and Ryan was informed that he if took a seat over in the lobby then he would be with him shortly.

"Thank you," he said as he turned and headed towards the white marble behind him. Around ten to fifteen minutes later a youngish man appeared with slick black hair, a cheap suit on and name badge pinned to the right-hand side of his jacket. Straight away Ryan knew that was him. As he looked around Ryan stood and waved to get his attention and he bounded over like a puppy.

"Good morning, sir, my name is Lex and I'm the manager here. I understand you wanted to speak to me about something?"

Ryan removed his wallet and handed Lex a business card.

"Correct. I'm Ryan Jackson, a lawyer from New York, and I wanted to ask you a couple of questions regarding a case I'm currently on. Is there somewhere a little more *private?*"

The color drained from the hotel manager's face and he didn't even know what the conversation was about yet.

"Erm, yes, my office would be best. Please follow me."

Lex spent some time looking at Ryan's business card whilst Ryan searched through his briefcase for some papers to make notes on.

"I have a staff meeting at 10.30 a.m. so whatever this is about can we make it quick, please?"

"How long have you worked here, Lex? That's probably the

most important question right now?" Ryan closed his briefcase and held four sheets of paper in his hand.

"Five and a half years altogether." He pointed to some plaques on the wall.

"As a manager?" Ryan didn't really take any notice of where he was pointing to.

"Not always as a manager. I was a trainee manager for two and a bit years, then assistant manager and I've been hotel manager now for about eighteen months."

That placed him as an employee of the hotel when Henry Craig's affair happened so Ryan placed a picture of Henry in front of him.

"Do you know this man?"

"Who doesn't? He's a legend in the sport of NFL." He then again pointed to the wall and this time Ryan looked up only to be met with a Dallas Cowboys calendar.

"Has he ever stayed here before? When he was playing?"

Lex flicked a lever on his chair and leaned back, throwing a small squishy ball in the air while doing so.

"Yeah, probably. I don't know. All the sports teams stay here when they're in town, so I guess so. Our old duty manager used to get weird with us not making a fuss, so everything used to blend into one."

"But you just called him a legend and you can't remember if he stayed in your hotel?"

"I'm sure he did. Is there a reason you need to know this so badly?"

Ryan handed him pieces of paper that had dates and game details of the night the alleged affair took place.

"Do you remember this game?"

The guy had already given himself away to be a massive Dallas Cowboys fan so if he said no then Ryan would know he was a liar.

"Of course, man. What a game. What a day that was."

Ryan was waiting for him to point to something on the wall but he never did.

"Great. Henry and the Giants stayed here whilst in town for that game – correct?"

He leaned back on his chair again and titled his head sideways.

"He did, you're right. Now you mentioned it I was on the nightshift and remember seeing a load of them drinking in the hotel bar."

Just what Ryan wanted to hear.

"Would the hotel have kept a record of who worked that evening?" It was Ryan's turn to point now and he drew Lex's attention towards the computer in the room. He put his hand on the mouse and moved it to bring it to life.

"We will probably have a record from that night but now you've jogged my memory I remember a lot of sickness and no shows from that day."

What Ryan took from that was people were actually out celebrating the Cowboys' win. He looked through a couple of folders and clicked here and there and turned the screen so Ryan could see.

"These were the people who were scheduled to be on. As you can see, nearly half of them didn't make their shift. It was all hands on deck."

"Do you mind if I take a photo of that?" Ryan got his phone out and lined up the camera with the information that was on the screen.

"You didn't get that from me, OK?" Lex said as he closed the document down from the screen.

Ryan took the pieces of paper back from Lex and put them back in his briefcase. Lex locked the computer again, stood up and ushered Ryan towards the door.

"Do you have a business card or a number that I can contact you on if I have any more questions?" Ryan was basically being pushed out of the office as he asked the question.

"I think I've done quite enough as it is already, Mr Jackson. Should you need anything else you'll have to speak with the owners."

By now they were back in the hotel lobby and after a quick shake of hands, the hotel manager departed presumably for the 10.30 meeting he'd previously mentioned. Ryan went to walk out but the same young lady who greeted him chased him down and tapped him on the shoulder before he could reach the exit.

"Lex said there's a complimentary breakfast for you if you'd like it, sir?"

Having only eaten three quarters of a very average pizza in the last eighteen hours Ryan more than obliged and followed her down to the dining area. There was only half an hour left on the buffet so Ryan quickly put what he wanted on his plate and went and sat down in the corner of the room.

Ryan cleared his plate quicker than he loaded it and as he got up his phone started to ring. An incoming call from a withheld number. He sat back down.

"Give it to me." Ryan was straight into the phone call.

"It's only been about twelve hours so it's mostly just an update call."

Ryan was only in town until Sunday morning so they were both up against the clock to uncover something.

"So, what's the update?" Ryan had sat back down in the dining area and was continuously checking his shoulder to make sure no one was around him.

"I'm looking into both the staff lists for the strip club and the hotel to see who was working that night."

"I've got the staff list for the hotel. Let me know where I

can send it to and I will." Ryan continued, "The manager said a lot of people called in sick though so I don't know how useful it'll be." Ryan's phone had already vibrated before he'd finished the sentence with an email address of where to send the picture to.

"Now for the good news, or at least the one thing I have found out since we last spoke."

Ryan waited with bated breath to hear what the PI had uncovered.

"The blog that you told me about. It doesn't exist anymore. It's gone."

Ryan didn't see that as good news in the slightest. There was a slight pause between the pair as maybe Ryan was expected to answer but he continued to wait for the *good news* he was promised.

"A friend who's good with IT managed to find the blog's old posts and domain."

"OK, we can work with that. Do we have a name of the person who ran the blog?"

"We don't, no. But what we do have is this local blog never posted on or after the date you gave me so they must have been shut down after the Matt Woodman incident."

Maybe DeShawn scared her off? Maybe it was part of her deal that she had to stop?

"OK but we need a name so I can see if I can track her down whilst I'm here."

"I'll get onto that but I have more about the blog." Ryan took the information he already knew and started writing it down. "It gets weirder, all five of the previous posts were posted in the run-up to this woman meeting Matt. The website address was only registered six days before the date you gave me."

"Do you think the blog was a fake? She pretended to be a blogger?"

"That's another possibility that we're looking into. I'll call you tonight once I have anything more concrete."

Before Ryan could answer the line was dead and the PI was gone. Time was starting to get on so he jumped to his feet and headed back to the lobby to catch a cab back to his hotel.

Ryan was back in his hotel room in no time with two new key pieces of information to add to what he'd drawn up last night. He had the list of who was working in the hotel and also that the blog used to blackmail Matt Woodman was effectively fake. He started making his way through the list of staff firstly crossing off all the men. That ruled out around forty per cent of the people working and once you considered the female members of staff that didn't show for their shift Ryan had it narrowed down to around thirty people. He quickly snapped a picture of what he'd done and sent it to the PI's email. He opened up his laptop and began searching for the local blog just to make sure that the information he had been given was correct. He started to search other local blogs too and reference the people running and writing for them to see if any of them matched the description that Matt had given about the woman from that day. They didn't. Were any of their names on the staff list from that night? They weren't. He really needed the PI to come up with some kind of name that he could cross-reference. He was thinking it could be a sister of an employee or a friend but how then did that link to DeShawn? He now had less than forty-eight hours to figure it all out.

Ryan's phone started to vibrate and he grabbed it hoping it would be the PI with more information. It was Emilia. Ryan breathed a huge sigh of relief and although it wasn't who he had first hoped, he was happy to see his wife's name.

"I'm sorry," he said picking up the phone before it rang out.

"You're in Dallas?" Emilia decided to ignore her husband's apology and instead prioritized why she was calling.

"Yeah, I got in late last night. I'm here for the case."

"Where are you staying?"

"Straight to the point today, I see. I'm staying in a place not far from the airport called Hampton Inn & Suites and coming to and from town when I need to."

Emilia seemed to have some pretty solid questions lined up regardless of how Ryan was answering.

"I just can't believe you're here. What does Dallas have to do with your case in New York?"

"It's where all the key events took place. I overlooked it because everyone kept referring to teams as their franchise name but I'm sure something has happened here." It sounded as if Ryan was still trying to convince himself that Dallas was indeed the link.

"I just can't believe you're in Dallas, that's crazy." She knew Ryan's job was very full-on with twists and turns but it'd never taken him halfway across the country before.

"I know, right. On another day it could have been Denver and I would have been able to see you."

"I'm in Dallas too, Ryan, remember." Emilia sighed as it was just another example of Ryan not listening to her when they were at home.

"Really? Can I see you? I need to make it up to you and explain the other night." Ryan's voice was tinged with excitement now at the thought of being able to see Emilia.

"I'm working, as are you. That's the only reason we're both here. I might be able to squeeze in seeing you tomorrow night, maybe."

"Maybe is good enough for me right now. Listen, I need to go, talk tonight?"

"OK, love you."

Emilia hung up and with that Ryan's trip to Dallas now had two meanings; uncover the truth and also make it up to his wife.

Ryan didn't know what time the strip club opened so he was heading back into the city early afternoon and if it wasn't open, he was going to just wait around until it was. He figured the earlier he got there after it opened then the quieter it would be, so he'd probably be able to talk to the people he needed to. If they still worked there. Just as Ryan when to turn his attention back to his work his phone vibrated next to him. It was a text message from Macpherson:

*How's it going? Found anything substantial yet?*

## 19

# FRIDAY 23RD OCTOBER, 7.58 P.M.

Ryan checked his watch again, 7.58 p.m. He found it hard to believe that a strip club on a Friday night wasn't opening until 8 p.m. but that was the situation he currently found himself in. He had been in the center of town for several hours now and had passed the time meandering around parks and drinking several cups of coffee. He had heard nothing further from the PI, Emilia, or Macpherson since he caught up with them all earlier. He glanced down again, 7.59 p.m. He was becoming rather impatient with his current surroundings as he wanted to gather more information, go back to the hotel and get back to trying to link everything together. As he went to look down again the door swung open and rather large man appeared. The gentleman was six-foot four, white, with a bald head and dressed in all black. He brought out some rope and small poles with him to form a barrier for a queue line and flicked a switch on so that the club's name lit up above the doorway. It seemed it was officially open for business.

Ryan headed on over immediately knowing that once inside he would be the only non-employee in there. He understood he may look a little seedy but at the same time he was planning on never returning again so it didn't matter. As he got within a couple of steps of the front door the man outside, who it was now clear was the bouncer, stopped Ryan in his tracks and asked him for his ID. Ryan produced his driver's license and in doing so unveiled the rest of the contents of his wallet.

"New York, huh? So, what are you doing all the way out here in Dallas?" The bouncer looked down at Ryan after removing the license from his eyesight.

"Business," Ryan replied confidently.

The bouncer gave the card back to Ryan.

"Let me see your wallet, please."

Ryan handed it over, confident that it was protocol for the club to do this. After rummaging around, the man pulled out Ryan's business card that revealed he was a lawyer. The man handed everything back to Ryan.

"Not tonight." He escorted Ryan away from the door.

"I just want a couple of drinks, that's all. I'll be in and out within an hour. No funny business."

The man looked Ryan up and down. He probably had a good half a foot on him and a hundred or so pounds.

"You have a maximum of sixty minutes and any trouble then you'll have me to answer to."

He unclipped the rope from one of the barriers and allowed Ryan to enter the club.

It was just as Ryan thought it would be. Once inside he paid his fee to get in. The club was desolate apart from a few people behind the bar and a handful of exotic dancers as the sign above the door called them. He approached the bar and ordered a large whiskey with no ice so he didn't draw attention to himself. He sat on one of the bar stools and waited for his order to arrive. A gentle tap on his shoulder came.

"Hey, sugar, you want to go somewhere a little more

private?" As he swung around a scantily dressed woman stood in front of him. "I haven't seen you in here before," she said, as she ran her fingers over his arm.

Ryan removed her hand from his arm promptly.

"I'm just in here for a few drinks this evening but thank you."

He swung himself back round to face the bar. Moments later his drink arrived and he exchanged money with the bartender and told him to keep the change. As he went to walk away Ryan called him back.

"How long have you been working here?" he said as he waved a $100 in the guy's face.

He snatched it and shoved it under a UV light to make sure it was real.

"About three years now. I started whilst I was working through college and I stayed in the area so I stayed on here for a little extra money."

Similar to the hotel manager he would have worked when the incident took place.

"What about your manager? How long has he been here?"

The guy leaned in towards Ryan.

"She has been here since it opened. She's not just the manager though, she owns it."

"Is she in tonight?" Ryan pulled another $100 dollar bill from his pocket and placed it on the bar. The guy looked around and glanced over his shoulder. He was blocking a CCTV camera.

"See the door to the left of the stage, through there, up the stairs and her office is the first door on your left. You didn't hear that from me." He put his hand over the $100 bill and slid it along the bar.

Surprisingly to Ryan it was fairly easy to make his way through the door. It wasn't locked, there was no one standing guard and no code to get through. A number of customers had started to arrive at the club as well so he was able to slip through unnoticed. The stairwell was fairly dark and narrow but you could see the light at the top as a door was slightly ajar. Ryan made his way carefully and quietly towards the office. As he reached the top he paused to listen as he could hear a conversation taking place. Whoever was inside was on the phone.

"It was good to see you the other night, don't leave it too long next time. Safe trip back, Love you."

Ryan gave it a couple of seconds before he firmly knocked on the door.

"Come in," the person replied with a sniffle in her voice. As Ryan entered the room, the woman stood up from her chair as she clearly didn't expect it to be him entering. "I've got a gun in my drawer," she said hastily. "Are you a cop?"

Ryan put his drink down on the side and held his hands up.

"My name is Ryan Jackson; I'm a lawyer from New York and I just have a couple of questions to ask you. It doesn't involve you, it's about the club."

Ryan continued to hold his hands up to gesture he wanted no trouble. The lady sat back, opened the drawer and placed the gun on her desk.

"I'm leaving this here for my piece of mind. I don't usually talk to your kind but I like the balls you've shown to get into my office. You've got ten minutes."

Ryan picked his drink back up and sat on the chair opposite.

"Sorry, I didn't catch your name?"

Ryan's eyes scanned the desk and walls behind to see if he could see anything to help him.

"Latesha Rhodes," came back quickly. "But I know you didn't come in here to ask me that, so what do you really want to know?"

"Do you follow sports, Latesha?" Ryan reached into his jacket pocket and pulled out the same pieces of paper he had from earlier.

"I know a little about NFL and NBA but not a lot." She tapped her fingers on her desk anxiously.

"Do you recognize this man?" He handed her a picture of Luke Best. She looked over it for about ten seconds and handed it back.

"I can't say I do, unfortunately."

Ryan asked her if she remembered the date that Luke was in the club.

"Are you kidding me? I can't remember what goes on in my club two weeks ago let alone years ago."

"The Mavericks played the Celtics; Celtics won and won the Eastern Conference. I know you said you don't know much about the NBA but does that ring any bells?"

Latesha rolled her eyes at Ryan when he had finished.

"Why does it always have something to do with sport? Every damn problem around always comes back to sport."

"I assume that nudged your memory about the date?"

"Whenever there's a big sporting event in town, I always have to call in backup to open this place. The girls try and party with the athletes, and the bartenders get drunk off tips and celebrate the win. Nothing changes."

Ryan handed her another piece of paper and tried to bring her back round from her mini rant.

"Do you remember the Boston Celtics players that came in here that night?"

This piece of paper had several faces on it.

"I'm sorry, Ryan, they all blur into one the number of

times they com—" She stopped mid-sentence. She turned the paper and pointed at one of the faces. "That's Kyle Rayner. He used to play in Dallas but moved to another team. He used to be a regular in here."

With that the door slung open and the rather large man from the front door stood covering the hole where the door was.

"I knew I shouldn't have let you up here. Get up, fool."

He grabbed Ryan by his shoulder and launched him towards the door. Latesha stayed quiet and didn't say a word; Ryan was tumbling down the stairs before he could even say another word. Being frog marched through a strip club wasn't how Ryan envisioned his Friday night ending, but this was how it was. Slung onto the sidewalk he looked up at the bouncer from lying on his back.

"If you come here ever again, it will be a lot worse next time."

Dusting himself off Ryan hailed down a cab and headed back to the hotel. He had pretty much wasted a whole day because he'd barely got any information out of Latesha, just that sports stars went there all the time and she didn't recognize Luke Best. Apart from that, his trip was pretty pointless. He stopped en route home to get some food and drink as he sensed he was in for another long night. He got back to the hotel around 10 p.m. and after eating half a bag of crisps and three quarters of a chocolate bar, got back to work trying to connect the dots. What did a fake blog, a plush city hotel and a dingy strip club in Dallas have in common? They were all in their separate columns on Ryan's TV with nothing whatsoever linking them yet. He started to head towards the toilet when his phone vibrated. He ran across the room and saw an incoming call from a withheld number. Hopefully the PI would have something to help.

"Please tell me you have something substantial that will help. I'm losing my mind." Ryan sat down on the toilet whilst talking to the PI.

"I do have something that may help although I will need some information from you too. Did you go to the strip club?"

"I did and I got thrown out within about thirty or forty minutes of being there." Ryan looked in the mirror and he had a scratch on his forehead and some grazing on his right arm from landing.

"Did you find anything useful before this happened? Did you get who was working that night?" The PI tapped away at whatever he was doing his end whilst talking.

"I didn't, no, the trip was of little worth if I'm honest with you." He made his way back into the other room cautiously stepping over everything on the floor. "All I got was the owner's name, Latesha Rhodes. She also manages the place and it's notorious with athletes but she couldn't put a name to Luke's face."

"That's not good, not good at all but I can still run some checks on her."

Ryan put the onus back on the PI.

"So what did you find out in the last twelve hours?"

"Two things, actually." The typing stopped. "This blog that blackmailed Matt was a fake but one thing really stunned me about it."

"Go on," Ryan said urging more information out of him.

"When I ran a check on the IP address for the website it seems as if it was created here in New York. I couldn't link the direct address, but it was showing up as Manhattan."

Ryan was silent. The reporter that blackmailed Matt was from New York and not Dallas. He was deep in thought about the new information he had just received.

"Do you think DeShawn could have set the website up?"

"That I don't know yet but it could well be a possibility right now."

Ryan scribbled on a Post-it note what he'd just found out and added to the notes his end.

"The second thing?" Before the PI could reply a knock came at Ryan's door. "Bear with me, room service."

"So, what's the second thing then?" Ryan had thrown his burger and chips on the table and almost ran back to his phone on the bed.

"This one relates to your trip to the hotel this morning," he replied. "When you sent me the rota for who was supposed to be working and who didn't show up, I did a bit of digging on the hotel."

"Right," Ryan said nodding his end. "Digging such as?"

"A hotel that size couldn't function on the amount of people that turned up so I got a friend to hack into their email system and that night it seems they made several calls to an agency for temporary staff." Now this could be very useful. Now the PI was earning his substantial fee as far as Ryan was concerned. "I'll have that list of staff for you by the morning."

"Good work." Ryan continued jotting all of this down on more colorful Post-it notes.

"That's all from me at the moment. Do you have anything to add?"

Ryan started to rack his brains to see if he did. He did.

"Now you mention temporary staff, the owner of the strip club did say that they always had to call in backup workers when there's a big game in town. Can you look into them the same way you did with the hotel?" The PI proceeded to double check all the necessary information he needed. "That is all correct," Ryan confirmed.

"Perfect, if you leave that with me, I'll have everything for you in the morning, OK?"

"Talk, then." Ryan put the phone down.

Ryan had taken the notes he scribbled during the phone call and placed them under their rightful columns. What he had been told about the blog was good. If it linked back to New York in some way, shape or form then that was a step closer to tying this to DeShawn. Putting it altogether and actually convicting DeShawn was still a very long way off, though. He looked around the room and noticed his food was still on the table and by now would probably be lukewarm at best. He dropped the pen and walked over to eat what he could.

As he finished, the phone in the room rang. Ryan answered it to be told there was someone waiting for him down in reception. He didn't know anyone in Dallas apart from Emilia and she told him she was working that night and tomorrow they'd see each other. Puzzled by the thought of who it could be, Ryan got dressed and headed down to reception. When he arrived, he was pointed towards somebody waiting just outside the lobby.

"Can I help?" Ryan said as he approached the figure from behind. Turning round to answer, the person removed their hood. Ryan recognized the face straight away. It was the bartender from the strip club earlier on.

"What are you doing here? Better question, how do you know where I'm staying?" Ryan fired the second question at him before he could even answer the first one.

"It's more what I can do to help you," he said with mischief filling his voice. "As for knowing where you're staying, the cab driver who brought you here is a regular at the club so I bribed him with one of the $100 bills you gave me." *Impressive for a bartender*, Ryan thought. "You're the lawyer representing the sports stars in New York, aren't you?"

"Yes, that's me. How do you know about that?"

"It's all over the news channels and I follow the NBA and NFL," he replied laughing. "It's kind of hard to actually not know about it."

Ryan didn't take the sarcasm very well.

"Why are you here? What do you want?" Ryan said, getting impatient. If he wasn't going to find out anything useful, he might as well try and get some sleep.

"The guy you're up against, DeShawn Arlington."

"What about him?"

"He's been at the club a whole bunch of times before. He knows Latesha from somewhere; I've seen him there since that day I started."

"You are sure it's him? It's a pretty dark place unless someone is right in front of you." By this point Ryan had his phone open taking down notes so that he could transfer them later.

"I'm a hundred per cent sure it's him. He's been in when the club isn't even open." Ryan was thrilled with what he was hearing. He finally had something concrete to tie DeShawn to being in Dallas. Although at the moment it was just a random bartender's word.

"Excellent, here, put your number in my phone, I might need to call you later on." As the guy tapped his number into Ryan's iPhone, he put his hand in his pocket and unfolded some crumpled bills. "Here take this." He handed him another $200. "Just make sure you pick up the phone if I need you."

He turned back and walked into the hotel; he was desperate to tell the PI the new information so he could look into it further.

As he reached the room, he fired off an email on his phone requesting a call from the PI and set about writing up what he'd just found out to add it to the TV. DeShawn had been to the strip club several times before and the blog's IP address was in Manhattan, but what about the hotel? His phone lit up and Ryan grabbed it thinking it was the PI but in fact it was a message from Emilia:

*We're all good for tomorrow night. See you then xx*

## 20

# SATURDAY 24TH OCTOBER, 8 A.M.

Just like yesterday Ryan's alarm went off but once again he had been up long before it. He was hoping to get a better night's sleep than the previous one, however when the PI didn't reach out, he spent the majority of the night trying to piece everything together himself. He wanted to, or more so needed to, tie everything together in the next twelve hours otherwise meeting Emilia wouldn't happen and after how things were left in New York, spending time together that evening was non-negotiable. Ryan had also been thinking on how they could get DeShawn on the stand for a third time given the new information he knew. He could tie him to two of the three dates now but still had nothing on the hotel but truth be told none of it was substantial evidence. A bartender's story and a mystery IP address were the best he had but it wouldn't be good enough for Judge Sullivan. He opened his phone and fired off another email to the PI asking for him to call him ASAP to discuss. It was Saturday but Ryan thought that the person he was trying to get hold of hardly worked a normal Monday to Friday job. He stared at his phone hoping for it to ring and as he was about to put it down to jump in the shower when it did.

"Why didn't you call me last night like I asked? I've got new information." Ryan barked down the phone as he picked it up after not even one ring.

"So do I," the PI responded. "I wanted to make sure it was legitimate before I told you about it."

Ryan stopped. Hopefully both pieces of information lined up rather than contradicting each other.

"OK. I'll go first and we can see how it lines up, that OK with you?" The PI waited for Ryan to continue and reveal the information he'd been so desperate to share. "DeShawn makes regular trips to Dallas. More importantly he's a regular at the strip club where Luke was pictured with the drugs."

"Good work, Ryan, but I have to ask, is that from a credible source?"

Given the fact Ryan was in Dallas and had his boots on the ground he thought the PI would have been pleased to hear this.

"It's from the bartender at the strip club. He came to my hotel last night after we spoke."

"Interesting," the PI replied slowly. "What I'm about to tell you all makes sense now." Ryan thought having two pieces of information link together was great but he had hoped it was related to the hotel as that was the missing piece. "Have you got something to write this all down?"

"So," the PI took a deep breath as he started. "What I am about to tell you must not under any circumstances come back to me. I said I would help you as a favor to José but in all honesty, I didn't think I'd actually find something."

He must have found something fairly substantial to start off with that. Ryan answered back, "I don't even know your name for it to come back on you."

"Right, I looked into the strip club as I agreed to last night and it turns out that they use the same temporary staffing company as the hotel." Ryan was frantically trying to note all this down as fast as the PI was talking. "I cross-referenced the agency database as to who was sent out to work on both of those nights and there was only one match. One female." He paused. Ryan paused. This was the moment that he had been waiting for. "The name that appeared on both was Tiffany Maddison." Ryan started to repeat the name in his head, over and over again. Over and over again. Tiffany Maddison. "Does that name mean anything to you? Has it come up in the case before?" Ryan was busy still repeating the name in his head. "Ryan, you there?" The PI was concerned by Ryan's lack of response.

"Sorry, yeah, I'm here." Ryan finally answered after digesting the mystery name. "The name doesn't ring any bell—" He paused. It clicked. The name. "Wait there, hold on." Ryan put his phone on loudspeaker and went into his emails. He scrolled through until he found what he was looking for. Bingo. "The name Tiffany came up in the first day of the trial. DeShawn's former assistant Isobel said Tiffany handled DeShawn's private affairs whilst she handled his business affairs." His voice got louder and louder; you could picture him smiling like a kid on Christmas just by hearing the tone of his voice.

"Did Isobel mention Tiffany ever being in the office?"

"I think she did, in fact I'm ninety-nine per cent sure she did."

"Well then, she's the one who connects the dots, isn't she? She was at both venues the nights the incidents took place and she could have created the blog when she was in DeShawn's offices."

Ryan jumped to his feet immediately and continued to jump, screaming in jubilation on the inside.

"But why Dallas? What do DeShawn, Tiffany and Dallas have in common?" Ryan grinded to a halt and glared over at his phone. "Ryan, why Dallas?"

He suddenly came crashing back down to earth. "I don't know yet but this is enough to start the ball rolling."

"With the case going as it is? You're mad, Ryan. Whatever you come up with needs to be airtight."

Ryan knew the PI was talking sense in what he was saying. It took DeShawn not even a week to tear down a case his firm and multiple lawyers had spent months working on.

"You've got another twenty-four hours, so get out and see what you can find out. I'll call you at 8 p.m."

Just like that Ryan was alone again.

Ryan was torn in two. Was it enough? Wasn't it? Would a man like DeShawn really cave under questioning from what he'd found out so far? Nobody even knew who this Tiffany was, let alone be able to get her onto the stand. After lying down and contemplating everything, he decided that the bartender was his only chance of getting any further information whilst in Dallas. He cyphered through his phonebook to find his number and called it. No answer. He started to write out a text when the number called him back. The exchange was very brief and Ryan organized for them to meet in town for a coffee to see if he could get anything else out of him; something a little more concrete to add to the Tiffany information. He headed into the shower to freshen up having already been up several hours. The organized meeting time was in one hour.

As the cab pulled up down a side street Ryan got out and looked at the meeting point. The coffee shop that the bartender had requested was a boutique one and not your usual Starbucks or Tim Hortons. As Ryan crossed the road, he saw the guy sitting in the window and made his way inside. At first, he didn't acknowledge him but once he had ordered and received his drink, he made his way over to the table and sat on the one beside the bartender.

"I didn't expect you to call so soon. I have a shift at my other job that starts soon. What's up?"

"I'm only here for another twenty-four hours so if you really want to help like you said I need more." Ryan tried to keep his voice hushed enough that others wouldn't hear it but firm enough so his acquaintance knew he meant business.

"What more can I do? Isn't it enough what I told you last night?" The bartender's voice cracked as he finished his sentence. A worried expression was written on his face. "I could get into a lot of trouble for this, you know." He scanned around the shop and looked out onto the street.

"I need more on DeShawn. Why did he keep coming to the strip club? How does your boss, Latesha, know him?"

"I don't know, I'm just a bartender. I've never spoken to him. I just see him."

Ryan sipped at his large cup of coffee whilst he pondered his next question.

"Did you ever see them together? On the club floor? When going into her office?"

"Once," he replied fairly quickly. "But as soon as I opened the door, they stopped their conversation straight away."

"And their conversation was about what?" Ryan reached into his jacket pocket and removed a small pen and paper and started to write some notes.

"I don't know. I briefly heard them talking about buying something together but the music was loud so I could be wrong."

"Why would they buy something together?"

"You don't know much about Latesha, do you? What she does? What she owns?"

Ryan had a puzzled look on his face; he thought she just owned the strip club. The bartender stood up and squeezed past Ryan and made his way towards the door.

"Wait, where are you going? It's only been ten minutes," exclaimed Ryan as he noticed where he was heading.

"I told you, I have a shift to get to. The mood you put Latesha in last night with your little stunt I do not want to be late and piss her off."

"Latesha? I thought you said you were going to your other job?" Ryan still had the puzzled expression etched all over his face.

The bartender chuckled, "I did. The Rosewood Hotel. Maybe now you'll understand what I mean about Latesha." He pushed the door and left the coffee shop and in doing so left Ryan with another dot to now connect.

Ryan stuck around in the coffee shop for probably another half an hour trying to piece together how what he'd just been told fitted what he already knew. Now he had Latesha owning the strip club and the hotel. He had DeShawn's assistant Tiffany at both those locations and the blog originating from New York. He also knew DeShawn and Latesha knew each other, but how? There was clearly one key piece of information missing that finished the puzzle. He finished his coffee and made his way towards the exit whilst frantically typing on his phone. The email was once again to the PI and he asked him to look further into Latesha Rhodes, her background and if there were any direct links to New York and DeShawn. As he stepped out onto the sidewalk Ryan went to slip his phone into his pocket but it pinged before he could do so. It was a text message from Emilia:

*Change of plans my end, I can't do tonight. See you back at the apartment tomorrow xx*

Ryan looked left and right and headed in the same direction as the bartender towards the Rosewood Mansions to see if he could find out anything else. It was about a fifteen-minute walk all in all and after asking a local for directions he made it safe and sound. Walking towards the lobby, a familiar face was there to greet him. The bouncer from the club the night before was now standing on the door to the hotel. He noticed Ryan and puffed his chest out and took a step in Ryan's direction.

"Not you again."

Ryan knew they would be the first words out of his mouth. He changed direction and headed for another door on the left-hand side. The bouncer followed suit and headed over to the door.

"Not today, Ryan," he said. Ryan made a beeline for the door hoping to make it in before he was cut off but in one swift movement of the bouncer's left arm, he found himself lying on his back on the floor again. The scenario seemed all too familiar from last night. He bent down and grabbed Ryan by the scruff of the neck.

"You've been treading a fine line in the last eighteen hours, my friend, so if I was you, I'd make myself scarce before you get really hurt."

"Is that a threat?" Ryan scampered backwards and got back to his feet.

"It's a promise. Now fuck off."

He pointed in the direction away from the hotel and stood firm until Ryan finally started to retreat. Ryan walked away far enough that the guy went back to the main entrance of the hotel.

Several hours passed and Ryan was waiting for a glimpse of either Latesha or the bartender but neither came. The door was still heavily protected and without one of them walking out of the hotel he wasn't going to be able to speak to either. The day was running away from him and he still needed to gather his belongings and safely store everything he'd written since he arrived. He checked his watch; it was getting on for 4 p.m. He debated with himself whether it was worth staying on for a little longer but very quickly made the decision to head back to his hotel by the airport. He hailed down a cab and departed Dallas for what he'd hoped would be the last time this trip.

Ryan collected his things in the small bag he'd brought with him and started to take down all of his notes and findings to take back to New York. He genuinely believed that what they'd discovered was enough for Macpherson to allow him to continue the case. If only the PI would now call with the news that he'd been able to link Latesha and DeShawn then Ryan truly would be back in the driving seat. As he sat on the old wooden chair in the corner of this room he looked out of the hotel window and into the parking lot. His mind and thoughts flicked to Emilia. He couldn't believe he had let a case come between them. They swore they'd never let work do that but for some reason this one was different. Ryan couldn't control himself during this case. The internal phone rang, snapping him out of his daydream, and he walked over to pick it up.

"Hi, Mr Jackson, it's reception, we just wanted to let you know that the hotel bar is showing the Dallas Mavericks Brooklyn Nets game this evening. Tip is in about an hour."

Ryan had completely forgotten about the game in the midst of everything.

"Thanks, I'll be down."

Ryan made his way down just before tip and sat at the bar directly in front of one of the four small screens they had dotted around the room. He was the only person in there at this point and there was only one bartender as well.

"Two Heinekens, please," Ryan said as he was approached by the member of staff. He settled in and the game got underway. With most of the weight off his shoulders Ryan enjoyed the opening quarter of the game and was knocking back the beers as if he had something to celebrate. The Nets went 34-27 up through Cam Thomas and it seemed like the tide was turning finally. He gorged on the bar snacks provided and as the buzzer went for half-time, he turned to make his way to the toilet. In doing so he noticed that he had company. A blonde lady was sitting alone at a table across the other side of the room. He laughed on the way to the toilet as he thought about Henry's and Matt's stories – could this be the elusive Tiffany Maddison?

He returned to the bar; he couldn't notice any distinguishing features on the woman. She was blonde, wearing plain clothes, no glasses or rings and was drinking a single glass of red wine whilst she read a book. As he sat back down on his seat, he noticed that his empty bottles had been replaced by two new ones.

"Thanks for the refills," Ryan said as the member of staff working walked past.

"Don't thank me," she said. "The lady over there ordered them for you."

Ryan turned but the woman still had her head buried in the book, so he shrugged and turned back to the game which was a minute or two into the second half. The game was starting to get a little closer and as usual when it did Ryan started to drink quicker. Still in the third quarter Ryan had drunk one of the beers and was on his way to finishing the second one when he was approached and another two beers were placed in front of him.

"It seems as if you have got someone's attention," said the bartender, glancing in the direction of the mysterious blonde. Ryan turned around but once again wasn't able to get her attention.

As the game approached the final six minutes the Mavericks had started to pull away from the Nets and held a ten-point lead, so Ryan decided it was time to call it a night. To his surprise he didn't feel great and became lightheaded when he stood from his stool. He beckoned the member of staff over and pointed towards the lady.

"What's she drinking?" All of a sudden Ryan started to slur his words.

"Are you OK, sir?" She put her hand on Ryan's arm as he put both hands onto the bar.

"Can you please get me a glass of whatever she's drinking?"

More concerned for Ryan than making the drink he'd asked for she kept both eyes on him as she poured the red wine into a large glass.

"Can I get a whiskey as well, please?" Ryan's slurring was even worse by now; he sounded as if he'd already drunk a bottle of whiskey.

"I'm sorry, sir, but I can't serve you any more alcohol this evening, not in your current state."

Ryan's hand slipped from the bar and he fell face first into it and slid down it like something from a cartoon.

"Sir, are you OK? Shall I call you an ambulance?"

Ryan dragged himself up and realized that he was in a worse state than he may have originally thought. But how? He'd only had maybe eight or so beers which was a fairly normal night for him.

"Can I please have the drink and then I will be heading back to my room." Stumbling from the bar over to the table he placed the drink carefully down ensuring not to spill any. "Thanks for my beers earli—"

## 21

# SUNDAY 25TH OCTOBER, 9.21 A.M.

Checking in and slowly making his way through the airport Ryan looked and felt horrendous. Something wasn't right with him after last night. He'd woken up late and missed getting breakfast, his phone was dead and his phone charger was missing. Adding those on top of how he felt, this wasn't a good morning so far. He couldn't work out why he barely remembered much from the previous night when drinking a normal amount. He even had to ask the receptionist when checking out how the game finished up that he was watching. Much to his surprise the Nets had taken the game to OT and gone on to win. Ryan squinted his eyes and looked around the terminal for one of the portable charging machines to see if he could give his phone some life. He spotted one tucked away to his right-hand side and ambled over. On the way he stopped to grab a breakfast deal in the hope the greasy food and orange juice might perk him up but the smell of it initially made him feel even worse. He plugged in his phone and sat down on a chair a couple of seats away and started to eat. Within a few minutes his phone came back to life and with it, hundreds of notifications. He shot over to it amongst the glares of his fellow travelers as beeps rang through the boarding gate. Every important name in his life at the moment presented itself: Emilia, Macpherson, Daniels, José and even several missed calls from a withheld number.

Deciding to leave his phone to charge and check everything in the queue for the plane, Ryan returned to his seat and continued eating. He still didn't feel great, but the food was filling his empty stomach. As he turned his back, his phone started to vibrate again. Another call from a withheld number. Ryan didn't feel like an intellectual conversation right now but considering the amount of missed calls he'd already had he thought he'd better answer this one.

"Where have you been? I've been trying to get hold of you since last night." Ryan could hear the PI's voice before he could even put the phone to his ear.

"I don't actually know, last night is a bit of a blur at the moment." It was evidently clear from his voice Ryan wasn't himself.

"Great, I'm glad you had a good night. I'm here risking my life and you're out all-night drinking. Glad we're both aligned on this."

"Calm down. It was only a few beers. I think I must have been spiked."

Ryan mouthed to the person sitting beside the charging port if he could pass him his food, which he duly obliged.

"I've found out something big. Something that could win you the case. I found the missing link."

As if by magic Ryan all of a sudden perked up upon hearing these words. Hiring this PI was very expensive at his own cost but it seemed as if it had now paid off. Ryan finished a mouthful of breakfast.

"Go on," he said when he was finally able to.

"So, from everything we have learned so far, you asked me

for the connection between Latesha, DeShawn and this Tiffany woman. Correct?"

"Correct." This time Ryan didn't wait to finish his mouthful of food.

"Well, after digging on the pair of them with an old friend of mine, Latesha was—"

Ryan waited with bated breath for the PI to finish his sentence. He waited. Nothing came. He looked at his phone and the call had dropped. With no way to call him back Ryan just sat there staring at his phone waiting for a call back.

The final call had come for Ryan's flight, but he still stood at the charging port trying to give his phone as much battery as possible and hoping the PI would call back. He'd also sent him an email and then a text message to Emilia. He finally unplugged it and made his way over to the doors. With the queue virtually gone he could walk straight onto the plane. He now had just over three hours to sit and digest his time in Dallas and hope that the PI would contact him as soon as he had landed. Ryan was planning on going to Macpherson's house straight away and start to work out a way to win this case once the trial reconvened on Tuesday. Ryan was in fact the last person to board the flight, so shortly after taking his seat they were off back to JFK.

As the plane landed slightly earlier than it should have, Ryan was up like a rocket taking his bag out of the overhead locker and making his way to the front of the plane; despite the seat belt sign being on.

"Somewhere to be in a hurry, sir?" one of the air hostesses said from behind him as he waited by the plane door. Ryan didn't reply. Instead he had his head buried in his phone checking his emails and messages. Coming to the end of them, there was still nothing from the PI. It was so strange. Just as he was about to reveal what Ryan was waiting for the call dropped and he'd not heard from him since. Ryan looked up and the doors were being opened so he headed off the plane and towards the terminal building. He made his way through passport control and with no luggage to pick up was already walking out of departures. As he paced through the terminal, one of the boards being held by drivers caught his eye. *Ryan Jackson, Macpherson & Daniels*. He diverted his way towards him. He hadn't ordered anything personally.

"Hi, I'm Ryan Jackson," he said as he approached the smartly dressed man.

"Great, let me take your bag for you." He leaned in and took Ryan's bag from his grasp. "Follow me."

Not asking any questions he assumed that Macpherson had sent the driver to take him straight to meet her from the airport. As they entered the lift to the car park, Ryan sent another email to the PI asking for him to ring him urgently as he wanted to know what he did before seeing his boss. He jumped in the back of the car, and they set off for Manhattan.

Each driver had their own way of getting back to Manhattan from JFK, so Ryan wasn't too concerned with which way the driver was going. He would occasionally glance up and look out of the tinted window, but he spent most of the time looking over the notes he'd made in the hotel room to prep himself to see Macpherson. As he went through what he would say to her, what he'd found out and what he wanted to do next, he found himself talking to himself in the back of the car and acting out both parts. The miserable weather that they were experiencing wasn't helping get back any quicker. Ryan noticed they were in Brooklyn and continued doing what he was doing. He checked his phone and there was still nothing from the PI. He was starting to get a little worried and nervous now but remembered that these guys basically did what they wanted for a living, so he would reach out eventually. The car came to a halt. Ryan continued in his own little world thinking it was traffic. The car door flung open where Ryan was sitting and he was grabbed and thrown out of the car. Two stocky, older men stood over him and clutching one arm each they marched him into the building. He managed to get a quick glimpse of his surroundings and it wasn't somewhere he was familiar with. All he knew was he was still in Brooklyn.

As he was dragged through what he now realized was an abandoned run-down building he asked a range of questions to the two men holding him but was met with complete silence. Every question fell on deaf ears and Ryan even tried offering them money to tell him where he was or where he was going but again, he got nothing back. Light shone through a smashed and missing window, but it was fairly dark as the trio moved quickly through a tight corridor. As they turned the corner a brighter light shone from a different room and the three of them came to a standstill. They freed Ryan from their grasp and grunted at him to go forward. He stood freely and dusted himself down after his recent trip on the floor. He had nowhere to go other than forward with behind him blocked, so he slowly edged in the direction. As he reached the door he looked back and the men were still there. He looked up, said a little prayer and twisted the doorknob to enter.

Two people sat round a circular table in the middle of the room. One had their back to Ryan and the person he could see looked as if they had a bag over their head.

"Don't be afraid. Come and sit, Ryan."

He instantly recognized the voice that echoed around the room. It was DeShawn. He remained behind him and didn't follow DeShawn's request.

"I said come and sit down, Ryan."

DeShawn's voice was a little louder this time. Two guys stepped out from the shadows of the room and made their presence known so Ryan decided to do as he was told. He was outnumbered four to one if you counted the guys outside the room so ultimately, he didn't have much of a choice. As he made his way to the table, he tried to work out who could be the person under the bag? Emilia? The PI? Macpherson? He sat down in the middle of DeShawn and the unknown person. Sweat dripped off his forehead; he wasn't tired or exhausted any more but nervous. The case seemed to be getting deeper and deeper as it went on but this was a whole new experience for him in his legal career. Never before in his life, let alone his career, had he found himself in a situation like this one. DeShawn leaned forward and got a little closer to Ryan.

"So how was Dallas?"

Ryan sat there and wanted to think clearly before answering the question. He didn't want to give a smart answer and be beaten up, or worse killed. He also didn't want to lie as DeShawn clearly knew he'd been there. So, he took a few seconds before he answered.

"It was successful for why I went there."

Not a lie, not too much information. DeShawn stood up from his chair and walked towards the other person at the table.

"And why did you go there, Ryan?" Again, he didn't want to lie but before he could answer DeShawn continued, "Maybe this guy can tell us before you do."

He took the bag off to reveal the PI that Ryan had been using to help him gather information. He looked a little battered and bruised since the last time Ryan saw him. DeShawn ripped off a piece of grey duct tape that had been covering his mouth and he took a huge gulp of air. After a few seconds he launched into an outburst claiming that he didn't know DeShawn was involved, he didn't know Ryan's case and that when he found out, Ryan had forced him to help him. Ryan sat and digested the lies, thinking of what he could tell DeShawn whilst their lives looked to be hanging in the balance. The PI finished talking and took another huge gulp of air. DeShawn sucker punched him from behind with a shot to his kidney. He winced in pain but couldn't move for being tied to the chair.

"You fucking little liar. Not a single word of what you just said was true."

He walked round to the front and this time he landed a punch to his face. Ryan heard something crack. This was getting more and more uncomfortable by the minute.

"I'll ask again, why were you in Dallas, Ryan?"

Ryan looked at the PI as the blood poured from his nose down onto his white shirt. He needed to make sure his next answer was the right one or the PI would probably end up even worse.

"Is he distracting you?" DeShawn placed his hand on the bloody and beaten man's shoulder. "Guys, come and get this no-good, lying low-life out of here so Ryan and I can talk alone."

The two men Ryan had previously seen made their way to the table and dragged the PI and the chair off towards a door at the far end of the room. DeShawn sat back down.

"Great. So where were we?"

DeShawn asked Ryan one more time why he was in Dallas and sat back down and patiently waited for an answer.

"I went to Dallas to dig deeper into our case, but you already know that, don't you, so let's cut to the point as to why I'm here."

"And what did you find out, Ryan? I'm intrigued to know what you think you know."

"That your assistant Tiffany took the photo of Luke and the drugs. That your assistant Tiffany had the alleged affair with Henry. That your assistant Tiffany bribed Matt into throwing the game."

DeShawn stood up and started to clap his hands.

"Bravo, Mr Jackson, bravo." He walked behind Ryan and placed his hands on his shoulders. "Bravo. I must admit of all the lawyers I've faced over the years no one has ever got this far."

Ryan thought he was about to be hit after finding himself in a similar uncompromising position to that of his PI minutes before. DeShawn reappeared in front.

"So what's the next move? What are you going to do with this new information you have?"

Ryan thought it was pretty obvious what he was going to do with it, but he'd spell it out for DeShawn anyway.

"It'll become public knowledge in court on Tuesday." In such uneasy circumstances Ryan was still able to crack a slight smile when he said it out loud.

"And that's exactly why you're here today. I can't have you doing that because it would ruin a lot of things for me and cost me a lot of money." DeShawn was now back behind Ryan again.

"Is this your tactic to scare me into keeping quiet like you did to Macpherson all those years ago?"

DeShawn chuckled at Ryan's accusation.

"I didn't scare her; I simply gave her a choice. A choice which I'm about to give to you." DeShawn reached into his pocket and pulled out a brown envelope that he threw onto the table in front of Ryan.

Ryan's attention was immediately drawn to the sealed envelope. What on earth could DeShawn have mustered up now, that would stop Ryan from revealing what he had found out?

"Open it, Ryan," DeShawn said. "I want you to see the choice you've got to make."

Ryan grabbed the envelope and tore it at one end. A handful of photos fell out onto the table. Some were face up, others face down. Ryan saw himself in two of the photos. He collected them and started to look through them, a little closer one by one. The color drained from his face. DeShawn started to laugh.

"I... I... I don't get it. When were these taken? How?" Ryan continued to look at the photos, shuffling from one to another quicker and quicker.

"Last night my assistant Tiffany was in this pokey little hotel by Dallas Airport when who should she lay her eyes on but you." Ryan couldn't believe that the blonde in the bar he vaguely remembered was actually Tiffany Maddison. "So, she bought you two beers whilst you were in the toilet and the open one she laced with something that would make you feel a little... queasy, shall we say?" Ryan could feel the anger starting to build up. How could he have been so stupid. "So, when you went over to thank her and you couldn't stand or speak, she took you back to your room to make sure you got there safely."

Ryan stood up and his chair flew towards a wall. He banged on the desk with his fists clenched.

"Shut up," he shouted. "Just shut up."

You could see DeShawn revel in Ryan's fury and the fact that all of his work had been for nothing.

"Don't worry, Ryan. These pictures stay secret if you don't tell anyone about your little jaunt to Dallas. If I lose the case, however, from information you've gained, then your wife, Emilia, will have copies of these."

Ryan remembered his talk with Macpherson and now realized what his boss would have gone through with DeShawn when she lost her case.

Ryan had picked the photos back up and started looking at them again. He noticed little things in the pictures like food and drink he'd bought which would link to his bank statements. The pictures really were real.

"So, Ryan." DeShawn picked up his coat from the back of his chair and slipped it on. "You have a simple choice to make. Lose the case and keep your wife or win the case and I destroy your marriage." He turned to leave heading towards the far exit where the PI was dragged out by his men. "You have forty-eight hours to decide and think carefully. I know all that you know so if you decide to pass any information on, I will know."

Ryan slowly picked up the chair and sat back on it and screamed at the ceiling; no words just a scream of pure frustration. Now alone in the room his phone vibrated. It was a text from Macpherson who was clearly waiting for him arrive at her house:

*Your flight landed hours ago! Have you got lost?*

## 22

# SUNDAY 25TH OCTOBER, 6.37 P.M.

Ryan didn't bother to text Macpherson back and he wasn't going to go to her house that day. Not after what had just happened with DeShawn. His focus was solely on Emilia and his marriage. He retraced his steps back to where he was dragged from the car and he was all alone. DeShawn was gone, so were his men and so was the car that brought him from the airport. Ryan's duffel bag was thrown at the foot of the door to the building. It had clearly been rummaged through and anything valuable to the case was gone. He tried to compose himself and work out where he was in Brooklyn. Not having much luck, he started walking aimlessly in one direction hoping to recognize something or find a subway station. After a couple of blocks Ryan saw a convenience store and worked out that he was in Mapleton. From there he planned his route back home. Emilia was on a later flight than him so he was hoping that he could beat her home and sort himself out before seeing her. He dived on the subway and boarded a northbound Q train which would take him back to Times Square.

The ride would be around an hour back so Ryan knew he would have time to think about everything just in case

Emilia was home. How on earth was he going to tell her what had happened? With everything that had gone on recently, how could Ryan now admit to her that he'd been unfaithful on a night he was supposed to meet her? Bearing in mind it was their anniversary in the coming week, Ryan knew that DeShawn had him bent over a barrel. Any decision he would make ultimately, he would make it alongside Macpherson and the firm, but they wouldn't ask him to risk his marriage for a case, surely. Ryan knew that taking this case would define his career, but he didn't think that it would end up defining his life too. As the train crossed the Hudson back into Manhattan something dawned on Ryan. What if DeShawn didn't stop with this case and every time he needed a favor or wanted legal advice, he'd use this against him? Ryan thought Macpherson would be the best person to answer so that would have to wait until tomorrow at the earliest. He zoned out for the remaining few stops of the train. He still had the walk from Times Square to the apartment so for now that was enough thinking.

As Ryan walked his route home his phone vibrated in his pocket and every time, he took it out to see it was either Macpherson or Daniels ringing him. As he got closer to his apartment, he finally went to switch his phone off but as he unlocked it the vibrating stopped and his battery died. Ryan breathed a huge sigh of relief. He walked past Mulligans and for the first time in as long as he could remember had no urge to go in. It was Sunday so he usually squared up his weekly tab, but he knew if he went in, he'd end up staying in there. He stopped off to grab some beers to try and be as normal as possible when Emilia returned and within minutes he was at the foot of the building. As he went up, he took deep breaths. In, out, in, out. For someone who was a high-profile lawyer you'd think that he'd be used to being stressed and under pressure, but Ryan was by no means comfortable in his current situation. Ryan entered the flat and luckily for him all the lights were off which meant he had beaten his wife home. He ran to the bedroom and plugged his phone in to give it life again and turned the TV on. He wanted to paint the picture that he had been in for a while when Emilia got home. He opened one beer and put the rest in the fridge. He sat on the sofa and grabbed the remote to put on some sports channel and he heard a knock at the door. Ryan walked slowly towards the door knowing when he opened it that he was going to have to start living his lie. Getting to the door, it flung open and knocked him back into the wall. In stormed Macpherson with a scowling look on her face and marched towards the living area.

"I thought you were dead!" Macpherson turned and shouted at Ryan as he joined her in the room. "I thought you were dead and buried, or missing, or hurt or something!" She looked around the flat to notice everything in order. "Here you are having a beer and watching the fucking sports network."

Ryan walked over towards his boss.

"It's not as simple as that, I promise you. It's not what it looks like."

Macpherson was absolutely raging with Ryan.

"It's not, no? So then why didn't you come to my house as we agreed but instead left your two bosses waiting around like a pair of fucking interns."

"Calm down, will you? I just needed a little time and space to think before I saw you." Ryan edged towards the fridge to get a drink for his guest but she closed the door before he could even take it out.

"We need to know what's going on, Ryan. You upped and disappeared to Dallas. We've barely spoken and the trial starts again in thirty-six hours."

Ryan knew that his boss was talking sense and he needed to give her some glimmer of hope otherwise she'd continue.

"I have something really good; something concrete that will win us the case, but I can't talk right now. We can discuss it tomorrow in the office." Swigging at the beer he had opened, he signaled towards the door. "Now you know I'm OK, can we leave this tonight? Emilia is due home any minute and we're not on the best of terms." "Why? What's up? Everything OK?" Macpherson's anger turned to concern for her protégé.

"This case is what's up, if I'm honest. I should have taken everyone's advice and stayed well clear of it but here we are." He again signaled towards the door and this time Macpherson started walking. As she got to the front door she turned and looked Ryan dead in the eye.

"I'll give you until 10 a.m. tomorrow. Not a minute later."

Ryan closed the door and realized he had now put himself in a no-win situation.

Not even half an hour had passed and Ryan heard the front door unlock. Emilia was home. He collected the three empty beer bottles beside him and took them over to the kitchen and waited to greet his wife. She walked into the room, suitcase trailing and jumped at Ryan, wrapping her arms and legs around him.

"I've missed you so much these last couple of days. Can we agree never to argue again?"

Ryan's guilt crept in immediately. He hugged his wife tight but didn't reply to her. She took her head from his shoulder and gave him a kiss.

"So how was Dallas?" she said as she jumped down back to her feet.

"Yeah, Dallas was OK, thanks. Bit of a weird place, isn't

it? Or maybe it was weird because of why I was there." Ryan reached into the fridge to grab himself another beer. "What about you? Good trip?"

"Great trip! I can't believe you don't like Dallas, it's amazing!" She reached into her bag and pulled something out and gave it to Ryan. "Open it. I got you a surprise."

Ryan looked at the little white bag and wondered what it was. What he pulled out he truly wasn't expecting. Unfolding it in all its glory it was a Brooklyn Nets jersey signed with Kevin Durant 7 on the back.

"I bumped into them at the airport this afternoon and got this from the kit manager. Think of it as an anniversary present. You can hang it in the office." She leaned back in for another kiss and Ryan's guilt doubled instantly. How was he going to live his life like this when he was struggling to last the first ten minutes? Emilia wandered off into the bedroom to unpack her suitcase and do whatever she had to do and Ryan made his way back to the sofa to continue watching TV.

By the time Emilia had finished in the bedroom, Ryan had ordered their favorite Italian takeaway and had dimmed the lights and lit some candles. He was fueled by how he felt but she would be none the wiser and probably thought he was doing it to make up for last week.

"Ah, this is cute," she said as she joined him on the sofa and snuggled into him for a moment before sitting back up. "So do we need to talk about the more pressing matter?"

Ryan's guilt topped out even though he knew she wasn't talking about anything in Dallas. He was on edge.

"We don't need to talk about it, it's in the past. It's done. Let's move forward."

Emilia looked slightly confused but then the penny dropped; Ryan was talking about Thursday night. She started to laugh.

"No, you idiot. Where have you booked for our anniversary?"

"Ohhhhh, yeah. That. I forgot about that." Ryan side-eyed Emilia knowing full well she wouldn't take kindly to that reply. She playfully slapped his arm.

"Stop playing, Ry, I want to know where we're going. A girl has to prepare for these things."

"It's a surprise, Em, just know that you're going to love it."

"Is it Chinese food?" Her face lit up before Ryan could even answer her question.

"Maybe," he said through an emerging grin. "Maybe it'll be food courtside at a Nets game." He shot bolt upright and grabbed a pillow for protection as Emilia playfully launched herself onto him.

"Where are we going?" By now she was fully on top of Ryan hitting him as he covered his face with a pillow. As he stayed silent, she continued digging into him but the doorbell rang which seemed to save Ryan.

"Food is here. Get off me, you little rapscallion."

Ryan easily pushed Emilia to one side and jumping to her feet she jogged to the door.

By the time Emilia returned, a bowl and a plate were on the side for the pasta and pizza. A large glass of red wine sat next to the bowl and Ryan had opened himself yet another beer despite having most of his previous bottle left when the food arrived. Emilia placed the food down on the side and Ryan's eyes were met with a brown envelope resting on top of the pasta box.

"What's that?" he said nervously having flashbacks to his afternoon with DeShawn.

"I don't know," Emilia replied. "It wasn't the normal delivery guy; he just said he'd been asked to give this to us."

Emilia pressed her nail to break the seal and ran it across to open it. As she lifted it to reveal the contents Ryan dived for the envelope, snatched it out of her hands and crashed onto the kitchen floor. He was instantly in pain from the fall and it was etched all over his face.

"Oh my god, Ryan. What is wrong with you?" Emilia bent down to her husband's side to see if he was OK. "Why would you do something like that?"

Ryan had to think fast.

"I'm in the middle of a trial, Em, who knows what this could be!"

She rolled her eyes at his reply.

"Not everything is about you, Ryan, it's part of a pizza delivery." She grabbed it back out of his hands and started to withdraw the contents.

"Let's have a baby!" Panicking at what was inside, Ryan blurted out something that he knew would make Emilia instantly stop what she was doing.

"Sorry? What did you just say?" She sat down, cross-legged and dropped the envelope immediately. Ryan joined her despite clearly in a lot of pain.

"Let's have a baby."

After an awkward minute where neither of them spoke, Ryan and Emilia were now back on the sofa with dinner and drinks. He knew Emilia wouldn't take his comment lightly but at least he had got her attention off the brown envelope. They both started to eat without addressing the elephant in the room. After a few mouthfuls of their dinner, Emilia finally restarted the conversation.

"Ryan, did you mean what you just said?" She put her bowl and cutlery to the side of her. "That's something quite serious; you know I've always wanted us to start our own family."

Ryan stopped eating as well. Although in the future he also wanted to start his own family, he only said what he did in fear of the envelope coming from DeShawn. He realized if he had to act impulsively every time he thought his secret was about to come out, then eventually Emilia would work out something was wrong.

"I know you do, Em. Do you not think now is the right time?" Ryan thought if he put the onus back onto Emilia and she agreed then he would just have to go with it. "We're not getting any younger, are we? Don't you want children?"

"I do but I never thought we'd start the discussion in pajamas, eating an Italian takeaway on a Sunday evening." Emilia started to cry. "I do want a family, Ryan. Of course I do, I thought you'd never ask." Similar to earlier she threw herself at Ryan but this time there was no play fighting. She buried her head deep into his lap and started to cry more. "You don't know how happy you've made me. Seriously, this is the best thing ever."

After the tears had dried up and they had finished their dinner, Emilia took the bowls and cutlery over to the sink and Ryan continued to watch the same sports headlines for the eighth time in the past couple of hours. Emilia returned with a big bowl of ice cream and two spoons.

"If we're going to have a baby then we would need a garden," she said as she passed him one of the spoons.

"One thing at a time, Em, one thing at a time." They both laughed as she reached over Ryan to grab the TV remote.

"I'm sick and tired watching this, can we watch a fil—" Ryan knew the question before she'd even finished it.

"Put on what you want, I've got some bits to do relating to the case." Ryan stood up and made his way towards his bag that was in the hallway.

He was unsure how tomorrow would go when he returned to the office. Ryan decided to piece everything back together, present it and then tell them his predicament and make it clear his priority was his marriage. He knew something similar had happened to Macpherson so maybe she would understand. Ryan had proved that he *could* have won the case against DeShawn but they'd have to settle for losing publicly and winning privately. He only had about fourteen hours to wait to find out what they wanted to do.

"I'm taking this to the bedroom. I'll finish it in there and then I'm probably going to sleep. It's been a long weekend."
"OK, babe, no problem. I'll come in soon anyway."

Ryan maneuvered round Emilia as she turned back to finish her program. He shut the door and let out a deep breath. He sat down with a notepad, sellotape and a pen and started to scribble out everything to replace the notes DeShawn's men had taken earlier. It only took him a few minutes to do what he needed but when he stood up for an aerial view of everything, he was mightily impressed with himself. Considering the case had been taken off him the last time he was in the office this was an unbelievable turnaround. He grabbed his phone to take a picture just in case anything happened overnight but regardless it was all in his memory. He carefully picked it all up and placed it into his briefcase for the morning and headed off to the shower before bed. He was in and out but when he returned Emilia was already sitting on the bed. She had a weird smile on her face, like a mischievous one.

"Can I help you?" Ryan said as he applied his moisturizer and sprayed his deodorant.

"Me? How could you help me?" Emilia replied putting her hand on her chest and making her way over to Ryan. "I thought maybe we could start to make this baby this evening?" She wrapped her arms around her husband's waist from behind.

"Yeah, I, erm, good idea. Let me just go grab an orange juice."

Ryan slid out from Emilia's grasp, grabbed his phone and headed towards the refrigerator. On route he opened up his emails and fired one off to Macpherson:

*Just me and you tomorrow morning. No Daniels.*

## 23

# MONDAY 26TH OCTOBER, 5.02 A.M.

It was completely pitch-black as Ryan crept around the apartment trying not to disturb Emilia sleeping. He'd been tossing and turning for a good few hours and just decided to get up and get on with the biggest day of his career. As he sat on the sofa and slipped his shoes on, he sat on the remote and the TV lit up the room and filled the flat with sound. He quickly grabbed the remote, turned it off and sat still hoping to hear nothing from the bedroom. Nothing came. He stood and tiptoed over towards the front door, grabbing a banana and switching the bathroom light on as he passed. As he made his way out the bottom of the building, he opened his phone to book an Uber. It was just gone 5.20 a.m. Ryan looked at the sky. With no clouds in sight it was starting to get light so he decided to walk. He would be the first one in the office that day regardless of how he got there.

Ryan crossed through Central Park and decided to walk down the Upper West that morning for a change of scenery. It was busy but still quiet enough that he could get lost in his thoughts without bumping into someone. His thoughts were all over the place at that moment. The case, the new evidence and the meeting with DeShawn were at the forefront of his mind but agreeing to have a baby last night after being caught cheating on his wife kept creeping in. With everything going on at the moment maybe he shouldn't fight Macpherson to keep the case after all. It would probably be better off with her given she could give it her full attention, or full attention without fear of it ruining her life. As Ryan approached the corner of 5th and 59th near The Plaza Hotel he decided rather than cutting across and through Times Square that he would continue his walk down 5th past the Rockefeller Centre before going into the office. There was a really good takeaway breakfast bar he knew of in that area that he for once had the time to visit. The streets and roads were starting to get busier by the time Ryan reached his destination, just gone 6 a.m. He ordered what he wanted to and watched life go by as he waited. After around five minutes a slight tap on the shoulder came and he was presented with a little bag.

"Egg and sausage bagel, sir."

Bag in hand, Ryan set off and headed towards the office.

As Ryan strode through the office the automatic lights started to brighten up the dark office. It had been a long, long time since he was the first one in the office so to beat the interns in on a Monday morning was a big thing. He pushed open his office door, threw his briefcase onto a chair and sat behind his desk. Opening the bag, the smell filled his nostrils and he leaned back with a big cheesy smile filling his face. As he started eating the bagel, he felt his phone starting to vibrate in his pocket. It could only be one person at this time in the morning and that was Emilia. Sure enough she had woken to find Ryan gone and was worried about where her husband was at 6.30 a.m. in the morning. He busied her call and proceeded to send her a voice note of where he was and why. As he put the last piece of his breakfast in his mouth, he noticed that the lights had come back on outside which meant he wasn't alone any more. He walked over to the door and peered out to see if it was anyone worth talking to but it was only interns. He could see them mulling around in the bull pen. Ryan decided that although his meeting with Macpherson wasn't for another three hours, the quicker he sorted everything out the quicker he could start to take care of some emails and look forward to his next case. He walked down to the boardroom and wheeled the whiteboard out and into his office to transfer everything onto that so visually it would be easier to talk through his findings. He got out everything he'd prepared last night and got to work.

It had just gone 8 a.m. when Ryan finally finished getting everything ready. He had decided to include all information from the opening day of the trial until right then, not just what he had found out in Dallas. A whole overview would paint a clearer picture in order for them both to make the correct decision about how to move forward. The office was now thriving with people so Ryan flipped his work so nobody could see or read it and returned the whiteboard to the boardroom. As he came back out, he noticed that the light was on in both his bosses' offices. 8 a.m. was still an alien time for him to be in the office but at least it was nice to know his bosses were both treating this seriously. He decided to walk towards Macpherson's office just to make it known that he was in. As he got there Daniels was in there but Macpherson beckoned him in to join them.

"Look at you in the office before 9 a.m. You must be taking this seriously," she said as Ryan shut the glass door.

"I've been here since 6.30 a.m. I'll have you know."

"Well I never. I saw your light on when I got here about fifteen minutes ago but I just assumed it was the cleaner and not you."

All three of them laughed knowing that what Macpherson had just said was the most lighthearted thing they'd say today.

"Anyway, it was just a flying visit, I just wanted you to know that I was in."

"Shall we move the meeting forward to 9 a.m. then?" Macpherson quickly replied as Ryan turned to leave.

"Works for me," said Ryan who was now halfway out the door.

"Works for me too," Daniels chimed in.

Ryan didn't acknowledge his reply but he made it blatantly clear to Macpherson yesterday evening that he didn't want Daniels in this meeting. It was a late text and it was only 8 a.m. so maybe they hadn't caught up about that but either-or Ryan wouldn't tell all with him in the room.

The next hour went incredibly slowly, or so it seemed that way to Ryan anyway. He filtered through, replied and deleted all his unread emails. He caught up on social media, deleted a bunch of photos from his camera roll and even had time to clean up his set of fantasy basketball line-ups for the week. It was still only 8.40 a.m. He decided that he would just go and wait in the boardroom for the meeting to start. As Ryan walked down towards the room he diverted and made himself a strong coffee. As he took a seat, he had fifteen minutes to wait. After a couple of minutes, he got up and flipped the board so he was ready to go over everything when his boss arrived. Another couple of minutes passed and he changed his mind and flipped it back to a blank board. As he turned from doing so Macpherson and Daniels finally entered flanked by Daniels' assistant who was carrying various things amongst a voice recorder and her laptop. Ryan didn't say anything but caught Macpherson's eye and it seemed that his boss knew that Ryan wasn't happy. As they all took a seat, Daniels' assistant seemed to set up to take notes, placing the microphone in the middle. Daniels was the first one to talk.

"So then, let's get everything you know out in the open and we can work on a plan to move forward."

Ryan and Macpherson exchanged glances again as Daniels folded his legs and waited for Ryan's response. Ryan walked over to the blank whiteboard at the opposite end of the room and started writing.

"This is what I found out when I went to Dallas." Ryan stepped away to reveal the word *NOTHING* in capital letters in the middle of the board. Both Macpherson and Daniels sat there puzzled waiting for Ryan to do or say something to follow up his opening statement.

Ryan's silence filled the room. Everyone was on edge waiting for his next move. He put the lid back on the pen and returned to sitting on his chair.

"I found out nothing," he confirmed.

"What do you mean you found nothing?" Macpherson opened her mouth to respond but it seemed as if Ryan was going to continue to reaffirm what he'd just written on the whiteboard.

"I mean what I said. When I went to Dallas I found nothing out about the case. Just dead ends."

"So why the fuck are we having a meeting if you know nothing?" Daniels had now unfolded his legs and was leaning forward, angling his body towards Ryan.

"I don't know, boss; you wanted the meeting. You tell me."

Macpherson now understood Ryan's angle after their exchange the evening before so she stayed silent and let her partner continue.

"Macpherson, I thought you said he had something?"

"That's what he led me to believe but it seems as if he doesn't now."

Daniels stood up angrily and started to wag his finger in Ryan's face.

"You younger generation think the world owes you a living. Well, it doesn't. Fucking waste of my time. Macpherson, take the case; I'm done with this bullshit. You can deal with him." He stormed out the room with his assistant in tow and once the door had shut Macpherson burst into laughter.

"Did you really have to do that?"

"I wouldn't have if you had just told him that I only wanted to speak to you about it."

"We're partners, Ryan. I've told you before it's not as simple as that."

Ryan walked back over to the whiteboard and flipped it to reveal everything to Macpherson.

"Depending on how the next hour goes I might be as well," Ryan replied.

Macpherson didn't immediately answer Ryan's comment as her eyes now scanned what she could see as she tried to take everything in.

"My good god," Macpherson said as she leaned back and put her hands over her mouth. "My mind is absolutely blown." She sat staring at the ceiling for about thirty seconds before bringing herself back to the conversation. "You have really let the cat out the bag here, haven't you? This is going to kill DeShawn's career if this is all true." Macpherson's words slowed down as she finished the sentence as she looked over at Ryan. "This is all true, isn't it? It's not made up?"

"No, of course it's not made up. What do you think this is? Hollywood?"

"Well, reading all that, can you blame me for asking?" Macpherson stood and started to walk over towards the whiteboard next to Ryan. "So let me get this straight so we're on the same page here; DeShawn set up all these scenarios with the help of someone called Latesha Rhodes and one of his PAs Tiffany Maddison?"

"Correct," Ryan nodded as he confirmed Macpherson's statement.

"So, the waitress in the strip club, the woman behind the bar in the hotel and the journalist that interviewed Matt were all Tiffany?"

"Mind blowing really, isn't it?" Ryan could barely contain his smirk.

"How does Latesha link to this, though? How does a business owner from Dallas link to a sports agent in New York?"

"That is the one piece of information I haven't worked out yet."

Macpherson and Ryan were shoulder to shoulder as Macpherson went over everything one more time in her mind. She turned and put one hand on Ryan's shoulder and extended the other for a handshake.

"Welcome to the big leagues, Ryan. This is going to be some arrival for you." As they finished shaking hands Macpherson pulled out her phone. "I'll call Judge Sullivan now. Tell him you're still on the case after new evidence has come to light."

As she unlocked her phone and entered the call log, Ryan put his hand over her phone to stop her.

"It's not as straightforward as that," he said begrudgingly. Macpherson locked her phone again. A nervous look covered Ryan's face which was now also drained of color. "That's why I didn't want Daniels here. DeShawn has dirt on me."

Macpherson turned and walked back round the table to her chair. Slowly sinking back into it, she looked towards the window. A distant look filled her eyes; Ryan's words were still the last to be spoken in the room.

"This seems all too familiar, Ryan, all too familiar. Nothing is ever as easy as you think with this man." Macpherson let out a huge sigh and looked everywhere in the room bar at Ryan. "So out with it, then. Come on. What does DeShawn have on you?"

"The last night in Dallas I watched a Nets game in the hotel bar. Next morning, I didn't remember much and then it turns out DeShawn has very suggesting photos of a woman and me in my hotel room from that night."

Macpherson picked up an empty glass on the table and threw it into the wall, smashing it into a thousand pieces. "How could you be so stupid!"

"I didn't think something would happen whilst I watched a basketball game for a few hours."

"Why?" Macpherson snapped back angrily. "Do you think Matt thought that when he went for an interview? Or Henry when he went for a drink that night?"

"No but I—"

"No, Ryan, it's pure naivety. You have an active case against him and you'd just confronted who we think to be his accomplice. Just being in Dallas you were closing in on the truth. What did you expect?" Jubilation had quickly turned to disappointment.

"I don't know. I didn't expect—"

"That's the issue right there. That's why you have a lot to learn in this game. Now I'm going to have to go into court tomorrow and get my ass handed to me or settle and lose the case." Her face now as red as her shirt, Macpherson stood up and stormed out the room. She was absolutely furious with Ryan.

Ryan left it a few minutes and then decided to follow Macpherson back to her office. Unsure of the reaction he would get he entered quickly and shut the door promptly.

"I'm not finished," he said the moment the door shut. Turning round from looking over Manhattan, Macpherson couldn't believe that Ryan had followed her.

"I don't have anything to say to you right now. You went from hero to zero in minutes. I don't want to hear any more." She walked towards Ryan presumably to open the door so Ryan could see himself out.

As she got halfway, Ryan cleared his throat and confidently said, "Was it worth it?" Macpherson stopped in her tracks.

"Was what worth what?"

"Losing your case to DeShawn all those years ago. Was it worth it?"

Macpherson retreated a little and perched on her desk, taking a mouthful of coffee before replying.

"Not really," she responded before finishing the remains. "It eats and eats at me every so often. That a smug bastard like him is walking around still being shady and getting away with it." She got up and poured herself a stronger drink and drank it in one. "But that's life, isn't it, Ryan? As he's proven again with this case, in life there are winners and losers and he's the type of guy that'll always end up winning."

"What if we don't let him win this time?" Ryan took the glass from Macpherson and poured himself a whiskey, drinking it as quickly as he poured it. "What if we call his bluff and win the case? Do you really think he will tell Emilia?"

"110 per cent," Macpherson said taking her glass back. "He is not the type of person to mess with, Ryan, so don't take his threats lightly."

"He can't keep getting away with this. Someone has to make a stand."

Macpherson sat silently and pondered Ryan's latest comment. She looked deep in thought.

"He can't but let someone else sacrifice their life to take

him down. Your future is too bright." Macpherson stood up and put both her hands on Ryan's shoulders. "You've done so well in this case. I know that and so will Daniels. It doesn't matter what anybody else thinks."

"It matters to me. It matters so much." Ryan shrugged off his boss. "This is my first big case and it's going to look like I shit the bed to everyone else."

"Like I've already said, it's life. Look at me now. When I gave up the case and lost to DeShawn all those years ago, did I think I would end up a named partner? Absolutely not."

"I'm not you, though, and there's no guarantee I end up where you are."

Something had suddenly switched in Ryan and it seemed his decision to let everything go was now changing. Macpherson had a concerned look upon her face. As much as she wanted her company and employees to be successful, she also didn't want them to do it at the expense of potentially ruining their personal life.

"Whatever you're thinking you'll need to clear it with me," she said looking concerningly towards Ryan. "Remember we are where we are because Judge Sullivan granted me continuance. He doesn't expect to see you tomorrow."

Macpherson was a hundred per cent correct but it wasn't what Ryan wanted to hear. Last night he was set on losing but now he was debating throwing his entire life away to win.

"I've got to go. I need some time alone to clear my head. This is all too much."

Ryan exited the room before Macpherson could say anything to stop him and he headed towards the elevator. As the doors opened for Ryan to enter, his phone pinged. It was Macpherson:

*Think carefully, Ryan. You have until 8.30 a.m. tomorrow morning.*

## 24

# TUESDAY 27TH OCTOBER, 3.45 A.M.

Another sleepless night where there was no need for Ryan's weekday alarm. It was inevitable with the trial restarting today but at least he managed to get a couple of hours' sleep before deciding to get up. He was still arguing with himself in his head about what to do and now he had less than five hours to make a decision. As he crept out of the bedroom he paused for a moment and looked at his wife lovingly as she slept. Could he really make a decision that jeopardized all this? He collected his clothes off the chair and made his way out of the room quietly shutting the door behind him. He flicked on the TV. *Moneyball* was on one of the film channels. Ryan knew the film off by heart so muted it and went over to the ceiling to floor window and peered over New York life. A couple of cabs went past below followed by a convoy of meat delivery trucks but Ryan was more daydreaming than looking for anything specific. As he gazed over the treetops and onto the illuminated skyline he slipped into a trance-like state and started thinking about various different outcomes from the case. Named partner at his age was unheard of but it would mean Emilia would divorce him. But could he live the rest of his life knowing he basically threw the case? After ten to fifteen minutes Ryan turned from the window and started to get ready. He wasn't going to the office, but he knew that lounging around and doing nothing wasn't the best thing to do. He did his hair, fixed his tie, put on his shoes and headed for the door. It was 4.45 a.m. by the time he was ready, so he now had under four hours to decide what he was going to do with his life. He shut the front door as quietly as he shut the bedroom door so he didn't wake Emilia and within minutes he was walking out of the building into the crisp October morning air.

He decided Central Park would be the best bet despite the lack of light. He didn't get a chance to run on Sunday due to travelling back from Dallas and although he wouldn't be running in his current attire either, at least he could take a brisk walk around the park whilst it was quiet. As he set off in a fairly central place in the park, he headed north towards the Queens end so he would finish up in Manhattan. Although the park was still dark at this time, Ryan didn't mind as he knew it like the back of his hand. As he made his way round, he could think of nothing else but what he knew and what to do come 9 a.m. After making up his mind and then changing it again during his conversation with Macpherson he was still split between head and heart. Head said take DeShawn Arlington down and change the future for a lot of people, including himself. Heart said there would be another opportunity and Emilia and his life were more important. Time was ticking away quickly.

By the time Ryan had walked where he needed to, he was heading down towards the south entrance of the park at around 6.50 a.m. He was heading straight down to the Supreme Court after his walk but with still no decision, it seemed as if the next ninety minutes would determine the rest of his life. The avenues were starting to fill up with commuters so Ryan became a bit more aware of his surroundings but ultimately, he was the definition of 'lights on, no one's home'. Bar stopping at a Starbucks to get a double espresso, Ryan followed a straight path all the way down to his destination and by the time he arrived it was 8.05 a.m. He had twenty-five minutes before Macpherson made her way into the judge's chambers and confirmed that she was taking over the case and taking the fall for Ryan. As usual he entered through a side door of the court to avoid the media coverage and after security checks, was inside. As he walked down the corridor of the courthouse, he was very tempted to go into the room where DeShawn and William would be to talk to him. Confront him. Have it out one last time so DeShawn really knew how Ryan felt. After briefly pausing outside the room, Ryan decided what he wanted to do was the last thing the case or the firm needed so he continued on past the room. A few steps later he felt a hand on his shoulder. He spun round to see DeShawn standing within a few feet of him.

"Ryan, it's a pleasant surprise to see you here."

Ryan grinned through gritted teeth, "I'm here to support my boss for the rest of the trial."

"So, you've come off the case altogether now then?" DeShawn's usual creepy grin was even wider and he resembled the Cheshire Cat. "That's a shame I was looking forward to continuing our dual this morning."

"I have another case to focus on. Macpherson will take it from here on in. You know her, don't you? From the Austin case?" The sarcasm in Ryan's voice was prominent but he was never going to have the upper hand in this exchange.

"Ah, I remember her. Another person I comfortably beat who wrongly tried to prosecute me."

"Wrongly or you blackmailed her into losing like you are me?"

At this time of day there were plenty of people lining the courthouse corridors who could hear that accusation and the answer DeShawn was about to give but he wouldn't be so stupid as to answer how Ryan wanted. He gasped.

Covering his mouth partially, he said, "Blackmail? Me? Whatever do you mean?" He took a few steps towards Ryan and whispered closely, "Once you lose once in life, Ryan, you become a loser. You've chosen the life of a loser where I chose the life of a winner. Get used to your new life."

He very gently slapped Ryan's face two or three times and turned to walk back to the room that was allocated for him and William. Ryan stood like a statue and didn't move; his blood was boiling. If they hadn't been standing where they were he'd have lunged for DeShawn. He glanced down at his watch and the time was 8.31 a.m.

"STOP!"

Ryan burst into the judge's chambers at around 8.35 a.m. with Judge Sullivan, Macpherson and William all in conversation. Judge Sullivan hastily jumped to his feet.

"Mr Jackson, what are you doing here? I thought you'd been removed?" He glared over at Macpherson looking for confirmation.

"It's not too late, is it? Can you change it back?" Ryan was hunched over, hands on knees panting as he asked questions.

"Too late for what?" the judge responded.

"I haven't been removed from the case yet, have I?"

"Well, no. Not yet. We were just agreeing to appoint Ms Macpherson as the new counsel but I granted continuance on the basis you were being removed."

"There's damning new evidence against Mr Arlington that was presented over the weekend. She knows all about it, I told her yesterday."

Ryan was now pointing at Macpherson. Judge Sullivan

turned and a nod of the head from Macpherson was enough confirmation for him. "It'll convict him hands down. It'll convict DeShawn of all the charges and more."

"Do you know anything about this evidence?" The judge flicked his attention to William.

"No, Your Honor, this is news to me. I would like time to confer with my client."

"Confer all you want. He's bang to rights," Macpherson chimed in and then addressed the judge. "With you permission I'd like to leave Mr Jackson on the case to finish what he started. You have my word; this case will be wrapped up today."

He pondered ever so slightly but the answer was almost immediate.

"I have no problem with that. Mr Jackson, you're still on the case. Mr O'Neill, you have twenty minutes to confer with your client before the proceedings recommence."

He fled the room so he could take as much time as he possibly could with DeShawn.

"You'd best be right about this conviction otherwise I'm going to get annihilated by my peers," Judge Sullivan said as he signaled for the remaining two to also leave his chambers.

William and DeShawn were already in the courtroom waiting for Ryan and Macpherson to enter. Macpherson grabbed Ryan's arm just as they got to the doorway.

"Are you sure you want to do this? If you prosecute him there's no going back. He will ruin your life."

"I understand but this needs to be done. He can't keep getting away with this."

"I know that and we've said that before but it doesn't have to be you that brings him down." Macpherson was sounding like a broken record but she wanted to make sure Ryan really knew what he was about to do.

"The world needs this. I am a winner and I will continue winning not for this firm but for myself. This is my life. I'll explain everything to Emilia and if she walks away then so be it."

She let go of Ryan and he immediately brushed down his suit sleeve. He fixed his tie one last time and looked over at Macpherson.

"You ready to do this?"

"More ready than you could ever imagine."

As they pushed the doors open DeShawn turned and he wasn't sporting his usual smug look as they walked towards him. Instead a worried look was etched onto his face as if he'd seen a ghost. Ryan appearing to continue the case was certainly not in his plans. As they both took a seat they almost instantly stood back up as Judge Sullivan entered the room.

"Please be seated," he said as he sat down himself. "Mr Jackson, the floor is yours."

"We would like to recall DeShawn Arlington to the stand."

"Do you solemnly swear that you will tell the truth, the whole truth and nothing but the truth?"

"I do," DeShawn replied nodding.

"Mr Arlington, I am sorry to drag you up here a third time during this trial but new evidence has come to light and I believe it's very damning against you."

"If that's what you believe, young man, then please ask away."

"Do your or your family's or your extended family's business interests venture outside of the state of New York? To say, I don't know, Dallas?"

"I'm afra—"

"Let me remind you, Mr Arlington, that you're under oath to tell the truth and you could be found in contempt of court and sentenced to five years if you're found to be lying."

DeShawn's smug grin had now found a new home on Ryan's face.

"If you let me finish, I was going to say I'm afraid it does, yes."

For this first time in this trial DeShawn didn't answer with a question of his own. Surely a man of his magnitude wasn't to go down without a fight.

"So, the example I used in Dallas – is that true? You have business interests in Dallas?"

"Had/have depending on how you look at it but yes is probably the most suitable answer."

Ryan turned to face the jury at this point.

"And could you tell the jury what they are, please?"

"My ex-wife, Latesha Rhodes, owns multiple businesses in Dallas – hotels, an adult entertainment bar amongst other things but I don't see why that's relevant to this case."

There was the missing link Ryan had longed to hear since Sunday.

"It will become evidently clear as to why in just a moment." Ryan returned to his desk and picked up some paper. He held one in his hand; he gave one to DeShawn's representation and then gave one to the judge. "For the jury's sake, we're going to recap the key points in this trial and your ex-wife's businesses."

"You mentioned your ex-wife owned a hotel. Is that the same hotel where Henry Craig supposedly slept with one of the female members of staff?"

"I guess it is, yes. But a lot of tea—"

"And the adult entertainment bar that she owns – is that the same adult entertainment bar in which Luke Best was pictured with illegal substances?"

"Do your clients know you're doing this?"

Judge Sullivan stepped in and requested that DeShawn answer the question.

"Again, yes, I suppose it was."

"Finally, the blog that questioned Matt Woodman and offered him money to make something happen during a game. Was that blog made from your office?"

"I have no idea what you're talking about with this one, Mr Jackson."

Ryan produced another piece of paper and handed copies to the relevant people.

"We have traced the website's origin to the New York area. Do you need me to find its exact location?"

DeShawn looked narrow-eyed at Ryan. For the first time in his lengthy career the threats hadn't worked and he was on the verge of losing the case but worse, being exposed. He knew that this could cost him millions in lawsuits if he lost this one.

"Your Honor, I would like to enforce my right to plead the fifth."

Gasps came from the people watching the trial and Macpherson clenched her fist in a quiet solo celebration. After multiple sessions of being embarrassed by DeShawn and his clients' secrets, Ryan now had the upper hand. He wasn't done there however and continued to press DeShawn whilst he had the chance.

"So just to clarify, my clients' supposed *problems* that you covered up for millions of dollars all happened on sites owned by your ex-wife?"

"Supposedly, I guess so."

"Supposedly? Mr Arlington, do not make me subpoena your ex-wife and personal assistant Tiffany Maddison. That's if anyone can actually find Tiffany."

"Why would you subpoena Tiffany? What's she got to do with all this?"

Ryan chuckled as he turned to the jury.

"As if you don't know already, Mr Arlington, Tiffany was

the person who took the photo of Luke, allegedly slept with Henry and bribed Matt."

Macpherson could not believe Ryan was continuing the attack on DeShawn; he was clearly going for the confession.

"Your Honor, I would like to enforce my right to plead the fifth."

"You've just proven you can answer questions so pleading the fifth is only making it a lot worse for you, DeShawn."

"Objection, Your Honor, badgering the witness." William jumped to his feet in a feeble attempt to divert Ryan's questions.

"Overruled. Sit down, Mr O'Neill."

"Thank you, Your Honor. Now, Mr Arlington, are you going to answer any further questions of mine or are we done here? Did you and your ex-wife, along with one of your PAs, create compromising situations to frame my clients and then steal millions of pounds from them covering it up as settlement money to make it go away."

"Your Honor, I would like to enforce my right to—"

"Just answer the question, DeShawn. For everyone's sake it'll make it a lot easier."

Ryan and DeShawn locked eyes and the courtroom fell silent. There was no objection from William. You could have heard a pin drop as everyone waited for DeShawn's answer to Ryan's most black and white question of the trial. Something or someone had to give soon. Judge Sullivan went to speak but as he did the words came out of DeShawn's mouth.

"Yes, it was all a set-up."

The court descended into anarchy after DeShawn muttered those five words. William hung his head and Macpherson's private celebration became a public one. Judge Sullivan slammed his gavel to regain control of his courtroom. Ryan hadn't moved from in front of DeShawn and was still staring at him. Eventually a hush fell back across the room and Ryan was urged to continue. He pondered his next move. DeShawn looked disheveled.

"No further questions for the witness, Your Honor."

Ryan turned back to Macpherson, grinning from ear to ear. He was caught in the moment with victory in reach making everything seem worth it. He took a seat back next to Macpherson and his boss leaned in.

"Welcome to sleeping with one eye open. How did it feel?"

Ryan didn't care because in that moment he felt untouchable.

"Just get that name changed to Macpherson, Daniels and Jackson, will you?" he responded as he squeezed Macpherson's hand in pure elation.

"Mr O'Neill, the floor is now yours."

Judge Sullivan beckoned him out to cross-examine his client now Ryan was finished. William stood but DeShawn shook his head from side to side. That was it, the trial was officially over. William sat back down muttering, "No further questions, Your Honor."

DeShawn sluggishly walked back towards his lawyer after being dismissed from the stand. After his confession during Ryan's questioning, it seemed as if the jury could start deliberating a verdict straight away.

"Mr Jackson, do you have any further witnesses to call to the stand?"

"No, Your Honor, I don't. The prosecution rests."

"Mr O'Neill, does the defense have any further witnesses to call to the stand?"

Ryan waited anxiously for William to answer. If he had learned one thing in the past two weeks, it was that with DeShawn it was not quite over until it was over. William stood.

"We have no further witnesses to call to the stand, Your Honor."

Ryan breathed a huge sigh of relief.

"Perfect," said Judge Sullivan as he turned to face the jury. "Members of the jury, you have heard all of the testimonies concerning this case. It is now up to you to determine the facts. Once you decide what the evidence proves, you must then apply the law. The bailiff will now take you to the jury room to consider your verdict."

The courtroom stood to allow the judge and the jury to exit, both teams stood and made their own preparations to leave. As Ryan collected what he needed to, he opened his briefcase and his phone lit up. It was a text from Emilia:

*Hope today goes well, I can't wait for our anniversary meal tomorrow xx*

## 25

# WEDNESDAY 28TH OCTOBER, 8.12 A.M.

"No, don't leave, can't you stay here for the day?" Emilia wrapped her arms around Ryan's waist as she sat on the edge of the bathtub and he cleaned his teeth. "We can stay in our pajamas and order lunch to be delivered before tonight."

Ryan spat out his toothpaste, rinsed and dried his mouth and wriggled away from his wife.

"Em, you know today's the day. This whole chapter will close and we can move on from the last two weeks."

Ryan knew in the back of his mind that it wasn't going to be the end with what DeShawn now held over him but if he couldn't enjoy winning the trial then he might have lost it instead.

"Hopefully the jury doesn't deliberate for much longer today, then I can come home and we can spend the rest of the day together." Ryan's phone buzzed and Macpherson's name popped up meaning that she'd be downstairs waiting in the car. "I've got to go now but your present is in my wardrobe in the bottom drawer and I'm so excited for this evening." He leant in and kissed Emilia's forehead. "Love you."

She smiled back and repeated her husband's words as he set off towards the front door. Ryan stopped with his hand on the handle, took a deep breath and caught a glimpse of himself in the mirror. This would hopefully be the day that he had spent his entire life working towards. Emilia noticed he was still there but before she could say anything he was gone and the next time she'd see him the trial would be over. As he headed out the building Macpherson's car was parked right outside. The window rolled down.

"Today's the day your life changes, hotshot. Climb in." She opened the door to the car and shuffled over as Ryan got in.

As Ryan sat silently staring out of the car window Macpherson tried to break the ice by starting the conversation.

"How are you feeling? Nervous at all?"

It took a few moments, but Ryan turned his attention back to his boss and started to engage in conversation.

"Kind of. I think the trial is definitely done. I'm more concerned when I will face Deshawn's backlash."

Macpherson knew deep down from experience that Ryan should be worried, but she tried her hardest to get him back focused on the positives he could take.

"Daniels called an emergency stakeholder meeting last night and has cleared the partnership if the jury rule in favor of us today."

"He's cleared it already?" Ryan looked taken aback by the gesture of his other boss especially considering the frosty relationship the pair of them had.

"See, he's not so bad after all, is he?"

They both laughed together as the car rolled to a standstill. Macpherson took out her phone and started to check emails whilst Ryan sat there quietly pronouncing the firm's potential new name, "Macpherson, Daniels, and Jackson. Macpherson, Jackson, and Daniels." Looking up at Macpherson he exclaimed, "I like it, don't you?"

"Let's get today out the way and then you can shout it from the rooftops. The first version by the way."

After taking a side road or two their car pulled up outside the courthouse with around twenty minutes until session started and they could be called for the jury's verdict. Macpherson opened the door and jumped out and held it open for Ryan to follow.

"You go ahead, I'll meet you inside in a minute." Ryan shut the door from the inside and watched as his boss disappeared into the crowd outside the courthouse. He opened his phone and started to flick through the photos he had of Emilia and him. Macpherson called him but he rejected it as he continued to flick through memories. Macpherson called him again and again over the next few minutes, but every time Ryan sent her straight to voicemail. Realizing the time, he stepped out of the car and finally picked up the phone as he barged his way through the crowd and onto the court's steps.

"Meet me inside? What, inside the actual court?"

Macpherson snapped at Ryan frantically, "Why haven't you been picking up your phone?"

"Calm down, it's only been fifteen minutes, what's wrong?"

"DeShawn wanted to change his plea to guilty and offered to cut a deal. I've just spent fifteen minutes in Judge Sullivan's chambers."

Ryan started to panic that Macpherson had cut a deal without consulting him.

"What did you do? Please tell me you rejected it?" Ryan was now in the corridor and walked past Macpherson putting the phone down, heading towards the stairs to the judge's chambers. Macpherson turned and grabbed his arm.

"Yes, I rejected it but wouldn't you have liked to have been in the room to watch them squirm?" Ryan breathed a sigh of relief. "Now get your ass in that room over there. Hopefully we haven't got to wait much longer."

As the time approached 11 a.m. Ryan started to pace up and down the small room whilst they still waited for the jury's verdict.

"Sit down, will you, you're making me nervous." Macpherson reared her head from whatever she was doing and kicked the chair Ryan should have been sitting on.

"Why is it taking so long? He basically admitted it on the stand!"

"I know he did but they still have to go through everything thoroughly. Come on, Ryan, you know this it isn't your first trial."

Ryan huffed and puffed as he finally took a seat opposite his boss.

"I just know someone on the jury is going to be corrupt and then he'll get the win as he always does."

"If he does then he does, that's life, Ryan. I've said it so many times to you already. We know what's happened and what hasn't. Both Daniels and I couldn't be happier with you."

"And I've told you so many times already, I am not losing this case."

"Well, it's out of our hands now. So, what will be will be." Those words switched a light bulb in Ryan's mind and an idea filled his head.

"There's one more thing." He got up and walked towards the door. "I'll finish the job."

As he opened the door, he was greeted by a court official blocking his exit.

"Mr Jackson, Ms Macpherson, the jury have reached a verdict. We're ready for you."

The moment had arrived. Ryan turned and looked at Macpherson who was already standing behind him ready to leave the room.

"Whatever you had planned is going to have to wait now. Let's go." She picked up her suit jacket, put it on and squeezed past Ryan into the corridor. "Come on," she signaled for Ryan to follow her.

Ryan's brilliant idea didn't matter now the jury had reached a verdict. He still hadn't acknowledged his boss and continued to stand in the doorway to the room.

"I said come on. The longer we're out here the longer it'll be until we find out the verdict."

As she finished her sentence DeShawn and William walked past them heading for the courtroom themselves. Whilst William looked at the floor when passing, DeShawn looked up and directly in Ryan's direction. No emotion on his face, not a word spoken, he just looked. As they faded into the crowd outside the courtroom entrance, Ryan finally started his own walk.

"Now smile the biggest smile you've ever smiled," Macpherson said as she led Ryan into what should be his thirtieth and biggest victory.

As Ryan walked into the courtroom hush fell over the room. He looked directly ahead of him and tried not to make eye contact with anyone in the room. He quickly noticed that Luke Best, Henry Craig and Matt Woodman were all sat in chairs near to those that would accompany him and Macpherson. He pushed his way through the gate and sat down at the chair closest to the jury and the judge, but not before shaking all of their hands.

"I suppose you know something about this?" Ryan leaned back and whispered into Macpherson's ear.

"Well, I called them all, told them what happened and they all said they wanted to come for the end of the trial. I mean, you're about to win them millions."

"I would have called them myself but—"

"But you've been preoccupied. I know, that's why I did it. That's what partners are for."

She smiled at Ryan; Macpherson's confidence had been sky-high since Ryan had DeShawn on the stand yesterday. This would almost be like winning her own case against the accused all those years ago. As Ryan turned to scan the room, he was now feeling slightly more confident but was interrupted by the bailiff.

"All rise for Judge Sullivan."

"Please all be seated." Judge Sullivan wasted no time when seated in addressing the jury. Ryan didn't know where or who to look at. "Jury, have you reached a verdict?"

A small Latino lady in her mid-forties stood to announce what everyone was waiting for.

"We have, Your Honor."

"In the first case of the financial mismanagement against Luke Best, how do you find Mr Arlington?"

"Guilty, Your Honor."

Muffled voices came from the crowd immediately, but Judge Sullivan's loud tone brought hush back to the room.

"In the second case of financial mismanagement against Henry Craig, how do you find Mr Arlington?"

"Guilty, Your Honor."

Henry stood on his feet and pumped the air.

"Come on," he shouted. "You conniving son of a—"

"Mr Craig, please refrain yourself and be seated in my courtroom." Macpherson tugged at his trousers to get him to sit down. "Finally, in the third count of financial mismanagement against Matt Woodman, how do you find Mr Arlington?"

"Guilty, Your Honor."

This time it was Ryan's turn to stand up as he clapped and turned to hug Macpherson. He shared a brief embrace with all three of his clients and turned back to face the judge and the jury.

"Thank you, Jury, for your service throughout this trial. You're dismissed."

As the jury exited the room, keyboards tapped, cameras clicked and short conversations took place before Judge Sullivan's next words.

"Mr Arlington, please stand."

DeShawn dragged himself to his feet. Slowly. For the first time in countless cases against him for various different things, he had been found guilty. He found himself in unchartered territory. William stood alongside him despite not being asked to.

"Mr Arlington, due to the guilty verdict delivered by the jury just a moment ago I will be imposing the following sanctions." Ryan was almost crouching as he sat on the edge of his seat waiting for the judge to deliver his penalties. "You will repay Mr Best $7.3 million, Mr Craig $5.1 million and Mr Woodman $3.6 million in full. However, you will also pay them a further thirty per cent damages which will amass to another $4.5 million."

Ryan turned to Macpherson.

"That's one part done. Now let's hope he punishes him even further."

"In addition to the financial sanctions, your sports management license will also be suspended for eighteen months pending a review after nine months."

Ryan side-eyed his boss; this would inevitably kill DeShawn and his business. It could cripple him. Ryan had been the umpteenth lawyer to try and the first to succeed. His entire empire could crumble.

"Furthermore, I will also be ordering an independent investigation into the last fifteen years of your company's end of year financials and any further misconduct could result in jail time."

"But, Your Honor, that's incredibly harsh." Speaking out of turn William objected before DeShawn could accept everything the judge had said. "That is arguably one of the most severe punishments ever given to someone in a finance-related trial."

"And you're very lucky that it is not more, Mr O'Neill, but I'm sure there will be many more repercussions for your client after this case."

"Now, Mr Arlington, do you understand the sanctions I have imposed?"

"Yes, Your Honor, I understand."

"Brilliant. In that case we have no further business with this trial. Case closed."

William's briefcase was already packed, and he exited the room immediately after the decision not even waiting for the judge to leave. DeShawn stayed seated. After digesting what the judge had sanctioned, he knew deep down that this could completely cripple his main business. On the opposite side it was jubilation all round as Ryan's victory meant that Luke, Henry and Matt got all their money back and more.

"I told you to trust me, didn't I? Imagine if you'd all told me the truth from the start."

It was something that they could laugh at now, but it could have been a very different outcome.

"If you ever want tickets to any Knicks game."

"Any Giants tickets then."

"Any Islanders tickets, call me straight away."

"I should be good thanks, guys, but if I ever need tickets don't worry, you'll be the first three people that I call for them. Except you, Luke, I don't want Knicks tickets."

They all laughed as they filtered single file out of the courtroom. Some were met by partners, some by their club reps but ultimately within two minutes the only people left in the room were the bailiff, DeShawn, Macpherson and Ryan.

"I'm going to call Daniels. Deliver him the good news. Make sure that he has the sign ready to go up. Drinks later on, partner?" She placed her hand on Ryan's back and patted it as she walked past him.

"Not tonight, I've got a celebration of my own with Emilia. It's our anniversary so we're going out for dinner."

"I'm sure she'll be delighted to hear the good news. Send her my love. I'll see you in the office in the morning then."

Since the trial had ended Ryan's back had been to DeShawn the whole time so you could have forgiven him for not knowing he was there. Thinking he was the only one left in the room bar the bailiff he stood tall as he was ready to leave, closed his eyes and looked towards the ceiling. He wasn't a particularly religious man but with the happenings of the last fortnight he felt like he could definitely become one. After a reflective moment or two Ryan opened his eyes after thanking God for his victory in the trial. As he turned to leave, he was met with DeShawn's voice.

"That'll only be a temporary thanks, will it not, Ryan?" He quickly stood up so the pair were now face to face. "It was a brave decision you made to win this trial. Well, I see it as a stupid one, but everyone will have their own views."

"It is not stupid to win a trial that I should have won because you have done something illegal."

"It's stupid of you to throw away your marriage in the process though." DeShawn reached into his jacket pocket and pulled out a business card, or what looked like one anyway. He tore it in half and proceeded to offer half of it to Ryan. "This is a debt card. If you accept this, then I can call upon you whenever I want help or you to do something for me. Fulfil this and then your dirty little secret stays safe with me."

Ryan pondered the initial proposition. He tried to quickly think of what DeShawn could make him do to keep it quiet. He then realized not only would he be making a deal with the Devil, but DeShawn wasn't a man to just ask once.

"Be in debt to you? I think I'd rather take my chances with Emilia." Ryan leant his shoulder into DeShawn and barged past him heading towards the door.

"You're making a big mistake, Ryan. You may have won this in court but it's a different ball game out there."

Ryan slowed his walk down and went to respond. As the words were on the tip of his tongue, he shut his mouth again and continued walking. He knew getting no response would play on the mind of someone like DeShawn. He put his hand out to push the door and one last time a voice filled his ear.

"Hope you have a nice anniversary meal this evening."

As Ryan got to the front entrance of the Supreme Court he peered through the window and saw twenty or thirty media people all out front on the steps with camera and microphones shoved in Macpherson's face – she was doing a good job of orchestrating them. Not wanting to be thrust into the limelight until tomorrow, he turned and headed for the side entrance of the building that he'd used so frequently throughout this trial. Being their anniversary Ryan just wanted to get home and spend some quality time with Emilia especially after the trials and tribulations of late. A familiar face greeted him as he exited the building and congratulated him on winning; news was spreading fast. As he exited onto the sidewalk it was buzzing but there were no journalists to greet him. Looking left and right he crossed the road and headed towards Chambers Street Station. As he opened his phone to call Emilia, she beat him to it and a message from her popped up:

*I've just seen the news – congratulations! It's a double celebration tonight xx*

## 26

# WEDNESDAY 28TH OCTOBER, 7.57 P.M.

"Em, come on, we're going to be late if you don't hurry up."

Ryan threw himself onto the sofa and huffed as he continued to wait for his wife to get ready to leave. He found it so hard to believe that despite the fact they had both been home for a large part of the day and been doing nothing but lounging around, she wasn't going to be ready on time. He flicked through the endless channels that were on their monthly subscription but ultimately found himself watching some version of sports news like every single day. The same headlines scrolled the bottom of the TV from when he was watching a couple of hours ago. He decided to jump back up and get himself a beer from the fridge to pass the time. He wasn't planning on drinking beer this evening as he wanted to celebrate sharing expensive wine with Emilia in the restaurant, but desperate times called for desperate measures. He popped the cap off and put it on the kitchen side as he walked back to the sofa. Glancing down at his watch and realizing their ride to the restaurant had already been downstairs waiting for over twenty minutes he shouted out to hurry his wife again. Just as he was about to sit back on the sofa a gentle cough came from the bedroom doorway. Ryan glanced over.

"Woah."

His eyes were met with his wife in a revealing red dress with a plunging neckline and red high heels to match it. Her long brown hair sat straight on her shoulders, and she was clutching a little white bag.

"You look absolutely amazing," he said as he tried to collect his jaw from the floor.

"Well, it's our anniversary after all so I thought I'd remind you of why you married me."

"I married you for more than your looks, but I suppose when you look as good as that it helps." Ryan walked over and planted a kiss on his wife's lips and placed his hand on her back. "Now get a move on, we're going to be late." He steered her towards the hallway and towards the front door before she even had a chance to put some perfume on.

"We're going to have to get a cab down to Nolita if we're going to make it there on time."

Ryan rolled his eyes as they were exiting the building.

"So now you want to hurry up after me nagging you for the past thirty minutes. No need for a cab when this is taking us." Ryan pointed to the blacked-out Mercedes parked just across the road with a man in a suit leaning on the driver's door. "Macpherson gave me her company car for the evening after I won the trial, so we have privacy there and back."

The driver opened the back door to the car as they both crossed the road.

Moments later they were southbound heading towards Nolita. Holding hands in the back of the car, Emilia thrust her other hand into Ryan's face and pretended to be a reporter. Putting on a deep voice she asked, "So, Mr Jackson, how does it feel to be the first lawyer to successfully prosecute DeShawn Arlington?"

He playfully slapped her hand away.

"Get that out of my face, will you?"

Quickly she thrust it back into his face and continued, "So how will you be celebrating your momentous victory?"

This time he grabbed her hand and pinned it down.

"Can we try not to talk about work this evening, please? Can we just talk about us and our future?" He slowly let go of her hand and this time she didn't put it back up and instead rested her head on his shoulder.

"I'm so proud of you, Ry, so, so proud." She looked up and into his eyes. "You beat a man like DeShawn and didn't back down. I know how conniving and deceitful he can be."

Ryan accepted the praise without thinking about it too deeply, it was another time Emilia had spoken about DeShawn. He leant in and kissed her on the forehead. As he looked back up and beyond the driver, he noticed that they were almost at the restaurant he had booked. As the rain started to come down ever so lightly the driver pulled over on the opposite side of the road and offered Emilia an umbrella, but Ryan's jacket looked as if it would do the trick.

As they entered the restaurant there was no queue and a waiter stood at the front desk waiting to greet them. As Ryan approached, Emilia hung back and had spotted a toilet sign.

"I'm just going to pop in here to freshen up," and she walked off before Ryan could object.

"Good evening, sir, do you have a reservation?"

"Yes, under the name Ryan Jackson for two people."

The waiter didn't even check the reservation list.

"Ah, Mr Jackson, your table is for three people and not two."

Ryan looked very confused at the waiter's response. "No, it's booked for two people. My wife and me for our anniversary."

"Mr Jackson, you called earlier on and changed it to three people? Your first guest has already arrived and is sitting waiting for you."

Ryan continued to be confused.

"Are you sure? The booking under Ryan Jackson?"

The waiter looked down this time and found the amendment and turned the tablet to face Ryan.

"Yes. Ryan Jackson for three people. Would you like me to show you to your table?"

Ryan looked back for Emilia. She hadn't returned so he nodded and followed the waiter into the busy restaurant. As they weaved through the tables Ryan scanned the restaurant looking for someone sitting at a table on their own but initially, he couldn't see anyone. As he continued to look, he nearly bumped into the back of the waiter as he stopped.

"Your table, Mr Jackson." His palm faced left towards a vacant chair. The mystery person immediately stood and emerged from behind the waiter.

"Happy Anniversary, Ryan," DeShawn said with smugness back on his face. "Take a seat, I'm looking forward to helping you celebrate."

Ryan sat slowly onto the chair opposite DeShawn which gave him a full view of the restaurant and more importantly when Emilia would be coming. DeShawn poured himself and Ryan a glass of red wine.

Taking a sip of the wine he'd just poured DeShawn started the conversation.

"I suppose you're wondering why I'm here, Ryan, aren't you?"

"No, not really. I'm surprised you're doing it this quickly, but I know exactly why." Ryan continued to look beyond DeShawn but still couldn't see his wife.

"I thought about leaving it. I thought about leaving you on edge for weeks, maybe even months. But then I wanted to send a message."

"You lost because you did something wrong. If you didn't do it in the first place, we wouldn't be here." Ryan was racked with nerves both inside and out.

"I think you'll find in tonight's situation, Ryan, you're the one who has done wrong." He reached inside his suit jacket pocket and removed a brown envelope and placed in on the table. "Inside this envelope are the pictures from the weekend in Dallas." He reached back in and pulled out the half of the business card that he offered Ryan in the Supreme Court. "Now this offer still stands," he said as he placed it next to the envelope. "I can ruin your life or you can be in debt to me." As DeShawn's sentence finished Ryan finally saw Emilia walk into the restaurant. It was written all over his face what he'd just seen so DeShawn leaned in.

"Tick tock, Ryan, it seems as if your decision just got a time frame."

Ryan watched as the waiter made his way towards the table with Emilia behind him. It was almost as if he'd forgotten DeShawn was there or what was about to happen. He didn't take his eyes off her. He was frozen. She got closer and closer. DeShawn sat there waiting for Ryan to answer him. Just a few steps from the table Ryan finally looked back at DeShawn but by now it was too late for anything.

"Madame, your table for the evening." The waiter moved out the way to reveal Ryan and DeShawn to Emilia.

"Hello, DeShawn," she said smiling.

Uncertainty replaced smugness on DeShawn's face as he stared blankly at Emilia as she stood there. Ryan, having listened to his wife greet DeShawn and not him, sat waiting for the situation to unfold. Emilia took a seat and sat in between the pair.

"Tiffany, what are you doing here? Also, your hair, where's the blonde gone?"

"Tiffany? Her name's Emilia," Ryan replied. "And she's my wife."

"I'm having an anniversary meal with my husband," Emilia pointed at Ryan. "And he's right, my name is Emilia, not Tiffany."

She proceeded to place her bag down beside the chair and poured herself a glass of wine. An air of confusion lingered over both the men on the table. Ryan flicked his eyes between DeShawn and Emilia, who was now sporting DeShawn's usual look.

"Can somebody please tell me what on earth is going on here?"

"It's probably best for me to explain in this scenario as I'm the common ground." Emilia took a mouthful of the wine she'd just poured herself. "Why this had to happen tonight of all nights I'll never know." She reached down to her bag and pulled out her purse and removed two driving licenses handing one to each person. "Ryan, meet Tiffany Maddison. Deshawn, meet Emilia Jackson."

"Wait," Ryan stuttered. "You're the person who set up Luke, Henry and Matt?"

"No, DeShawn is the person who set up those three. I just did what he asked."

"So, this whole time you've been working for me but actually working for Ryan?" DeShawn looked up from the card Emilia had given him.

"I don't work for Ryan, I'm his wife and as you can tell from his reaction, he's as new to this as you are."

Ryan had a million and one questions for his wife and her alter ego racing through his mind.

"So, I had an affair with you in Dallas?"

"Technically yes, but—"

"Hold on, so you had an affair with Henry Craig?"

"No, if you let me finish then I was going to tell you. I didn't actually have an *affair* with either of you, I just set it up to make it look like I did, took some photos and left." Emilia turned to face Deshawn. "You're unusually quiet for you. What's up?"

He started to shake his head.

"I can't believe what I'm hearing. I've trusted you for the best part of a decade and the whole time it's been a lie."

"Ten years," Ryan exclaimed. "You've worked side by side for nearly ten years with him!"

"Yes, so having worked alongside DeShawn for the time period I know a hell of a lot more than he would want others to know." She proceeded to pick up the debt card DeShawn had offered Ryan several times already and put it in her purse. "Now I'll have this, and you'll be in my debt for me to keep my mouth shut about all your wrongdoings." She looked over at Ryan and grasped hold of his nearest hand. "Then when *we* need something off of you, I will be in touch."

DeShawn, shell-shocked, stood up from his chair and turned to leave the table, but not before he stopped as he pushed his chair in.

"How? How have you led a double life for this long?"

"Let's just say it helps to have family in high places." Ryan straight away knew she was talking about her father, José. "Oh DeShawn, just in case you hadn't realized by now, I quit."

He started his walk out of the restaurant and Emilia moved herself, so she was sitting opposite her husband.

"Right, let's start this again, shall we?" she asked as she picked up the menu. Ryan still had so many questions to ask her but was stunned into silence by what had just happened.

As the starters arrived at their table Ryan still wasn't engaging massively in conversation with Emilia and it wasn't the meal that either of them was expecting to have on their anniversary. Instead of starting to eat her food, Emilia looked up and addressed her husband.

"Are you alright, Ryan? This is a supposed to be a double celebration."

"Alright? What do you think? I'm trying to digest my wife has been leading a double life!" He downed his cutlery. "I've just found out my wife has been working for one of the biggest crooks in the sports world, who's just caused me the most stressful two weeks of my life." By the end of his response Ryan's voice was raised and people around them were starting to look.

"Calm down and lower your voice, Ryan, people are staring."

"I'm struggling here, Em, I really am. One of the best days of my life so far has turned into easily the most confusing. The last however many years feel like they've been a lie."

"Nothing has been a lie; I'm still Emilia, your wife. That part of my life has been completely normal, you just didn't know who I worked for."

"You mean you didn't tell me you worked for DeShawn?" Ryan picked up his knife and fork and started to eat his food.

"Ryan, we're having a conversation. Can you wait?"

"No, I can still listen. I might as well digest my food as well as all this new information. Did you even work for whatshisname at all?"

"I did, yes, but that's how I met DeShawn and ended up working for him."

"And the reason you didn't tell your husband all of this was because? Because right now it's not really making sense to me."

"Steve befriended DeShawn in a big play for some property

down in Brooklyn. Part of his repayment was that I went to work for DeShawn."

Ryan, who still had Emilia's fake driving license next to him on the table, picked it up and handed it back to her.

"Why the Tiffany Maddison? Why not go to work for him as Emilia Jackson?"

She took the card out of his hand and placed it next to her cutlery and napkin.

"Mainly because I had almost been acquired – like a basketball trade. I didn't know who and what I was going into, so I wanted to protect myself."

"How did you become Tiffany Maddison?" She looked directly at Ryan, and he knew the answer after Emilia's hint to DeShawn earlier. "Your dad helped you."

As the pair of them finished their main courses the conversation was starting to pick up between them but still wasn't what it usually was. Emilia was the one constantly starting and probing, Ryan's answers more often than not closed ones.

"Please, we have about an hour here. Can we just talk normally? I'd even listen to you talk about the Nets right now."

"I just need a little time to process all this, Em. Can you imagine if it was roles reversed?"

"I can, I mean I can't. I mean I don't know. All I know is I love you and there's absolutely no malice behind this whole situation."

"I don't think there is malice, but I've just spent the best part of a week thinking my life is going to change for the worse and all along there was nothing to worry about."

The waiter arrived to take their dessert order; Emilia's eyes screamed at him to leave.

"I couldn't exactly have told you, could I? It would have jeopardized everything you worked towards in your career.

You won this case on your own." Those seven words rung true to Ryan. Almost instantly his mood went from confused and angry to happy and upbeat, his predominant thoughts now back on the trial win this morning. "Ryan, I promise you this, I am sorry for lying. Everything between us is amazing right now. Can we please start celebrating?"

Sheepishly, Ryan linked Emilia's hand.

"I will try to but there will be more questions."

Emilia nodded back in recognition and her eyes now found the waiter to order their dessert.

The rain was still coming down as they left the restaurant but just a lot harder now. The driver this time had managed to secure a spot right outside so there was no need for either of them to get too wet. As he pulled away, he did a U-turn and continued to head south from Nolita towards the financial district.

"Excuse me, you're going the wrong way, we're going back to the Upper West Side."

The driver looked in his rear-view mirror at Ryan who smiled back at him.

"We're just taking a quick detour. We won't be long."

Continuing down towards the bottom of Manhattan, Emilia asked Ryan repeatedly where they were going but he wouldn't budge on telling her. She kept guessing names of bars and late-night venues that she knew in the area, but he kept tight-lipped the entire journey. Eventually the car pulled over and stopped. Emilia looked around as she got out and very quickly realized that they were down by the South Ferry port. The parking spot gave them a nice view of the Statue of Liberty lit up in all its glory. Ryan took his jacket and placed it over her shoulders. They both stood and looked for a moment.

"Night trip to Liberty Island? It's just like the movies."

"Not quite," Ryan replied quite candidly. "Come this way."

He started to walk away from the ferry port and dragged Emilia with him. They walked east up South Street and moments later it was very clear where they were going. The pier nearby was a notorious hotspot for tourists and helicopter rides. One red helicopter sat on the helipad with a pathway to the door lit up by lights on the floor.

"It's still just like the movies, isn't it? Just a different movie." Emilia squealed in excitement and ran ahead of Ryan as he now strolled behind her. Everything was shut when they arrived, so Ryan had really pulled out all the stops for Emilia's anniversary surprise.

"You very nearly didn't get this surprise. About an hour ago I was tempted to go straight home to bed."

Emilia smirked, "But you didn't because you love me."

"Maybe I love Tiffany Maddison more?"

Emilia smacked Ryan on the arm before she was helped into the helicopter by the pilot. As Ryan grabbed onto the side to boost himself up his phone started to vibrate in his pocket. He stepped back down to look; it was a text message from Macpherson:

*Hope tonight went well. No rush in the morning, give yourself a later start.*

## 27

# THURSDAY 29TH OCTOBER, 9.10 A.M.

As Ryan stirred from his sleep, his eyes were temporarily blinded by the warm October sun as it shone through his bedroom window. He raised his arm over his forehead, sat up and stretched. He could hear the TV on in the other room and life going on outside. He grabbed his phone and the time showed 9.10 a.m. Ryan walked into the living room. Emilia was cooking breakfast in his shirt from last night. He walked over to the fridge and chugged from the open orange juice carton. Wrapping his arms around his wife he buried his head into her neck.

"Breakfast smells good," he said as he looked over at what she was cooking.

"Triple-stacked pancakes with maple syrup and bacon," Emilia replied as she wriggled free to re-open the fridge. "Breakfast of champions for my champion." Ryan leant on the side and watched as she juggled between trying to cook the bacon and making sure she didn't burn the pancakes. "What time are you planning on going in today?"

"I'm not sure, maybe just before lunch. I'll see how I feel." He extended a hand to take control of the pan that was cooking the bacon so she could flip the pancakes.

"Before you do, I want to talk about last night."

"No, let's leave last night where it belongs, please. Firmly in the past."

Emilia turned down the heat on the pan cooking the pancakes and wandered over to Ryan.

"Do you mean that, though? Will you actually leave it there?"

He took her hand.

"Yes, I will. If you promise never to lie again. I know you thought it was better but it really wasn't, so please no more secrets."

"No more secrets, I promise." Walking back towards the cooker she turned with a cheeky look on her face and her tongue poking out. "I do need a new job now, though."

She could tell by the look on Ryan's face that he was about to grab her.

As Ryan placed his plate down on the table beside the sofa, he noticed that he had a few missed calls on his phone from both Macpherson and Daniels. He cleared them from his screen and went back to watching the garbage morning TV show that Emilia had on whilst they ate breakfast. Moments later he sprung to his feet, collected the bowls and put them over on the kitchen side.

"I'm going to jump in the shower and get ready," Ryan said as he made a beeline for the bedroom.

"It's only 10.15 a.m., though, I thought you were going in late."

"This is late! It's not a day off. I've got to go in and get to work on whatever's next. Only one of us gets paid now."

Ryan disappeared into the bedroom and Emilia turned the TV up.

Ryan looked in the bathroom mirror after he finished brushing his teeth. He had on a normal suit and shirt but there was a glow to him he hadn't seen before. He almost felt like he had an aura surrounding him. He walked out and shouted, "I'm off now, I'll probably be home late after celebratory drinks."

Emilia came jogging from the bedroom and into the hallway to cuddle him.

"Have a nice day at work, if you can call it that today. What I mean is have a nice day drinking and celebrating." She leaned in to give him a peck on the lips.

"It's celebrations I've earned, don't you think? I mean you of all—"

"Ah. I thought we were leaving that in the past?"

Ryan shrugged his shoulders and leaned back in to give her a proper kiss.

"I'll try not to be too late, OK?"

Ryan exited the bottom of the building and was once again blinded by the sun. It was warmer than it usually would be in October, so he decided to walk to the office rather than getting the subway. As he walked down the side of Central Park, he walked with a big smile across his face and a spring in his step. He greeted strangers and even stopped to help an elderly woman pick up her groceries after her bag split. Just before the turn into the city Ryan crossed the road and looked down in the direction of Mulligans. The time was around 11.15 a.m. by now so no doubt they'd be open for trade. He decided to dart right and pop in as he remembered he had a debt to pay.

As he walked into the bar, he was right about them just opening. Similar to when he arrived there the week before, the place was absolutely deserted. A waitress was behind the bar restocking the fridge but as far as Ryan could see she was the only one in there.

"Is Freddie around at all?"

She stood up and dusted her knees off.

"Yes, he's down in the cellar. Bear with me one moment."

She walked over to the cellar door which was open and shouted for her colleague to come up. Around a minute later he reared his head carrying a crate of bottled beer.

"My man Ryan, I thought you'd done a runner and would never be seen again!"

"Ha, I had some personal things to deal with so it's a slight delay on the winnings."

"I know, I know. I saw on the news that you beat that guy and got everyone their money back."

Ryan reached into his trouser pocket to pull out his wallet. From that he pulled five $100 bills. He handed him the money.

"$500. Wow. I can't believe you actually paid me that bet."

"I'm a man of my word and you earned it! Now please don't waste it."

As the guy counted the bills Ryan turned and left.

"It's all there," he shouted as he pushed the door open to leave.

Looking at the quickest route into the office from where he was it would involve going through Times Square. He slipped in his earphones and started to walk quickly towards the office. As Ryan walked past the many newsstands that littered every other corner of the city, he noticed that his name and face seemed to be on the front cover of every paper he could see. DeShawn's image was always a little larger being the more well-known person in the case, but his photo and name were clear enough for him to make out. He started to notice that random people were smiling at him, and he could feel people looking at him as he got into Times Square. As he navigated his way through the mix of New Yorkers and tourists, he waited to cross the road perfectly placed under the Mega Screen and that's when he saw it. Himself. As the green man appeared and the rest of the crowd started to flow, Ryan stood fixated watching as his face covered the largest screen in the city. With that, even more people started to recognize him and immediately swarmed round him.

"Thank you, thank you, thank you, ma'am."

Ryan smiled his way through many thankyous, high fives and handshakes as it seemed a lot of people wanted him to win, or more so DeShawn to lose the case. Eventually he managed to cross the road but continued smiling at and thanking people. As he exited Times Square and headed south, his walk got a little calmer and he was able to compose himself before he reached the office. The late start meant only one thing, that Macpherson was probably planning to shut the office early and celebrate the landmark win, as she always did with big cases. Ryan had to act as if he didn't know his boss's intentions and it was a normal working day. As he got to the bottom of the building there was four or five paparazzi outside who immediately started snapping and shouting questions but one of the buildings' security guards rushed out to greet Ryan and get him inside quickly.

"Afternoon, Mr Jackson, quite the stir you've caused today."

"Reggie, it's Ryan, come on, you know this."

"I've been told that today it's Mr Jackson."

Reggie led Ryan to the elevator where there was another building employee ready to take him up to his floor.

"Champagne, Mr Jackson?"

Ryan took the flute as the elevator doors shut.

There was no big surprise as the elevator doors opened on the floor. No one greeted him from the firm and he walked into what seemed like a normal working day. As he edged out no one was there, just the two receptionists who were both occupied with calls. A little confused Ryan continued to walk in as office life swirled around him.

"Excuse me, could you hold the line? Ryan, could you wait there, please?"

The receptionist stopped Ryan in his tracks with no explanation and went back to her phone call. Ryan looked around. The bull pen was full of interns; the boardroom's lights were on and so were Macpherson's and Daniels'. Everyone was in. He waited for another couple of minutes and the receptionists were still engaged so he started to walk towards his office.

"Excuse me, could you hold the line please? Ryan, could you wait there? Ms Macpherson will be out to greet you shortly."

Ryan walked backwards and retreated to the lobby and took a seat as if he was a guest waiting for one of the lawyers. After a few minutes of puffing his cheeks in and out and checking his phone, Macpherson appeared and greeted Ryan.

"There's my superstar," she said as she leaned in for a hug.

"Good afternoon to you as well."

Macpherson noticed a little tensity in Ryan's voice.

"Are you alright? Bad morning?" she said as he came out of the hug.

"I just thought, that, you know, today would be a celebration of winning the case."

A perplexed look fell over Macpherson's face.

"You want us to celebrate you winning a case? Isn't that part of your job here? You know, the one we pay you very well for?"

With the day not seemingly going as he thought, Ryan started walking towards his office to start a normal day.

"Hold up. Hold up. Come back here." Ryan turned back to face his boss. "I've got something to show you." As Ryan rejoined his boss in the lobby, he was now facing the lobby wall that greeted employees and clients every day. A huge smile appeared across his face. "Well, do you like it?" Macpherson said brimming with pride. The sign on the wall read *Macpherson, Daniels and Jackson*.

"SURPRISE!"

A whole host of people marched out of the boardroom and headed towards Ryan and Macpherson. Led by Daniels they came over and congratulated Ryan whether it be through a kiss on the cheek or a handshake. He finished the glass he was given getting into the elevator and was handed another full one promptly.

"I knew you could do it. Well done you." Daniels clinked Ryan's glass to celebrate.

"No, you didn't," Ryan said laughing. "Don't lie. The pair of you set me up to lose this case. We'll discuss that more later."

Both of his bosses shrugged their shoulders in agreement with what Ryan said.

"But here we are now," Daniels continued. "Out the other side as winners and you being the first man to successfully prosecute DeShawn Arlington." He offered his glass up again to both his partner and Ryan. "I'll drink to that."

As the three of them clinked glasses amongst the celebrations, Macpherson remembered that they still needed to talk about Ryan's promotion to partner.

"Despite all of this, the three of us need to sit down and finalize your promotion. There are certain things you need to know at partner level."

"The finer details that come with a promotion – more money outgoing mostly." Daniels looked at the pair of them.

"Can we not wait until tomorrow?" Ryan was in the mood to keep the party going so nodded in Daniels' direction.

"No, let's get this done now. Aside from the money it's better you know what you're getting yourself into."

"I'm just going to pop into my office quickly to grab something. Can we say meet in your office in fifteen minutes?" Both his bosses nodded, and Ryan departed for his office.

As he walked into his office Ryan flicked the light on

and shut the door behind him. He made a beeline for one of his prized signed basketballs and picked one up and started bouncing it. As he walked around the office bouncing, he mimicked a step-back 3-pointer and said in a commentator's voice, "Jackson for the three, and it's good. He comes up clutch as he always does. It's official. Macpherson, Daniels and Jackson for the win." He then switched roles to be the crowd as they erupted into wild celebrations. Collapsing into his chair, out of breath from his little role play, Ryan grabbed his phone. He opened it and called Emilia. No answer. So, he opened a text message and asked her to call him as soon as possible. He wanted to share the good news with her, now it was official. He stood back up and wandered over to place the basketball back on its stand. As he did, he paused for a moment and looked out over the concrete jungle that he called home. Lost in thought Ryan couldn't get away from the fact he'd been born and raised in New York and was now about to sign a contract to become a partner in one of its biggest law firms. Beaming with delight, he turned and headed for the door. Just before he exited the room, he noticed a new bottle of whiskey on his table. When he picked it up it became apparent what it was immediately. A rare bottle of Suntory Yamazaki that was twenty-five years old. A single malt edition, this bottle was at least $25,000. Thinking the present was a gift from either of his bosses he started to carry it towards Daniels' office. With that his phone vibrated. It was a text message from an unknown number:

*I hope you like the present. Welcome to the team,*
*partner.*
*D. A.*